"*Fatal Trauma* asks big ques   d
meaning, all within the cont
ical

              author
              ckmate

"D   a mur-
der   ct and
kee   and a
hin

              author
              l series

"G   guar-
ant

              e Cross

FATAL
TRAUMA

RICHARD L.
MABRY, M.D.

Abingdon Press
Nashville

Fatal Trauma

ISBN-13: 978-1-6308-8116-0

Published by Abingdon Press, P.O. Box 801, Nashville, TN 37202

www.abingdonpress.com

The persons and events portrayed in this work of fiction
are the creations of the author, and any resemblance
to persons living or dead is purely coincidental.

Macro Editor: Teri Wilhelms

Published in association with Books & Such Literary Agency

Library of Congress Cataloging-in-Publication Data

Mabry, Richard L.
   Fatal trauma / Richard L. Mabry, MD.
     pages ; cm
   ISBN 978-1-63088-116-0 (binding: soft back)
   I. Title.
   PS3613.A2F38 2015
   813'.6—dc23
   2015004764

Printed in the United States of America

1 2 3 4 5 6 7 8 9 10 / 19 18 17 16 15

For the two wonderful women with whose love God has blessed me: Cynthia, who will never be forgotten, and Kay, who makes my life worthwhile.

Acknowledgments

It may not be evident, but I—like almost all my author colleagues—suffer from what we call the Imposter Syndrome. We're surprised when we get our first contract, even more when additional opportunities for publication come our way, and absolutely floored by honors and awards for our novels. Well, that's the story of my writing career, and all I can say to each of you who continue to read my work is, "Thank you."

I appreciate my agent, Rachelle Gardner, and my editor at Abingdon Press, Ramona Richards. Thanks for believing in me. The final version of *Fatal Trauma* is much better than it might have been thanks to the suggestions and support of my first reader, severest critic, and biggest fan—my wife, Kay Mabry. Teri Wilhelms took my manuscript and edited with just the right touch. The cover design by the Anderson Design Group was perfect. And, to top it off, Cat Hoort and her staff made sure people knew about the book.

None of this would happen without the dozens of authors who unselfishly shared their time and talents to teach me the craft. My family was kind enough to believe in me and encourage me in my writing. And God has continued to bless me with opportunities. I'm not sure what's around the next corner, but I can hardly wait to see.

As I have done in the past, I'll close with the words with which Johann Sebastian Bach and George Frideric Handel signed their work: *Soli Deo Gloria*—To God alone be glory. Amen.

1

Dᴿ. Mᴀʀᴋ Bᴀᴋᴇʀ ꜱᴡᴇᴘᴛ ʜɪꜱ ꜱᴛʀᴀᴡ-ᴄᴏʟᴏʀᴇᴅ ʜᴀɪʀ ᴀᴡᴀʏ from his eyes, then wiped his forearm across his brow. He wished the air-conditioning in the emergency room was better. Patients might complain that it was cool, but if you were hurrying from case to case for eight hours or more, it was easy to work up a sweat.

"Nobody move!"

Mark spun toward the doors leading to the ER, where a wild-eyed man pressed a pistol against a nurse's head. She pushed a wheelchair in which another man sat slumped forward, his eyes closed, his arms crossed against his bloody chest. Dark blood oozed from beneath his splayed fingers and dropped in a slow stream, leaving a trail of red droplets on the cream-colored tile.

Behind them, Mark could see a hospital security guard sprawled facedown and motionless on the floor, his gun still in its holster, a crimson worm of blood oozing from his head. Mark's doctor's mind automatically catalogued the injury as a basilar skull fracture. *Probably hit him behind the ear with the gun barrel.*

The gunman was in his late twenties. His caramel-colored skin was dotted with sweat. A scraggly moustache and beard framed lips compressed almost to invisibility. Straight black hair, parted in the middle, topped a face that displayed both fear and distrust. Every few seconds he moved the barrel of the gun away from his hostage's temple long enough to wave it around, almost daring anyone to come near him.

The wounded man was a few years older than the gunman—maybe in his thirties. His swarthy complexion was shading into pallor. Greasy black hair fell helter-skelter over his forehead. His face bore the stubble of several days' worth of beard.

"I mean it," the gunman said. "Nobody move a muscle. My brother needs help, and I'll kill anyone who gets in the way."

Mark's immediate reaction was to look around for the nearest exit, but the gunman's next words made him freeze before he could act.

"You the doc?"

Now the gun was pointed at him. Mark thought furiously of ways to escape without being shot, but he discarded each plan as fast as it crossed his mind. "Yeah, I'm the doc."

The gunman inclined his head toward the man in the wheelchair. "He's... he's been shot." He snatched two ragged breaths. "I want you to fix him, pull him through." He punctuated his words with rapid gestures from the pistol. "If he dies... if he dies, I'm going to kill everyone in here." The gunman turned back toward his hostage. "Starting with her."

Mark's eyes followed the gun as it traversed once more from him to the nurse pushing the wheelchair. To this point his attention had been focused on the gunman, but now that he recognized the hostage, he knew the stakes were even higher. Although her red hair was disheveled, her normally fair skin flushed, there was no mistaking the identity of the woman against whose head the gunman's pistol lay. The nurse was Kelly Atkinson—the woman Mark was dating.

———

Kelly gritted her teeth against the pain of the gun barrel boring into her temple. Her stomach clenched and churned with the realization that her life was in the hands of this crazed gunman. Her lips barely moved in silent prayer.

Mark's voice seemed remarkably steady to her, considering the circumstances. "I can see that he needs help, and I'll give it, but stop waving that gun around." He nodded toward Kelly. "First of all, I'm going to need some assistance, and the nurse certainly can't help me with you holding that pistol against her head. Why don't you put it down and step away? You can wait over there, and I'll let you know—"

"Shut up!"

Suddenly the pressure on Kelly's temple was gone. Out of the corner of her eye she saw the gunman turn his weapon and his attention once more to Mark. If she was going to act, now was the time. She looked down at the man in the wheelchair and put all the urgency she could muster into her words, "Doctor, I'm not sure he's breathing! He may be in arrest."

Ignoring the gunman, Mark took several steps forward and squatted in front of the wheelchair. He touched the wounded man's neck with two fingers, then placed his stethoscope on the man's chest. In a few seconds, Mark pulled back his bloody hand, straightened and said, "We need to get him into one of the trauma rooms. Right now!"

Ignoring the gunman, Kelly started pushing the wheelchair toward trauma room 2. "What will you need?" she asked over her shoulder.

She hoped Mark's reply would communicate the urgency of the situation and further distract the gunman's attention. He didn't disappoint her. "I need to intubate him and start CPR. Start a couple of IVs with large bore needles so we can push some Lactated Ringer's into him until the blood bank can cross-match him for half a dozen units."

After an emphatic gesture from her, Bob, one of the ER aides reluctantly fell in behind Kelly. Bob's ebony skin couldn't show pallor, but he was sweating profusely. As he followed Kelly, he murmured under his breath, "What does the doctor think he's doing?"

Kelly's answer was a hoarse whisper. "I think he's trying to save everyone's life."

⤛⤜

"Hold it right there, Doc," the man with the pistol said. "You don't move unless I tell you to."

Mark watched as the gunman's finger tensed on the trigger of his weapon. He fought to keep his voice steady. "Every second you keep me standing here makes it less likely I can save your brother's life."

The gunman gestured at the door through which Kelly was disappearing with the wounded man. "Okay, but I'll be right behind you." He glared, his brown eyes seeming to bore a hole through Mark. "And remember—if my brother dies, everyone in that room dies—the nurse, you, the aide—everyone."

Out of the corner of his eye, Mark saw the curtains flutter at the ER cubicle he'd recently left, and a faint spark of hope arose in him. To set this up, he had to move. After a split-second's hesitation, he strode swiftly to the open door of the trauma room where Kelly and the aide were already moving the wounded man onto the treatment table.

Despite the sweat that poured out of him a few minutes ago, now Mark felt a chill that went deep into his bones. He probably had one chance to make this end well, but to make that happen, everything had to work perfectly. Otherwise, he and several other people would die.

"Start some oxygen," Kelly said to the aide. "I'll get IVs going."

"Help him, Doc," the gunman snapped.

Mark, at a shade over six feet and a hundred seventy pounds, was larger than the gunman. But the pistol in the man's hand was a great equalizer. Besides, when he looked into the brown eyes of the man holding the gun, Mark saw a fire that was due to zeal for a cause or the effect of drugs or maybe both. It took every bit of courage he had to keep his own eyes from showing the emotion he felt—fear.

Mark turned to the gunman and said, "I'll help him, but we need some space. If you're determined to watch, at least step back." He jerked his head to the side. "Stand there by the door. You can see everything, but you'll be out of the way. I need to start CPR on this man."

"But—"

Mark's voice carried all the authority he could muster. "Move! Now!"

The pistol came up, and Mark felt his heart drop as he waited for that trigger finger to tighten one last time. Then the gunman shrugged and backed up until he was against the door. "Okay, but remember—I'm watching." His pistol traced a circuit from Kelly to Mark and back. "Get cracking."

Mark reached down even further for courage he didn't know he had. "Okay." He moved to the side of the wounded man, where his fingers felt the neck for the carotid pulse. He took a deep breath and looked up at Kelly. "Got those IV lines in yet?"

"Just finished one," she said. "About to start on the second."

"No time. Let it go," Mark said. "When you started the IV, did you get some blood to send to the bank for T&C?"

She patted the pocket of her scrub dress, producing a glassy tinkle. "T&C for six units, stat hemoglobin and hematocrit, everything. Got the tubes right here."

"Bob, take these to the lab—"

"Nobody leaves the room!" the gunman snapped.

Mark started to argue, but decided it would be fruitless. "I'm going to start chest compressions now." He glanced at Kelly. "Hook him up to the EKG so I can see if there's any activity. We may have to shock him."

Mark looked down at the man on the treatment table. The aide had cut away the patient's shirt, revealing three puckered entrance wounds where bullets had pierced his chest. They were grouped tightly right above the man's left nipple, close enough together that a playing card could cover them all. Now the bleeding had completely stopped.

Why wasn't he here by now? How long would it take? Mark had to keep going. "I'm going to start CPR now." He put one hand over the other, centering them on the patient's breastbone. He wasn't sure how long he could keep this up, though. *Come on. What are you waiting for?*

The door crashed open, sending the gunman staggering forward onto his knees.

"Police. Drop the gun!" The policeman held his service pistol in a two-handed grip. "On the floor! Now!"

Instead, the gunman, still on his knees, twisted to face the policeman, his own pistol extended. The next seconds were filled with gunfire.

When he heard the first shot, Mark reached across the patient and shoved Kelly to the ground. "Get down," he screamed.

It seemed to Mark that the gunfire went on for a full minute, but he knew better. It always seemed that time either sped up or slowed to a crawl in emergency situations like this. His ears were still ringing when he raised his head and looked around. The gunman lay sprawled on his back, open eyes unseeing, his gun a foot away from his outstretched hand. Mark had seen enough death to know the gunman no longer presented any danger.

The policeman was crumpled in the doorway, one hand clenched over his abdomen, a fountain of blood issuing from between his outstretched fingers. The other hand still clutched his service pistol. He was breathing, although his respirations were labored.

Mark took in the scene in less than a second. He jumped to his feet and called to Kelly, "We need a gurney. We have to get him to the OR, stat." To the aide, he said, "Stick your head out the door. Have them call for help. Alert the OR I'm coming up."

"He looks familiar. Who...who's he?" Kelly asked.

"Sergeant Ed Purvis. He brings patients here sometimes. I'd just finished with one when all this started." Mark moved to the side of the wounded policeman. "Now help me get him onto a gurney."

"What...what about the wounded man already on the table?" Bob asked over his shoulder as Kelly and Mark slid their hands under the fallen officer.

"Don't worry about him. He was dead by the time Kelly wheeled him into the ER."

2

IN THE OPERATING ROOM, A GERMICIDAL SOLUTION SPLASHED on Ed Purvis's abdomen by the circulating nurse turned the pale skin bronze. The scrub nurse hurriedly placed sterile green sheets around the operative area. While the anesthesiologist was still injecting medication into the patient's IV line to relax him, Mark, now clad in a sterile gown, reached out a gloved hand for the scalpel and made a vertical incision that opened Purvis's abdominal cavity wide.

"Is one of the surgeons on the way?" Mark asked.

"We've put out a call," the circulating nurse said.

"Guess it's up to me until one shows up," Mark said. He looked to the anesthesiologist at the head of the table. "Can you give me more relaxation?"

Dr. Buddy Cane nodded. "Coming up. You've got a pretty good head start on me, you know."

Mark worked on, assisted by the scrub nurse. His attention was riveted on the operative field when a husky contralto voice from across the room said, "Tell me what we've got."

Dr. Anna King stood in the doorway, dripping hands held high in front of her. The scrub nurse turned away from the table to help the surgeon gown and glove.

For a moment, Mark had almost forgotten that Anna was a surgeon. In his mind, she was an attractive blonde he'd dated occasionally. Of course, he'd heard rumors...Never mind. He wanted help and now he had it. "Multiple gunshot wounds of the abdomen," he said. In a few sentences, he related how Purvis had been shot. "He's hanging on by a thread. I think we need to—"

"I've got it, Mark. Thanks." This was a different Anna King from the one with whom Mark had shared dinner just a week ago. That one was funny, easy-going. This one was, in every sense, the surgeon. The attitude was "I'm in charge," and Mark had the feeling that if he crossed her, he'd regret it. He was already wondering what a long-term relationship with her would be like. Never mind. He'd deal with that later.

Within less than a minute, Anna was gowned and gloved. She moved to stand at the patient's right side, and Mark slid around to a position opposite her. Anna readjusted the self-retaining retractor and held out her hand. "Let's get some suction in here. Adjust that overhead light."

For a few minutes, the OR was quiet except for the murmured conversation of the surgeon and assistant as they bent over the operative area. Once, the circulating nurse darted in to mop Anna's brow with a cloth. When she eased up behind Mark, he shook his head and she backed away.

"How many units of blood?" Mark looked toward the head of the table.

The anesthesiologist checked his notes. "Six." He paused. "More coming. But his vitals keep slipping."

Mark's deep breath resonated inside his surgical mask. "Let's—"

"Mark, you called for help. I'm here. Let me be in charge, would you?" There was no anger in Anna's words, just a simple statement of fact.

Mark nodded, but didn't reply. He'd have to be careful not to cross Anna while she was in this mode.

His mind moved from the Anna he'd known socially to the surgeon, Anna King. So far she seemed to be doing fine. There were too many smells in the operating room for him to pick up any scent of alcohol drifting through her surgical mask. Still, Mark wondered...

Anna spoke without taking her eyes from the operating area. "Mark, I know you feel responsible for this patient, but you did your part by getting him up here as quickly as you could. Now it's my responsibility." She held out her hand and the scrub nurse slapped a hemostat into it. "We'll do our best. But we can't save every patient."

"I got him into this," Mark said, clamping off another bleeding point. "It's my fault he got shot."

"No," Anna said. "Like every police officer, he knew the risks the first day he put on that uniform. You took the only chance you had to save the lives of three people."

"And it cost the life of another one," Mark said.

"Not yet," Anna said. "Now, if you're going to assist, don't focus on assigning blame. Just help me."

———

Anna King pushed her surgical mask down to hang beneath her chin. She stripped off her latex gloves and tossed them in the designated waste receptacle, then turned around so the nurse could unfasten her surgical gown. "I'm sorry, Mark." She balled the gown into a mass and threw it after the gloves. "We did what we could. We just couldn't save him."

Mark opened his mouth, then decided he had nothing to say, so he simply shook his head. Let her assign whatever meaning she liked to the gesture.

Anna paused with one hand on the operating room's swinging door. "I'll see if his family's here yet."

"No!" Mark hadn't meant to bark the word, but, considering the state of his emotions at this point, he wasn't surprised at the way it came out. "No," he said more softly. "Let me go out there and talk with them. They need to know more than that he was shot dead." He swallowed hard. "I need to tell them that he saved my life."

"Mark, you can't take this personally. You see gunshot wounds in the emergency room all the time. Some of those patients we can save, some not. What's so different about this one?"

Mark knew what was different, but he wasn't prepared to say the words. Not yet. Instead, he snatched the surgical cap off his head and held it in front of him like a penitent presenting an offering. "When they come into the ER—makes no difference which side of the law they were on when the bullets hit them—when they reach the ER, they're mine. I'm going to do my best to save them. Some I do, some I don't. I accept that." He looked at the body of Ed Purvis, now covered by a sheet. "But this wasn't someone who showed up with a gunshot wound. This was a man I knew—admittedly, not well—a man that I literally asked to put his life on the line to save mine." Mark bowed his head.

Anna put her hand on Mark's shoulder, probably the closest she could come to a gesture of tenderness in this situation. "And he responded the way you hoped he would. He did what law enforcement officers do every day in this country. He did what he'd signed up to do, and in doing so he saved your life." She opened the door. "Come with me if you like. I know his family would appreciate it. But don't take the responsibility for his death on yourself. And don't think you have to spend the rest of your life making up for it."

———— ∞ ————

"Thanks for doing this, Steve," Kelly said. "The adrenaline from what happened has about worn off, but I just couldn't be alone...not for a while, at least. Besides, I...I think it might help if I sort of talked this out, and you're a good listener."

Before he took a seat in the booth opposite her, Steve Farrington, pastor of the Drayton Community Church, handed Kelly one of the two steaming cups he'd obtained from the service counter at this all-night fast food establishment. "No problem, Kelly." He blew across the surface of his cup. "When I heard about the gunman in the ER, I headed for the hospital. I found out you were one of the hostages, and after you were freed I stuck around to see if you needed anything." He took a sip of coffee. "But, to be clear, did you want me here because I'm your pastor or your friend?"

"Both, I guess," Kelly said. "So you can wear whichever hat you want...so long as you stay here with me for a while."

"I'm happy to sit and talk with you, but don't you need to call anyone else? Family, maybe?"

Kelly thought for a moment. "No. My family wouldn't understand or even care."

He looked into his coffee cup but didn't drink. "Why don't you tell me about it?"

Kelly leaned across the table. "I was at the triage desk in the emergency room tonight when a man came in, supporting a gunshot victim. I was about to call for an aide to get a gurney for the patient when the first man grabbed a wheelchair and told me to push his brother back into the ER. I started to argue. Then he pulled a gun..." She bowed her head, closed her eyes, and took several deep breaths. "Sorry. He pulled a gun, held it to my head, and said, 'Take my brother back there and get a doctor to fix him up, or I'll kill you.'"

"Obviously that was frightening," Steve said. "So what happened then?"

Kelly worked her way through the explanation of the next few minutes, ending with the shooting of the gunman by Sergeant Purvis. "We rushed the policeman into the elevator and wheeled him into the OR. The night crew had just finished an emergency case, and they took over. I went back down to the ER and spent the next hour or so talking with the police."

"How do you feel now?"

Kelly shook her head. "I'm still shaky, but it's getting better. Talking about it helps, I guess." She looked down. "Now that I have time to think about it, during that time I was as worried for Mark as for myself."

"About what?"

Kelly stared into her cup. "I didn't want him to die."

"Why is that? Is it because Mark isn't a Christian?" Steve asked.

"I...I'm not sure where he stands. I've broached the subject a time or two, but Mark always deflects the conversation. I get the impression he doesn't like to talk about religion." She drained the cup and shoved it aside. "He says he got too busy for all that when he was in medical school." Kelly patted her lips with a paper napkin. "I think talking about religion embarrasses him."

"You and Mark have been going out for a while, haven't you?"

"Several months," Kelly said.

"Is it serious?"

"It's not exclusive for him, I guess—he went out with one of the surgeons from the hospital last week—but I haven't dated anyone else since I started seeing him."

Steve started to stand. "Would you like some more coffee?" Kelly shook her head.

He sat down again and took a sip from his cup. "Is Mark's spiritual status the main reason you were concerned about him?"

"I . . ." Kelly shook her head.

"This probably isn't the time for you to talk with Mark about this, but that time will come soon. I think you'd better try to sort out your feelings before then." He reached over and placed his hand on top of hers. "Until then, maybe you should pray about it."

Kelly nodded silently. *Yes, for both Mark and me . . . because I didn't tell you the rest of the story.*

———

Mark struggled to keep his voice steady as he stood face to face with Dr. Eric McCray in a relatively quiet corner of the emergency room. "Tough night," Mark said. "Thanks for taking over down here."

"No problem, man. When I got the call from the hospital about what happened, when they told me you had to go up to the OR to try to save the policeman's life, I jumped into my car and headed here, praying all the way." He pointed around the ER. "Everybody pitched in. Jim's coming on duty in another hour, but I think I'll stick around to help him clear out the backlog."

"No need. I'm okay to get back to work."

"Forget it," Eric said. "I don't have anyone at home waiting for me. You need to clear out of here."

"I...I appreciate it."

"Listen, how's Kelly doing?"

Mark shrugged. "I don't know yet. The ER people told me she'd left as soon as the police were through with her. I wanted to talk with her, but they grabbed me when I got down from the OR."

"Well, give her my best, and tell her I'm glad she's okay." Eric clapped Mark on the back and walked away.

Mark's pulse still wasn't fully back to normal when he collapsed onto the sagging couch in the break room, holding in one hand a Styrofoam cup of what had to be the world's worst coffee. He'd retrieved his cell phone from his locker, but right now it was still in the pocket of his scrubs. He should call Kelly, but he wasn't quite ready to talk with her.

Mark thought about everything that went through his mind when the gunman first entered the ER. He was ashamed of his first reaction. Fortunately, it had all worked out in the end. Thank goodness the gunman believed his friend was still alive and might respond to treatment. Of course, that only worked because Kelly picked up on the idea immediately. Matter of fact, as Mark thought more about what happened, Kelly might have had the idea first.

If she hadn't...don't go there, he reminded himself. He'd survived, and so had Kelly. The gunman was on his way to the morgue to lie alongside his brother. As for the policeman who'd killed him...Mark pushed thoughts of Ed Purvis aside. Anna was right. The man knew the risks. And despite what his heart told him, Mark's head reminded him he couldn't save everyone.

As soon as Mark returned to the emergency room from the OR, the police had grabbed him for questioning, asking the same things again and again. No, he had no idea of the identity of the gunman or the patient. No, he'd never seen them before. No, he was pretty certain the gunman fired first, but it all happened so fast. Yes, Sergeant Purvis identified himself as a police officer and ordered the gunman to surrender. And on and on and on it went.

Actually, Mark had some questions of his own. Who were the men who'd invaded the emergency room—both the gunman and the wounded man? How did the shooter get past the metal detector at the ER door? What was the condition of the hospital security officer the gunman struck down? After his first couple of questions went unanswered, Mark decided the police weren't interested in giving out information. Maybe he'd learn more eventually.

The questioning was finally over, but Mark had the feeling there'd be more. But, for now, he was alone. He crumpled his empty cup and flung it toward the wastebasket in the ER staff lounge, missing by a foot. It lay amid two other cups and a wadded candy wrapper, a testament to poor aim by staff called away before they could pick up their trash. Mark started to get up to clean up the mess, then decided he'd do it in a moment. He leaned back on the couch and looked at his cell phone as though it could provide the answer to his frustration. Come to think of it, perhaps it might, if Kelly would only answer.

———

Kelly was relaxing—or at least, trying to relax—in a hot tub when she heard the ring of her cell phone. Her first instinct was to get out of the tub, wrap herself in a towel, and trudge into the bedroom to answer the call before it rolled over to voicemail. After all, that's one of the first reflexes instilled into medical personnel. It could represent an emergency. The hospital—or, in this case, the police—might need something.

Then again, the call might be from Mark. After it was all over, she wanted to hug him, tell him how brave he'd been, to say how glad she was that he was alive, to pour out her heart to him. But now Kelly wondered if that talk should wait until they both calmed down some more. She hadn't even dared share with her pastor what she'd really thought tonight. Maybe neither she nor Mark was ready for this conversation right now.

Kelly turned on the tap to run more hot water into the bath. She needed to relax muscles that were tense as bowstrings. She sighed, eased back into the water, closed her eyes, and went over the events of the evening for what must have been the twentieth time. Her pastor had been right. What happened tonight was a natural springboard for a conversation she needed to have with Mark. But there was more there than the pastor knew... and she wasn't certain she was ready to tell Mark everything.

<hr>

Mark's call went to voicemail. His message was brief: "Kelly, this is Mark. I'm sorry I couldn't see you right after the shooting. Please call me." But she didn't. Finally, after waiting as long as he could, he called again... and yet again. The results were the same, except that he didn't bother to leave a message on those occasions, although perhaps the chip responsible for voicemail picked up the sound of his grinding molars.

Even though Kelly, like Mark, relied on her cell phone, she had a landline number. He tried it now, but there was no answer. Many hospital personnel, including Mark, complied as inexpensively as possible with the hospital's requirement they have a landline by using a "voice over Internet protocol" or VoIP phone. Most of the calls Mark received on that line were either wrong numbers or telephone solicitors, so usually he simply ignored the phone when it rang. Maybe Kelly was doing the same thing. After what they'd been through, he certainly couldn't blame her.

Common sense told him to give up, go home, try to get some rest. But he wasn't in a mood to rest. He was as jittery as the cook in a meth lab right now, and he knew there was no hope of his getting to sleep until he came down from his nervous high. He could call Anna King—she'd probably still be awake—but for some reason he wasn't ready for another conversation with her. Mark wondered if their conversation in the OR hadn't revealed too much of her already.

He had a few friends, most of them doctors, but Mark hated to wake them up. His parents wouldn't understand, and his call would only upset them. He tried to think of someone else to whom he could talk, but Kelly's name kept coming to the forefront.

Mark knew that some of his colleagues drank to relax after a particularly difficult case. Anna was a case in point. Maybe he should call her, perhaps drop by her home to wind down with a drink. He squelched the thought as soon as it popped into his mind. That wasn't any kind of a solution. It would only make matters worse.

He couldn't escape the feeling that what he and Kelly went through tonight had somehow tightened the bond between them. What did that mean about his relationship with Anna King? Maybe tomorrow he'd think about it. He had to take things one step, one day at a time.

The clock on the wall in the break room hadn't worked since the Reagan administration. Mark abandoned the practice of wearing a watch when he started working in the ER. He looked at the time displayed on his cell phone and discovered that it was almost one A.M. He shrugged into the white coat he wore to cover his scrub suit as he went to and from work, pulled his car keys from the pocket, and headed out the door. Common sense dictated that he drive directly home, maybe stopping at an all-night fast food place for a burger or malt. But he knew that wasn't going to happen. There was no doubt in Mark's mind what his next stop would be.

Finally, Kelly could put it off no longer. She crawled into bed, but sleep eluded her. All she could do was lie there and stare at the ceiling. She tried closing her eyes, but the images kept coming. A hot bath and a bowl of Blue Bell vanilla ice cream with chocolate syrup was her usual bedtime prescription for nights when sleep wouldn't come, but tonight the remedy hadn't worked. She read a Bible passage, but the words kept running together, and she got no comfort from them. Her prayers were a jumble of thoughts and incomplete sentences stemming from emotions running rampant in her brain.

She'd seen the "missed call" messages on her cell phone: three calls from Mark. While she was in the tub, still winding down from her ordeal, she hadn't been ready to talk with him. Afterward, when she started to call him back, she couldn't bring herself to press the button. Was it too late? Or was she just not ready for the conversation? In either case, the call went unmade.

Now Kelly tossed and turned, seeking sleep that wouldn't come. She was about to get out of bed and turn on the TV, usually her last resort, when she heard a car pull up outside her house. That was unusual at this time of the morning in her neighborhood. The occupants of the homes around her were mostly older couples whose children had long since left home, and by this time of night the street was quiet and empty.

Kelly eased from her bed, wrapped a robe around her, and slid her feet into worn, comfortable scuffs. She tiptoed to the front room and parted the blinds far enough to see the white sedan parked in front of her house. The lone occupant sat unmoving, shrouded in darkness, for several minutes. When he opened the driver's side door, the car's interior light came on, and she recognized Mark. He hesitated for a moment before striding toward her front door, his white coat high-lighted by the light from the street lamp.

He paused on her doorstep, and she could almost hear the thoughts going through his head. It was late. There were no lights on in the house. Should he wake her? What would she say?

Kelly examined her own feelings. Should she remain quiet? If he knocked, would she answer it? Or would she let her inaction turn him away?

Almost without making a conscious decision, she moved a few steps to the end table in the living room and turned on the lamp there. Apparently that was enough encouragement for Mark.

He tapped lightly on the door. "Kelly, it's Mark," he called softy. "I know it's late, but I need to talk to you. May I come in?"

Kelly cinched her robe more tightly closed, then opened the door. She gestured him inside, still unsure of what to say, then locked the door behind him.

They stood awkwardly for a moment, then each reached out for the other, and the embrace that followed seemed to last forever. Kelly found there was a lump in her throat that made speaking difficult. "I'm... I'm so glad you're okay," she said.

"I know it's late, but I'm having a hard time unwinding, and I wondered if you were, too."

"I was trying, but without much success," Kelly admitted.

"I knew I couldn't sleep until I talked this out with someone."

Kelly's heart thudded in her chest. Would the things Mark wanted to say be the same ones that had kept her awake tonight? She motioned him to the sofa and eased down beside him. "Then why don't you tell me?" Kelly looked into his eyes and held her breath.

3

MARK SAT ON THE SIDE OF HIS BED, GROGGY WITH LACK OF sleep after thrashing about for most of the night, unable to rest and emotionally wrung out. He'd left Kelly's house about a quarter to two. Right now she'd be getting ready for church, but she'd promised to call him after the services. Until then, he was on his own.

After the shooting, Eric had offered to take Mark's Sunday evening shift in the ER, and Mark readily accepted the offer. At that point, he felt like he never wanted to see the inside of a hospital again. Now, less than twelve hours later, he wondered what he'd do to occupy himself if he didn't go to work tonight. There was a time when his life revolved around his shifts in the ER: sleep, eat, go to work, come home, eat, sleep, repeat the cycle. Since he'd started dating Kelly, the pattern had expanded to include time with her, plus an occasional dinner with Anna for variety. One of those relationships might eventually demand more of his time. He knew which one, but he didn't want to think about that right now.

Last night had changed a lot of things. Mark's thoughts seemed to be stuck on the shooting—and his emotions while it was going down. He hung his head, closed his eyes, and wondered why he hadn't confessed to Kelly. Maybe today…

The buzzing of his cell phone startled him. He picked it up and frowned when the caller ID showed "anonymous caller." Could it be a reporter? None had managed to find him last night, but he had no doubt they'd remedy that today. Surely a telephone solicitor wouldn't be calling at eight o'clock on a Sunday morning.

Oh, well. He had nothing better to do. Might as well answer it. "Dr. Baker."

"Doctor, this is Detective Jackson."

Mark wished he could clear the cobwebs from his brain. Like slogging through mud, the synapses slowly clicked. Jackson was the lead detective investigating the shooting. Mark had met him and his partner, Detective Ames, last night—or, more accurately, early this morning. His mental picture of Jackson was of a short, stocky African-American in a wrinkled suit, the almost laser-like intensity behind his dark eyes a warning not to mistake a disheveled appearance for carelessness. Mark had decided to walk carefully around Jackson.

"Doctor, are you there?"

Mark sat up and swiveled around to perch on the bedside. "Uh, yeah. What can I do for you?"

"I thought you might want to know that we've ID'd the two victims of last night's shooting."

ID'd the victims? He already knew who the chief victim was: Sergeant Purvis. Then Mark realized the detective was talking about the gunman and the man—didn't he call him his brother?—the man who'd been essentially dead on arrival in the ER. "Okay."

"They were brothers," Detective Jackson said. "The older was Hector Garcia. The gunman was his younger brother, Ignacio, aka 'Nacho.'"

The names meant nothing to Mark. "Who?"

"Yeah, I'm sure the names aren't familiar," Jackson said, "but this may help you. They were members of the Zeta drug cartel."

That information opened Mark's eyes like a cup of strong coffee. Generally, his newspaper reading was confined to the sports section, but almost everyone in Texas knew that the Zetas were the most feared drug cartel in Mexico. Even the Mexican police and military walked carefully around the Zetas. He'd heard they were operating in the state, but he figured it would be further south, near the border. On the contrary, these men had been in Drayton, right in the heart of north Texas.

"I wanted to let you know," Jackson went on. "Since Ed Purvis shot Nacho, we're going to give some protection to the Purvis family for a while. We can't do that for everyone involved in the incident, but I thought I should at least warn you. The Zetas have a strong sense of revenge, and you might want to be extra careful yourself."

"What about Kelly?"

"Who? Oh, the nurse who first interacted with Nacho." There was a rustle of paper. "She's next on my list to contact."

"I'll do it," Mark said. "We're supposed to talk later today." He paused. "I don't guess the people in the OR attending to Sergeant Purvis are at risk, though."

"We don't think so, but you can never tell what kind of twisted logic these people have about getting even," Jackson said. "Anyway, I've got to get going. I'll call if we need anything more from you."

"Detective, one thing before you go. I know you generally keep information like this confidential, but would you give me Sergeant Purvis's address? I want to go by later today and personally express my condolences to the family."

"Did you talk with them last night?"

"Only briefly, and frankly after Mrs. Purvis heard about her husband's death, I don't think she took in anything I or the other surgeon had to say."

It took a good bit of cajoling, but eventually Jackson gave Mark the information he needed. "But be sensitive," the detective cautioned.

"I will be." Mark remembered how it was when his brother died. There were a slew of people in and out of the house. Most were well-meaning and helpful, but some just wanted to focus on assigning blame. To Mark and his family, it didn't matter that the other driver was drunk, was driving with an invalid license. Joe was still dead, and his family needed sympathy and support. Mark figured the Purvis family was in the same situation.

After ending the call, Mark shuffled into the kitchen and put on a pot of extra-strong coffee. He had a hunch he'd need it—it promised to be a long day.

"Shouldn't you be home?" Tracy Orton asked.

"Why? To worry about what's already happened?" Kelly said. "No, it's Sunday, and I wanted to be in church this morning. Actually, I needed to be here."

The two women stood in a relatively quiet corner of the Drayton Community Church, out of the traffic pattern of people exiting after the Sunday morning service. Tracy's dark hair was pulled back in a ponytail. Her makeup was understated. She wore very little jewelry. Her dress was a simple white sheath. But, as always, what most people noticed first was the hint of mischief that gleamed in the eyes of Kelly's best friend.

"Well, how about some lunch?" Tracy asked. "We can lust over the menu items we can't have because they're fattening, and you can tell me about last night."

Despite her somber mood, Kelly smiled. "I'm not sure about the lusting, but...yes, I think I'd like to talk to somebody about what happened." She paused, considering her next words carefully. "And there's something else I'd like to run by you."

"Want to ride with me?"

"No, I'd better go in my car. I'll meet you there," Kelly said.

They turned to go, but stopped when a voice behind them said, "Kelly. Surprised to see you here today, but I'm glad you've come. I've been praying for you and Mark."

Kelly turned slowly to face the pastor. "I'm glad I came. The sermon was just what I needed to hear this morning. And thank you for your prayers."

"Is Mark okay?" the pastor asked.

"We talked late last night. He was pretty shaken, but I think he'll be okay." No need to go into details with the pastor beyond what she'd shared with him last night.

"Well, keep me posted on developments." He smiled and moved away.

Kelly nodded. *I will...with some of them. But not all of them. Not right now.*

⸺◦∞◦⸺

Kelly was already seated in a booth at the back of their favorite little cafe when Tracy walked in. "I ordered iced tea for both of us."

"Great." Tracy sat down opposite Kelly and dropped her purse on the seat beside her.

They made small talk until after the waitress took their order. Then Tracy said, "So, the account in the paper was pretty sketchy, and the TV reports didn't tell me much more. I want to hear all about what happened."

Kelly was surprised that it took so little time to relate last evening's sequence of events. "Mark got the gunman to back up toward the door of the trauma room," she said in conclusion. "Sergeant Purvis burst through, knocking the man off balance, ordering him to drop the gun. Instead he fired, and we ducked. When we looked up, the gunman was dead, and Mark was calling for a gurney to take Purvis to the OR, where he died."

"Wow!" Tracy reached across and covered her friend's hand with her own. "What was going through your mind when all this was happening?"

"I tried to be calm, tell myself that if he pulled the trigger I'd end up in a better place. Of course, I'm not sure the same could be said for Mark, and I didn't have any idea where the aide stood."

"So you prayed for them?"

Kelly bit her lip. "Actually, no. Instead, I found myself thinking, 'Mark can't die not knowing.'"

"Not knowing what?"

"Not knowing that I'm falling in love with him."

⸻

Mark hadn't been to visit a family in mourning since a college friend died years ago. At that time, he and three of his fraternity brothers had driven almost an hour each way to pay their respects. He didn't remember much about the experience, except that he was glad he had someone with him. The sickly-sweet scent of flowers, the people conversing in hushed tones, all made him wish he could hurry and get out of the house.

A year later, his own brother had been killed in an auto accident, his life snuffed out by a drunk driver. Mark had virtually sleepwalked through that experience, letting his parents deal with the people who came by. A few of Joe's friends wanted to talk, but Mark tried to avoid them. He didn't want to talk about what had happened to his brother. He wanted it all to be a bad dream, and if that wasn't possible, he just wanted to get through the experience.

Since that time, the closest Mark had come to death was in the emergency room. Visiting the bereaved and attending funerals weren't on his list. Nevertheless, for reasons he couldn't explain, Mark felt the need to express his sympathy to Sergeant Purvis's family in person. He figured that most people there would be dressed informally, but after he'd donned khakis and an open neck knit shirt, Mark decided that felt wrong. He wasn't the average person coming to say, "Sorry for your loss." No, Mark was there to say, "I'm responsible for your husband getting shot." Somehow, it seemed that called for him to wear something different.

He pulled his dark suit from the closet. He found a clean white shirt in his dresser drawer. His stock of ties was laughably small, but he finally found a muted maroon-and-gold striped one that should be solemn enough. Mark looked in the mirror and decided that he was as dressed for the occasion as possible. If he ended up going to the funeral—and that was a very big "if"—he'd wear the same thing. He doubted that the Purvis family was going to notice much about his attire, either today or later. No, they had other things on their mind.

As Mark turned the key in the ignition of his white Toyota Camry, he wondered if he really should make this visit. Would Purvis's widow even talk with him? Would the family be in church this morning? No, it was more likely that if they weren't home they'd be at the funeral home, making final arrangements.

Mark decided that if he didn't do it now, he'd worry about it until the visit was behind him. He punched the address he'd wheedled from Detective Jackson into his car's GPS and pulled away from the curb. Suddenly, his collar was too tight. His throat was dry. He adjusted the car's climate control, but still he felt rivulets of perspiration running down his back.

Mark wished he could believe that praying would help. No, it had been too long since he'd even tried. Instead, he called on a meditation exercise he'd learned from a med school classmate. In a few moments, he decided that it—like so many other things in his life—wasn't working.

⸺⁂⸻

As soon as her declaration that she was falling in love with Mark was out of Kelly's mouth, the waitress served their lunches. Tracy was almost beside herself by the time the dishes were on the table and the waitress gone. She ignored her food, leaning forward toward Kelly and dropping her voice. "You're in love with him? Are you sure?"

Kelly picked up a half of her tuna sandwich, then returned it to the plate. "Pretty sure."

"And you suddenly decided this last night while a man was holding you and Mark at gunpoint?"

"I know," Kelly said. "It sounds crazy. Mark and I have been dating for several months. I knew I was growing fond of him, but finally, last night, when our lives were in danger,

I discovered…" She grimaced. "This is hard to say out loud, to hear myself admit it."

Tracy met her gaze but remained silent.

"I couldn't imagine life without him."

"Does he—?"

"No. I haven't said anything to him yet. Last night, he came by my house sometime after one. He was having a hard time coming down from the experience, and frankly, so was I. We talked for almost an hour about what we'd gone through, just letting our feelings out. Mainly we kept on rehashing the situation, saying the same things again and again until we finally ran down like a train engine out of steam. A couple of times he seemed as though he wanted to say something more, but each time it was like he hit an emotional wall and clammed up. And I couldn't bring myself to tell him what I was feeling, either."

"I see." Tracy shoved her salad aside. "Well, do you want some advice?"

Kelly shook her head. "Not really. I just had to share this with someone I could trust to keep my secret."

"Well, I'll give you my advice, whether you want it or not." Tracy paused to drink deeply from her iced tea. "Tell Mark how you feel."

Kelly felt her stomach twisting. She didn't want to hear this. "But what if he doesn't feel the same way?"

Tracy shrugged. "Only one way to find out. You know what your feelings are. Dollars to donuts, Mark hasn't examined his own. The only way to help him do this is to tell him what you discovered last night."

"But—"

"I know. He may not feel the same way. But you need to let him know where you stand, so he can figure out how he feels. You've got to make this a two-way street."

Kelly looked down at the almost-untouched sandwich on her plate. She knew Tracy was right. But another factor that no one had mentioned—the elephant in the room, so to speak—was Mark's dating Dr. Anna King. How serious was that? How foolish would Kelly feel if she told Mark how she felt, only to have him say that he had feelings for Anna.

Maybe Kelly did need to make this a two-way street, but what if she discovered that she'd missed a directional sign and was on her way to a head-on collision?

4

CARS, PICKUPS, AND SUVS LINED BOTH SIDES OF THE STREET in front of the Purvis house, a number of them Drayton Police Department vehicles. Mark saw uniformed members of the police department, a strip of black tape across their badges, interspersed with the others moving in and out of the front door of the little house.

The door bore a navy and maroon wreath, and was opened by a middle-aged woman with casually styled blonde hair. She gestured with an arm loaded with bracelets, their jangling a discordant accompaniment to her husky voice. "Hi, I'm Shirley McCoy, Clara's neighbor. She's in the living room."

Mark moved through the crowd and found the widow seated on a sofa next to a younger version of Ed Purvis. Mrs. Purvis wore a simple black dress, with no jewelry except a plain gold wedding ring. The young man beside her appeared to be in his late teens. When Mark looked at him closely, it was easy to see the resemblance to Ed Purvis. He wore faded jeans and a dark blue tee shirt imprinted with the insignia of the Grateful Dead. Although this was probably young Purvis's idea of somber clothing, the graphics made Mark wince.

Mark hung back until the clot of people around the widow moved away, then eased forward, extended his hand, and said, "Mrs. Purvis, I'm Dr. Mark Baker. We met briefly in the OR waiting room after your husband...when he was shot. I want you to know that I owe my life to him, and I'm so sorry that Dr. King and I weren't able to save him."

Mrs. Purvis dabbed at her eyes with a sodden facial tissue. "Thank you." She cast her eyes down, obviously ready to end the conversation.

Mark turned to the son, but before he could speak, the young man glared at him, then leaned in and put his hand on his mother's shoulder, murmuring something Mark couldn't decipher. Apparently there was nothing to be gained by prolonging the conversation. Besides, a new group of people was forming up behind Mark to pay their respects.

At the door, Mark squeezed by a police officer, an older man who, in addition to a taped badge, wore a double row of medals on his dark shirt and four neatly spaced stars on his collar. "Chief Green," Mark mumbled as he passed the man and edged on out the door. He'd met the chief once before, when a critically wounded police officer had been brought into the ER. Today the chief showed no sign that he remembered meeting Mark. Understandable. Chief Green met so many people, why should he recall one ER doctor?

As he neared his home, Mark was deep in thought, wondering if he should call Kelly or wait for her to contact him. He was startled when a dark-colored vehicle sped through a stop sign on his left, heading directly for his car. Mark jammed on the brake, turned the steering wheel hard to the right, and barely managed to avoid a collision. The speeding vehicle skidded around a corner and disappeared before Mark could focus on it. He'd been intent on avoiding a T-bone crash that would have put the front of the other vehicle into his lap. He wasn't even certain if it was a car, an SUV, or a pickup. And as for getting a license number, forget it.

Mark pulled over and stopped his car. He'd wait until his heart quit racing before moving forward. In normal circumstances, he might have figured he'd simply had a close call avoiding an accident with a driver who wasn't paying attention. But Jackson's warning came back to him all too clearly: "These people have a strange concept of revenge... You might want to be extra careful." He had supposed that meant that he'd have to be more aware of his circumstances in the future. But if this was what he had to look forward to...

Before he could start his car rolling again, his cell phone rang. Kelly was calling.

"Mark," she said. "I need to tell you something. Can we get together this afternoon?"

"Sure," he said. "When and where?"

They arranged a place and time, then Mark put his car into gear and drove away. Perhaps this call from Kelly was a sign. Maybe it was time for him to let her know the feelings that overwhelmed him when they were held at gunpoint.

Outside the abandoned warehouse on the outskirts of Drayton, a single vehicle rumbled down the crumbling macadam road. It was an older pickup with two men perched on the side panels in the back. From time to time, the truck would stop, one of the men would jump down, inspect what was piled at curbside, and hand a bit of salvage up to the man in the pickup bed where a table, two chairs, and an empty filing cabinet were already stowed. Then the vehicle moved on.

The action was repeated every half hour or so by a different vehicle carrying different men, but always with the same purpose. This was a typical Sunday afternoon activity in this neighborhood, and no one seemed to pay any attention to it. Likewise, the two pickups sitting in the otherwise empty parking lot at the side of the warehouse stirred no suspicions. One appeared to have been repainted by hand, dark blue except where red paint showed in a spot or two the brush had missed. The other pickup was a dirty white, had a cracked windshield, and tires that were almost bald. Its left rear fender had been painted with gray primer.

Inside the empty warehouse five men squatted in a far corner, smoking and conversing in low tones. A sixth man, armed with an assault rifle, stood near the door. Illumination was provided by rays of sunlight passing through several broken skylights, with a lesser amount filtering through the dirt and grime covering the intact ones. The men spoke in English, although there were sometimes pauses as they translated words and phrases in their heads.

"I have been able to confirm that Hector died in the emergency room. Nacho was shot by a policeman and is also dead."

The speaker was the oldest of the men, probably early fifties. Whereas the men to whom he spoke were dressed in dirty, wrinkled jeans and tee shirts, his clean khaki pants and shirt had sharply pressed creases. His engineer boots were shined. He was clean-shaven. His dark hair, although longer than current styles dictated, was clean and neatly combed.

"So what do we do now?"

"We do what *El Jefe* has told me to do, what the Zetas always do." The leader's voice dropped to a near whisper.

"We show everyone that we are in charge. And to do that, we kill the people responsible for the deaths of our brothers."

"I heard that the policeman who shot Hector was also killed in the same gun battle," said another man. "Maybe Hector was already dead when his brother brought him to the emergency room?"

One of the younger men piped up. "Perhaps. But then again, perhaps the doctor didn't want to put too much effort into saving the life of one of our people."

"The policeman who shot Nacho is already dead. Where are we to exact our revenge?"

"We will take the lives of everyone who was in that room with Nacho," the leader answered. "We start with the doctor and nurse."

"Do we have the names?"

The leader shook his head. "We don't know yet, but I expect to hear more soon from our source in the hospital where this took place."

"And when we find out—?"

The leader put his hand in front of him and slowly closed it into a tight fist. "We snuff out the lives of everyone involved."

"So we kill them all?" another man asked.

The leader grinned, but there was no mirth in it. "*Sí*."

Kelly looked at the clock in her kitchen. Mark had said he'd come to her house about half past two that afternoon, and it was already two forty. Had he changed his mind? Last night it seemed the most natural thing in the world for the two of them to fall into each other's arms for mutual support as they recovered from being held at gunpoint. Maybe he'd decided that he wasn't ready to talk again.

Tracy had been right, of course. Mark deserved to know about Kelly's feelings for him. But was this the right time to bring that up? Last night there'd been a couple of occasions when it seemed that Mark was also on the verge of saying something important, but each time he lapsed into silence, then changed the subject. She wondered if perhaps he'd made the same discovery she did—that losing her would leave a hole in his life he couldn't contemplate.

Kelly started to walk into the living room, turned around twice before going to the refrigerator, opened the door, then couldn't recall why she'd done it. She looked at her watch. two fifty—Mark was already twenty minutes late. She wondered—

The ringing of her doorbell interrupted Kelly's thoughts. She hurried to the front door, where, through the peephole, she saw Mark standing on the porch. He held a small white paper sack in one hand, two cans of Diet Dr. Pepper in the other. She opened the door, and he handed the sack and one soft drink to her.

"Sorry to be a little late. I remembered that Kroger's deli usually bakes cookies about this time each afternoon, and thought you might like some." He held out the sack like an offering. "They're still warm. Chocolate chip, your favorite."

"Thanks, Mark," she said, struggling to keep her tone light. "You always know the right thing to do."

They gravitated to the sofa and sat side by side. "I'm not so sure about always knowing the right thing," Mark said. He popped open his soft drink and took a long swallow. "I've been thinking about what I did last night."

Kelly frowned. "You're still upset because Sergeant Purvis was killed aren't you? It wasn't your fault. He—"

Mark stopped her with an upraised hand. "That's not it. The more I think about what happened, the more I realize that setting things up the way I did and hoping Ed would come to our rescue was about all I could do."

"And you handled it well," Kelly said. "I knew that if the gunman discovered that the wounded man was already dead, he'd go on a rampage and kill us all. That's why I yelled that the patient might be going into cardiac arrest. And you picked up on it immediately. You did exactly the right thing."

"That's... that's not really true," Mark said. He reached toward the sack of cookies on the coffee table in front of them, then pulled back his hand. "Yes, I picked up on what you started, and it turned out to be the only way we could stay alive until Ed took out the gunman. But that wasn't my immediate reaction."

Kelly paused, her hand halfway to her mouth with her can of soda. Was this going to be the time when Mark said he discovered he couldn't live without her? Did their near-death experience make it clear to him that he was in love with her? "Go on."

He half-turned, looking toward the blank wall to his right. "My initial thought wasn't about saving everyone else." He kept his gaze averted. "My initial thought was about my getting out of there... even if I left everyone else behind to die."

It was two-thirty in the afternoon when Tracy Orton closed her locker, gave one final look in the full-length mirror on the door, and walked into the operating room of Memorial Hospital. The first person she saw was the charge nurse for the day shift. "Want to give your report?"

"Sure," Barbara Scott said. "Pretty quiet, even for a Sunday. We had a couple of emergency cases earlier today, but they're finished. I haven't heard of anything brewing, but you never know."

"Well, I understand there was some excitement last night. Sorry I was off and missed it."

"I heard about it from the nurse who scrubbed on the case. About ten last night the ER called and said Dr. Baker was coming up with a policeman who'd been shot. Sandy and Candace were still here, so they set up." It took Barbara five more minutes to relate the story, and when she finished, she looked at the clock and said, "I guess it's all yours now." And with that, she disappeared into the locker room.

The three to eleven shift on Sunday could be an absolutely dead time, since there was no elective surgery scheduled, or the people working it might be kept hopping for eight straight hours or more with emergencies. Tracy preferred a mix—maybe a couple of appendectomies, a compound fracture or two—just enough activity to keep her busy, but not so much that she went home exhausted.

"Ready for this?" Carl Ortiz, the new surgical tech, flashed her a smile. Like Tracy, he was dressed in scrubs, with rubber clogs on his feet.

"Hope it's quiet," she said, adjusting the head cover she'd wear for the next eight hours.

"I understand there was some excitement here last night." Carl leaned against a doorframe, apparently ready to talk before getting down to the boring task of stocking the rooms for Monday morning's cases.

"Barbara told me it happened about ten o'clock."

"Tell me about it. What was it, who did the surgery, how did it come out?"

When Tracy finished her recitation, Carl shook his head. "Sorry they couldn't save him." He looked at the clock. "Well, time to get to work. Let's hope it's a quiet evening." He hesitated. "Oh, I forgot something in my locker. I'll be right back."

A moment later, when Tracy walked by the door to the men's locker room, she was certain she heard Carl's voice. She grinned. *Forgot something. Yeah, right.* He was making a phone call and didn't want her to hear it. It was probably his girlfriend. Tracy turned back to the list of supplies she needed to round up.

The words of Mark's confession were out, but they seemed to hang in the air and echo in his head. *My initial thought wasn't about saving everyone else.... My initial thought was about my getting out of there... even if I left everyone else behind to die.*

He started to say something more, but Kelly held up her hand. *You can sort out your emotions later. Right now, focus on saying the right things.* "Mark, in the heat of the moment, there's no telling what we'll say or do. So you were thinking of yourself. So what? What you ended up doing took courage. You bluffed that gunman, maneuvered him into position for Sergeant Purvis to break in and shoot him." She leaned closer to him. "You saved my life, you saved Bob's life... you saved your own life. It wasn't a matter of what you thought. It was all about what you did."

Mark shook his head. "Nice try, but I can't get over the fact that my first thought was self-preservation." He turned his gaze away from her. "At one time, I considered myself a religious person. I was taught that we're always supposed to think of others, put them before us. But apparently, when the chips are down I still think of myself first."

"Mark, listen to me," Kelly said. "You're not the first person to ever do something like this when faced with possible death."

"Maybe. But all I can think about are the stories I've heard about people putting themselves at risk to save others."

"Those were the end results, not what the people were first thinking." Kelly put one hand on Mark's shoulder. "Listen, I know you're not much on the Bible, and I guess that's a conversation for another day. But I can think of a story in there of a man who betrayed God himself, yet became one of the most revered saints in history."

"I know. You're talking about Peter's denial of Jesus. But that was thousands of years ago," Mark said, without looking up. "I'm talking about me. I didn't measure up when the chips were down."

"None of us do," Kelly said. "We all fall short."

Mark rose. "Thanks for trying, Kelly. But right now, I don't feel very good about myself. I've got a lot of thinking to do—about myself, about my relationship with others...even where I stand with God. Until I get a lot of that sorted out, I don't think I'm ready to be in a relationship with anyone."

Kelly started to speak, but Mark stopped her with an upraised hand. "I don't think we should go on dating...at least, for now." He kissed her on the cheek. "I hope you understand."

With that, he turned and hurried out the front door, leaving Kelly blinking away the tears forming in her eyes.

5

As Mark approached his house, he saw a black-and-white SUV parked at the curb in front. Even before he could read the wording on the rear, Mark identified it as a police vehicle from the light bar atop the cab. He pulled his Camry in behind the SUV and waited. Two uniformed officers emerged and approached his car, moving away from each other as they came near. The officer headed for Mark had his right hand on the butt of his service revolver. The other policeman veered toward the passenger side of Mark's car, his hand hovering near his holster.

Mark placed his hands atop the steering wheel and waited. The policeman stopped several steps away and called through the open driver's side window, "Are you Mark Baker?"

"Yes, I'm Dr. Baker. How can I help you?"

"Please step out of the car, doctor. Keep your hands where I can see them."

Mark complied. He noticed that the second policeman edged toward the front of the car, keeping the engine block as a shield between Mark and him. Both policemen had the retaining snaps of their holsters undone, although the guns remained undrawn. "May I ask what this is about?" Mark asked.

"Yes, sir, but first, if you don't mind, I'd like to see some ID. If it's in your wallet, please reach for it slowly and bring it out with two fingers."

Mark did.

"Now remove the driver's license and hand it to me."

Mark complied. "I can assure you that I'm Dr. Mark Baker, if that's who you're looking for. The question remains, why?"

"If you don't mind, sir, let me ask: are you carrying a weapon?"

"No, but feel free to check." Mark had seen enough TV programs to know what position to assume, and he did.

After a brief, impersonal, but reasonably thorough pat down, the first policeman handed him back his driver's license. "You can relax, sir. Sorry for the inconvenience, but you'll see in a moment why we're being cautious with everyone we approach about this case." He moved closer. "Would you like to talk inside your house or perhaps sit in our vehicle?"

Mark stowed his license in his wallet, which he returned to his hip pocket. "I think, until I know what this is about, I'm fine to stand right here, in full view of the neighbors, one of whom is probably already looking through her window at this little scene." Mark glanced to his left, and sure enough, there was an asymmetric tenting of the blinds in the front window of Mrs. Gordon's house. Good. If anything went down, she'd be a reliable witness.

The first policeman pulled a notebook from his hip pocket, flipped a couple of pages, and studied what was written there. Then he looked at Mark. "Doctor, are you acquainted with Dr. Buddy Cane?"

"Yes. Dr. Cane and I work at the same hospital, although I don't do surgery, so we don't work together. He's an anesthesiologist, and I—"

"How well do you know him? Do you see him and his wife socially?"

"Not really. Dr. Cane and I went to the same med school, so I knew him there. It was nice to find him on staff at Memorial Hospital when I came here, but we don't see each other outside the hospital environment."

The policeman looked back down at his notebook. "Can you account for your whereabouts for the past six hours?"

Mark looked at his watch: five fifty in the afternoon. "I was up late last night—"

"Just tell us where you were from before noon today to now."

"I was awakened this morning by a phone call from a Detective...Jack something...Jackson. Detective Jackson. I guess if you want to know what he told me—"

"That's okay. We'll check with him. What about after that?"

"After that, I had some coffee, ate breakfast, dressed. A little before noon, I went to Sergeant Purvis's home to pay my respects."

"Can anyone corroborate that?"

Mark remembered the glare Purvis's son directed toward him. "Well, Mrs. Purvis and her son should remember me." He thought a bit. "And maybe the Drayton Chief of Police. We passed each other as I left the house."

If the policeman was surprised, he didn't show it. "And after that?"

"I drove around for a while."

"Doing what?"

"Just thinking. Finally, I stopped for some cookies and took them with me when I went to visit a friend." He thought a bit. "If you'll let me reach into my pocket, I have the receipt for the cookies. I'm sure it has a time-stamp."

The policeman nodded, and while Mark rummaged in his pocket, the officer said, "We'll need the name and contact information for the friend." He looked at his partner, who pulled a notebook of his own from his pocket and clicked a ballpoint pen open.

Mark showed them the receipt, then gave the second patrolman Kelly's name and phone number. "What's this about?" Mark asked again.

"We're investigating the death of Dr. Cane. He was mowing his lawn this afternoon when someone shot him."

Mark felt his stomach in free fall and fought against the bile edging into his throat, knowing that the cookie on which he'd nibbled would be next.

Patrolman number two edged up next to his partner before speaking for the first time. "Do you have a gun, either pistol or rifle, doctor?"

"No." Mark was sweating, and it wasn't just the Texas summer heat.

"Would you mind if we search your vehicle and your house to verify that?" The second policeman's eyes were fixed on Mark, apparently observing his every expression. "We can get a search warrant if we need to."

Mark shook his head. "That won't be necessary." He held out his key ring. "I have nothing to hide."

He hoped that was true. He knew he hadn't shot Buddy. What worried him was whether his life was in danger now. Because he thought he knew who killed Buddy... and why.

Kelly read the caller ID and almost didn't answer the call. The truth was that Mark had hurt her deeply last night. She wanted to stand beside him, talk with him, help him through this period of doubt and searching. Instead, he'd pushed her away.

After three rings, Kelly decided she was being childish. Maybe Mark had a change of heart. Maybe he needed her. She pushed the button to answer the call. "I'm surprised to hear from you," she said in as neutral a voice as she could manage.

"I know. But this call is important. I thought you should know this so you can take precautions."

At the word, *precautions* Kelly's first thought was that she'd been exposed to some disease or other. Infectious diseases were always present in ER patients, but her mind went straight to the big one. Although she'd put on gloves as soon as she got the gunshot victim into the trauma room, she still had some blood exposure. Had he been found to be HIV positive?

"Yes?"

"There's no easy way to say this." Mark paused. "Buddy Cane is dead," he said in a matter-of-fact voice.

"That's terrible," Kelly said, immediately relieved that the news didn't mean she'd been exposed to some disease, yet guilty that her first thought had been of herself. Maybe she should share that with Mark—let him know that he wasn't alone in having such thoughts.

"It's more than terrible. It means that you and I and some other people are in danger. I think the Zetas shot Buddy. I think they're out to execute everyone who was involved in treating the Garcia brothers."

"Who?"

It took Mark a few minutes to explain to Kelly the identity of the two men at the center of the drama in the ER only a few hours ago. "And, according to the detective who called me this morning, the Zeta's idea of revenge is to go after everyone involved—sometimes even the families."

"I don't see how Buddy figures in this. I'd imagine that we might be in danger, but not the people in the OR who tried to save the policeman."

"Maybe they're going about it backward, getting the people in the OR first," Mark said. "But I think you should be cautious."

Kelly noticed she was holding the phone so tightly her knuckles were white. She switched it to her other hand. "So, do we get police protection?"

"I don't know," Mark said. "I didn't go into that when I talked with Detective Jackson this morning. I have his number, though. I'll check with him and call you back. In the meantime, keep your doors locked."

After she hung up, Kelly paced back and forth in her bedroom, occasionally walking to the front of the house and peering between the slats of the blinds. She knew she couldn't stay in her house forever. They were expecting her in the ER in—she looked at her watch—in less than twenty-four hours.

Maybe she should get a gun, learn how to use it, carry it to protect herself. She shook her head, as though to dislodge the idea. No, she knew she'd never do that. She'd often told others glibly that God protected her. But right now her faith had never felt so weak.

———

Mark paused with his cell phone in his hand. He needed to call Detective Jackson to see if this killing would change the plans of the police. Would they now protect everyone who'd been active in the shoot-out with the Zetas last night? Did the police have any evidence that Buddy's murder was a part of the Zeta's revenge? If the cartel appeared to be going after the OR staff first, Mark needed to warn Anna King. What about the scrub nurse—and the circulating nurse? There were too many variables, and Mark's head hurt trying to decide what he should do first.

While Mark was still pondering, the phone in his hand rang. He checked the caller ID: Anonymous Caller. Could it be a reporter? Maybe one of the cartel, calling to tell him his days were numbered? No, he'd better answer. It was better than missing the call and worrying later about who had tried to reach him. "Dr. Baker."

"Doctor, this is Detective Jackson. We spoke earlier today."

"Yes. I was just about to call you with more questions."

"Well, I have one or two of my own," the detective said. "I'd like to ask them face-to-face, though. Are you at home?"

Mark wondered what the detective wanted to say that couldn't be said on the phone? Was he coming with reinforcements to arrest Mark? *Should I call an attorney?* Mark remembered Kelly laughing at him once when inadvertently running a red light had him looking in his rearview mirror for hours.

"The Bible says, 'The wicked flee when no man pursueth,'" she told him.

Well, in this case, his conscience was clear...or, at least, should be. Why would he fear a visit from the detective?

"Sure, I'm home," Mark said. "Come on over."

⁂

Mark had almost given up on Jackson showing when he heard the doorbell. He punched the remote to turn off the television and was surprised to find he had no particular memory of the program he'd been watching for almost an hour. As he moved to the front door, Mark decided that golf on TV on a late Sunday afternoon was nothing more than an invitation to nap in front of the set.

Mark checked the peephole and saw Jackson on the step. Detective T. R. Jackson was about six inches shorter than Mark's own six feet plus, but he probably packed two hundred fifty pounds into that frame, enough of it muscle to make him a formidable opponent in a scuffle. His tie was at half-mast, and the wrinkles in his shirt were evidence of a long day in the Texas heat. Mark was surprised to see the detective without a coat, and even more startled by the absence of a shoulder holster and pistol. Weren't detectives supposed to carry a weapon, even when off duty?

"Come in," Mark said. He gestured toward the living room. "Can I get you something? Water? A soft drink?"

Jackson shook his head. "No, I'm fine."

When they were seated, Mark asked, "Where's your partner? I thought detectives always did interviews in pairs."

"I imagine Addison is home by now." He leaned forward. "As you may have guessed, this isn't an official interview. It's more...sort of an unofficial inquiry. A favor for a friend, you might say."

The detective crossed his legs, and Mark realized that his earlier assessment was wrong. Jackson was armed. A snub-nose pistol sat in an ankle holster on his right leg.

If Jackson saw Mark's gaze stray to the gun, he didn't react. Maybe he was used to people's eyes gravitating to his gun. Still, for some reason knowing his visitor was carrying a pistol made Mark a bit uncomfortable, despite his having nothing to feel guilty about.

"You said you had some questions. Why don't we see if I can answer them for you?"

Jackson crossed his legs the other way, and the ankle holster disappeared under the leg of his wrinkled pants. "Okay, let's start with this one. How drunk was Dr. Anna King when she operated on Ed Purvis?"

6

"How drunk was Dr. Anna King when she operated on Ed Purvis?"

The words hung in the air while Mark scrambled for a response. During his premed days, he'd played a bit of poker and been pretty successful. He hoped the neutral expression he pasted on his face would work as well now as it had when he was bluffing with only a pair of fives in his hand. "I'm not sure I know what you mean," he said.

Jackson jiggled his free foot. "Look, let's not dance around this. I interviewed quite a few staff members the night of the shooting, and it was pretty evident that Dr. King has had an alcohol problem in the past. Matter of fact, the consensus seems to be that's what broke up her marriage."

"I'm not—"

Jackson brought both feet down flat on the floor and leaned forward until he was eye-to-eye with Mark. "I read the divorce proceedings, doctor. You might think they were sealed because of the little girl involved, but this is part of a criminal investigation. I even got a clerk out on Sunday to get me the records. It's a proven fact that Dr. King had a history of alcoholism. That's why her husband got full custody of Hannah." He leaned back slightly. "Let me put it another way. Was King drunk when she operated on Ed Purvis?"

Then it began to make sense to Mark. "Unofficial inquiry... favor for a friend." This was a man who had known Ed Purvis, probably knew the whole family, and now he was looking into the circumstances of his friend's death. Maybe he was only doing it as a friend, but he was still a police officer. Mark realized that, although there was no doubt about who shot Purvis, another question remained unanswered: Did the doctors do everything they could to save him? The word that jumped unbidden into Mark's mind made him shiver inside: *malpractice.*

Even though he wanted to be cautious, Mark decided there was no sense lying. Sure, he'd gone out with Anna a few times, but it had never been serious. He remembered Mark Twain's admonition: "If you tell the truth, you don't have to remember what you said."

"I'm waiting for an answer," Jackson said.

"I honestly can't say if she'd been drinking," Mark replied. "I knew about Anna's history, of course. And when she was the surgeon who showed up in response to our call for help, I'll admit I was worried. But she and I were both wearing masks. There were the usual smells of the operating room that would have overpowered any alcohol on her breath. I can't criticize anything she did during the surgery. So if she'd been drinking—and I said *if*—it didn't seem to affect her surgical judgment or ability."

"And you'd swear to that, if it came to it?"

"Why would it?" Mark blurted out.

Jackson shook his head. "You never know." He rose slowly, shook his pants legs to settle the cuffs and make sure his ankle holster was hidden, and said, "No need to show me out. Thank you for your time."

Despite Jackson's words, Mark followed him to the door, mainly to make certain it was double-locked after the detective left. Then he wandered back into the living room, sank onto the sofa, and tried to convince himself nothing was going to come of this. Much as he'd like to believe that, the truth of the matter was that Mark was in it up to his neck. After all, he'd been the other doctor scrubbed in on the operation. If the Purvis family decided to bring some sort of malpractice suit, there was no doubt he'd be involved in the case in some way, either as a defendant or a witness.

He turned on the TV, but after fifteen minutes he snapped off the set, deciding that his life had a lot more drama in it than any soap opera the networks could put together.

Kelly turned down the burner under the soup she was heating before she pulled her ringing cell phone from the pocket of her jeans. Mark was calling again. "Yes?"

"I promise this will be my last call to you this evening, but I wanted to make sure you were safe."

Did he think she'd gone out jogging? Maybe shopping or at a movie? Ever since Mark had told her about the possible revenge sought by the Zetas, she'd been in her house, all the doors and windows locked, the blinds closed. Kelly took a deep breath and tried to make her voice calm, despite the emotions seething inside her. "I'm fine. I'm sure I'll be a bit twitchy when I drive to work tomorrow, but I'll be okay." She stirred the soup and turned off the heat. "Did you find out anything more about police protection for those of us involved in the incident in the ER last night?"

The silence on the line lasted a few seconds too long. Had he forgotten? Surely not. That wasn't the Mark she knew. If anything, he was obsessive about never forgetting anything. She'd heard him say, on more than one occasion, "A doctor can't make mistakes and can't forget. That's why it's so stressful."

Finally he said, "I'm afraid I don't know. I talked with the lead detective on the case, but he had some questions for me, and by the time I remembered what I wanted to ask him, he was gone."

Kelly felt the same sensation in the pit of her stomach that she experienced on a glass elevator during rapid descent. Although her air conditioner was working perfectly, she felt drops of sweat crawl downward between her shoulder blades. "So you don't know if the police are going to watch our backs? We're on our own?" She made no attempt to hide the bitterness behind her words.

"I'll check with him in the morning. But for now, I guess you're right. We have to be extra careful."

"Yes, you might say that," Kelly said, her words dripping with sarcasm.

"Look, I'm working the same shift as you tomorrow. Why don't I come by and pick you up?"

"What good would that do? That would be perfect for the Zetas if they wanted to hit us. Can you imagine? Both of us in one vehicle, so that however they wanted to do it—a well-placed firebomb, a crash with a stolen truck, a few rounds into the windows of the car—we'd be gone." She moved to the kitchen table and dropped into a chair. "No, I appreciate the offer, but no thanks."

"How does this sound? I've been thinking about it anyway. Why don't I go out tomorrow morning and buy a handgun? If I keep it in my car I won't need a carry permit. Until the danger is past, ride with me and I can protect us both."

And won't that be nice? First, the man she thought she'd fallen in love with tells her he can't date her right now. Then, in just a few hours, he offers to be her gun-toting protector. Not that being together that much would be awkward or anything. Oh, no.

Kelly discarded several responses before framing her reply. Then she had to unclench her teeth to speak. "I don't think so, Mark. But thank you."

After she ended the call, she sat with her head in her hands, her meager supper forgotten. *God, I have no idea where I'm going. Can you help me out here?*

<hr>

Mark didn't sleep well Sunday night. He awoke frequently from whatever light slumber he managed, startled by every noise, both real and imagined. Finally, he rolled out of bed at daybreak on Monday and padded to the kitchen. He turned on the coffeemaker, certain that he'd need it to get through the day.

At seven, a bit more awake after a shower and a cup of coffee, Mark sent a text message to Eric, thanking him for stepping in to finish his shift Saturday night and work for him Sunday, but saying that he'd take his normal shift today. If Mark stayed around the house with nothing to do, he would almost certainly go crazy. Sure, it was dangerous to drive to the hospital, but he'd take his chances against the Zetas. Anything was better than cowering in a darkened room, waiting for something that might or might not be coming.

Mark poured another cup of coffee, toasted an English muffin, and retrieved the morning paper from his front steps. He'd been intending to cancel his subscription for months, but had never gotten around to it. Now he was glad he hadn't.

The shooting in the Memorial Hospital ER had already been pushed off the front page by a crisis somewhere else in the world. Mark rarely paid attention to these. Instead, he turned to page 3, where a follow-up story confirmed that the police believed the men involved in the shooting were members of a drug cartel. According to the paper, the police were "following up several promising leads." In other words, they were working the case, but had nothing solid yet.

The obituary for Ed Purvis said arrangements were still pending. Mark remained undecided about whether or not he'd attend a memorial service. The response he'd received from Purvis's son when he visited yesterday had been somewhere between cool and angry, but Mark understood. He recalled how he'd felt when people came to pay their respects following his brother's death. Undoubtedly they were trying to be helpful, but some people just wanted to be left alone with their grief. He guessed that was the way Purvis's son felt.

Mark swept the crumbs from the table into his palm and threw them into the sink, then loaded his dishes into the dishwasher. He had at least six hours before he needed to leave for the hospital. Meanwhile, there were several calls he should make.

His first call was to the detective bureau, using the number on Jackson's card. Whoever answered said Jackson was due to be in court all day. Would Mark like to speak to his partner, Detective Ames?

Jackson had put his cell number on the back of the card he'd given Mark, but if he was in court there was no need to call him there. Might as well try Ames, who'd seemed like a reasonable person. Maybe he could help. "Yes, please."

Mark held for what seemed like forever until the voice came back on the line to say that Ames wasn't in yet. "Is there a message?"

"Please ask him to call Dr. Mark Baker." Mark added his cell number and an emphasis that the matter was urgent.

The voice on the other end of the call was polite enough, but Mark figured he wouldn't receive an immediate return call. Meantime, he had other things to do.

Next he phoned Dr. Anna King. He needed to tell her about Jackson's visit and its implications...for both of them. Contrary to what some people might think, Mark knew that surgeons don't spend all their time at the hospital. In fact, they spend more time in their office, seeing post-op follow-ups, pre-op evaluations, and consultations than they do in the operating room. So he played the odds and called Anna's office first.

The secretary who answered gave Mark both good news and bad. Dr. King was in the office this morning, but she was tied up with a patient at that moment. Could she call him back? Mark left his number and moved on to the next call on his list.

"MSI, how may I help you?"

MSI stood for Medical Specialists, Incorporated, and Mark wondered how a receptionist who must answer a hundred calls a day about medical malpractice could sound so chipper. Maybe the words didn't even mean anything to her anymore. Maybe they issued directly from her lips without any input from the cerebral cortex. He'd have to think about that some more. "This is Dr. Mark Baker, in Drayton,

Texas. I need to speak with one of your representatives about a potential claim against me."

"I presume you're insured with us," the receptionist said.

"You carry the insurance for our group. It's Emergency Physicians LLC. Dr. Eric McCray is the CEO."

Mark waited through three minutes of what probably passed for light rock before he heard a cheerful voice. "This is Buddy Blankenship. How can I help you, doctor?"

"I need to advise you of a situation that might turn into a malpractice claim. I don't think there's anything to it—" *Isn't that what all of us say when we first become aware we might be the subject of a suit?* "But I've been told many times to let you all know as soon as I become aware of a potential malpractice suit."

"That's the best thing to do," Blankenship said. "Tell me about it."

Mark did, trying to be as objective as possible in his recounting of an episode that still brought cold chills to him. When he'd finished, Blankenship said, "So all you have is a feeling that this Detective Jackson, acting on behalf of the family, is sniffing around to see if you did everything right to save the policeman's life?"

"Right. And I know I'm probably jumping at shadows—"

"Not necessarily. I've seen suits threatened or even brought in similar situations. And if what you tell me is true about Dr. King, she might be the principal person in such a suit."

"But just because she has a history of drinking—"

"That will be up to a judge and jury, of course." Mark heard a faint thud. "Sorry, had a sip of coffee and put the cup down too firmly," Blankenship said. "Have you told your group's CEO of this?"

"Not yet, but I will. All this is coming pretty fast."

"Okay. After you talk with him, I'd advise you not to say anything further about the threat of a suit. Simply leave it with me, and call if anyone else contacts you about the situation."

Mark hung up, hoping he'd done the right thing. Somehow, he felt he was being disloyal to Anna.

His main job now was to stay safe until the police put an end to the potential threat from the Zetas. And, if she'd let him, he'd do his best to protect Kelly as well.

The more he thought about it, the more convinced he was that he'd done everything he could to save the life of Ed Purvis. So far as he could tell, so had Anna King. He ought to let Eric McCray know about this. After that he'd follow Blankenship's advice and not talk to—

The ring of his phone interrupted his thoughts. When he saw the caller ID, Mark thought, "Oh, no." He'd forgotten that he'd called Anna. And now she was calling back.

Mark stood with his phone in his hand. His malpractice insurance representative had just warned him against talking about the possible claim to anyone. Did that include Anna? After all, she was the primary surgeon in the case. Besides, she was more than a colleague. She was a woman he'd dated. True, working with Anna in surgery the other night had shown him a side of her that wasn't as appealing as what he'd encountered on their dates, but maybe all surgeons behaved that way.

He squared his shoulders and answered the call. "Anna, thanks for getting back to me."

"Sorry I couldn't turn loose when you called. What's up?"

"Two things, I guess. I had a phone call from the detective working the shooting in the ER, telling me that the men who died were members of the Zeta drug cartel."

"Wow. I didn't know they had gotten this far north into Texas."

"Apparently they have," Mark said. "And the detective tells me they're pretty fanatical about revenge. Their usual reaction is to kill everyone involved. I guess that means you might be in danger, since you operated on the policeman who actually killed the gunman."

"That's silly. Why would they go after the surgical team?"

"I wasn't convinced either, until I heard that Buddy Cane was shot to death yesterday."

The silence on the other end of the line lasted long enough for Mark to wonder if he'd lost the connection. When Anna responded, there was a catch in her voice. "I heard that. Poor Buddy."

Mark took a deep breath. "You won't like the other bit of news any better. I got a personal visit from Detective Jackson to ask me if you'd been drinking when you operated on Sergeant Purvis."

Anna's voice cooled several degrees. "And what did you tell him?"

"I told him the truth—that I couldn't smell alcohol on your breath, and that you didn't talk or act as though you were impaired."

"Thanks," Anna said. "Matter of fact, I was stone-cold sober, and I can prove it."

"How?"

A woman's voice sounded in the background. "Look, I've got to get back to work. Why don't we have dinner together and I'll explain?"

"I've got the three to eleven shift in the ER tonight," Mark said.

"Okay, let's do this. It's a little before eleven A.M. now. Why don't you meet me for lunch about half past twelve?"

Although Saturday night's interaction with her had already made Mark decide not to pursue his social relationship with Anna, and he'd been warned only minutes ago not to discuss the possible malpractice suit with anyone, he didn't see a good way to turn down the offer. After all, what she had to say might be important. "I guess I can do that."

"Meet me at Bella's. I'll have my secretary call and ask them to put us in the back room so we can have some privacy."

He would have preferred something much more public, but he didn't think Anna would bend easily. She was showing more of the personality Mark had seen at the operating table, but never before in a social setting. He decided not to fight it. "Sure. See you then."

After he hung up, Mark stood there with the phone in his hand. *What have I gotten myself into now?*

Kelly looked at her watch. Almost noon. If Tracy had worked the three to eleven shift last night, she should be up by now. Since Kelly was going to ask her friend for a favor, she didn't want the conversation to start with Tracy upset by being awakened. But if she waited longer...

Kelly punched in the number, and breathed a sigh of relief when Tracy answered on the first ring, her voice betraying no evidence of sleepiness.

"Tracy, are you working in the OR again today?"

"Right. Three to eleven. Did you want to do something? I'll have to leave for work in a couple of hours, but—"

"No, I'm calling to ask if I can ride with you."

"Sure. Car trouble?"

"No. It's all a part of the shooting in the ER on Saturday night." Kelly wondered how much to tell Tracy, but decided that her best friend deserved to know what was going on and why she was asking this favor. So she told her.

"Of course you can ride with me," Tracy said. "I guess we don't know how long this will last, but that's okay. One day at a time."

"Thanks, Tracy. I hope it won't be long. And if you think I'm putting you in danger, we'll stop. Do you think that's the case?"

"I'm probably in more danger from someone running a stop sign and ramming my car than I am from a stray bullet aimed at you. Besides, that's what friends are for."

"Just let me know what time you want to come by," Kelly said.

"Why don't I pick you up at two?"

"I'll be ready."

"And when we leave work, I'll introduce you to Carl—it's really Carlos, but he's trying to adapt. He's the tech who works with me on the evening shift. I'm off tomorrow evening, but maybe Carl can pick you up then."

"Are you certain about that?" Kelly asked.

"No problem," Tracy said. "You'll be safe with him. I haven't known him all that long, but he seems nice."

"How he seems to you doesn't mean a lot to me right now," Kelly said. "I'm worried about someone trying to kill me."

"Don't worry," Tracy replied. "You can depend on Carlos. I'd trust him with my life."

7

MARK'S USUAL LUNCH WAS SOMETHING HE THREW together at home—maybe an apple and a container of yogurt or a couple of slices of leftover pizza. If he went out, Burger King was more his style than Bella's. The exclusive Italian restaurant in downtown Drayton had an extensive menu and a wine list that ran to two pages. Mark wondered if they'd have something light...both on his stomach and his wallet. He hoped his credit card could stand the hit if he ended up with the check. Maybe the cost would be worth it if Anna's news turned out to be important.

When he arrived, Mark discovered that the valet parking attendants he'd seen when he drove by Bella's in the evenings were sort of like vampires—active at night, absent during the day. He found a spot about a block away and left his Toyota Camry at the curb. He didn't know if Bella's required a jacket and tie, but just in case, he wore his blue blazer, a blue-and-red striped tie in the pocket. His shirt was white Oxford cloth with the button-down collar open. His khakis were clean and had a sharp crease. Maybe nobody would notice his Reeboks and athletic socks.

"Dr. Baker. I'm meeting Dr. King," he told the attractive lady behind the lectern right inside the front door.

She gave him a smile that was probably part of the job. "Of course. This way, please." The hostess led him through the restaurant, which was only about half full, and parted the maroon velvet curtains at the rear, gesturing him into a small private dining room. Anna was seated at the only occupied table. The lights were dim, but it didn't prevent Mark from seeing the oil portraits and lovely tapestries on the wall.

Anna didn't rise. "Mark, glad you could make it." She gestured to the chair opposite her at the table for four. "Please, have a seat."

Mark noted that the white linen tablecloth bore two place settings of heavy silverware plus goblets of ice water. Centered in the middle of the table was a basket of bread plus a shallow saucer of oily golden liquid with a swirl of dark brown in the middle.

"The bread is good, especially if you dip it in the olive oil and balsamic vinegar," Anna said. She gestured to the menu, which the hostess had deposited at Mark's place and which lay unopened in front of him. "Order anything you want. I invited you. You're my guest."

Mark tried not to make his sigh of relief too apparent. At that moment, the waiter approached. "May I get you folks something to drink?"

Mark nodded toward Anna, signaling for her to go first. "Just water will be fine."

Score one for Anna's sobriety. "The same for me," Mark said.

"We don't have a lot of time," Anna told the waiter. "I'm ready to order."

She looked at Mark, who nodded and opened his menu. Surely he could find something.

"I'll have a large salad with house dressing on the side," Anna said. "Mark, would you like to split the stuffed mushroom appetizer?"

"Sure. And the salad for me, as well."

When the waiter had gone, Anna said, "I promised you an answer to your question. Actually, there's someone who'll be joining us who'll answer it for you."

She apparently saw Mark's eyes stray to the two sets of silverware. "No, he won't be eating with us. I had to twist his arm to get him to join us for a minute or two."

The curtains behind them rustled. Mark turned and saw a man dressed much as he was, with the exception that the newcomer didn't have a jacket. Either he was more familiar with Bella's dress code, or simply didn't care. Mark suspected by the man's manner that the latter was the case.

The newcomer strode to the table, took the chair between Anna and Mark, and looked at her. "So, I'm here. What can I do for you?"

"Mark, forgive this gentleman's manners. Jack Tanner, this is Dr. Mark Baker." She looked at Tanner. "Mark asked me a question, and I promised him an answer. I think that answer would be more believable coming from you."

Tanner favored Mark with a brisk single nod. "Okay."

Mark frowned. The question he'd asked Anna could be embarrassing. "Are you sure—"

"Yes, Mark," Anna said. "Jack knows all about my problems. That will become clear when he responds."

"Okay." Mark took a deep breath. "Dr. King and I did emergency surgery Saturday night. The patient didn't make it. I was asked yesterday if she had been drinking at the time of the surgery. I posed the question to her, and she said she'd answer. But apparently she thinks it would be better coming from you."

"She wasn't drinking," Tanner said.

"I haven't given you the time frame."

"Doesn't matter. Dr. King is trying to regain partial custody of her daughter from her ex-husband. Part of that effort involves not drinking. She came to me on the advice of her lawyer, wanting to prove that she's staying sober."

Mark raised his eyebrows, but said nothing.

"Dr. King is wearing a SCRAM ankle bracelet. That's 'secure continuous random alcohol monitoring.' I monitor the results. She hasn't had any alcohol for at least the past eight weeks."

Anna turned and extended her left leg to the side so it was visible to Mark. She pulled up the hem of her fashionable black slacks to reveal a wide strap securing a small black box to her ankle. "This is the monitor. I was wearing it Saturday night, the same way I've done every hour of every day for two months." She turned back and let the pants leg fall into position. Then she nodded at Tanner. "Thanks for coming, Jack."

He rose and left without a word.

When they were alone again, Anna said, "I think that should answer the question. Don't you?"

Mark knew that implicit in Anna's statement was another question: "Does that satisfy you, too?"

"Sure," he said.

The waiter served the stuffed mushrooms and the salads, and there was little conversation as they ate. All physicians learn early in their training to eat when it was available, consuming the food rapidly, since they never know when the next opportunity will present itself. But while Mark took in the food, barely tasting it, his thoughts were on the Anna King who'd shown herself here yet again.

Anna consulted her watch. "I have to get back to the office. I've already signed the check, so we're good to go. Ready?"

Mark decided that perhaps the compliant, soft, easy-going woman he'd dated was a façade, a personality she could turn on and off depending on the circumstances. He contrasted that with the Anna he'd seen in the OR on Saturday night and again here today—the take-charge woman. Was this the real Anna King? And if it was, was this the type of person in which he was interested? All the votes weren't in, but for now he thought the answer was "No."

———

Mark thought he'd felt the buzz of his cell phone in his pocket during the meal, but it had come when Jack Tanner was delivering the news about Anna's monitor and he didn't want to interrupt the story by checking his phone. Now he stood outside the restaurant and saw two things: he'd missed a call from an unfamiliar number, and he had one voicemail.

He moved to a bench several steps away from the doorway where he could have some privacy. Mark checked the voicemail and heard, "This is Detective Addison Ames, returning your call. You can reach me at this number. It's my cell." That was it.

When he'd first met the two detectives in the ER, his impression was of an unmatched duo, the short, stocky, somewhat pugnacious Jackson paired with the tall, thin, blonde, easy-going Ames. Well, now he'd see how easy-going Ames was outside the presence of his partner. Mark pushed "redial" and in a minute heard, "Ames."

"Detective, this is Mark Baker. I'm the doctor—"

"I know who you are. How can I help you?"

So that was going to be Ames's style: brisk, to the point, not rude but not social. Okay, so be it. "Your partner contacted me yesterday to say that I and other people involved in the incident Saturday night might be at risk from the Zetas. In view of the shooting of Dr. Cane, I wondered if the police are taking any steps to protect the rest of us until you apprehend the gang members who might be responsible."

Was that a chuckle coming from the phone? Maybe Mark had been wrong about Ames. Sure enough, there was a smile in his voice when he replied, "Doctor, how much do you know about the Zeta drug cartel?"

"Only what I read in the papers and see on TV."

"In Mexico, they're the most powerful force there. Police and military give them a wide berth. The populace live in constant fear of them."

"But that's in Mexico," Mark said.

"Right," Ames replied. "And in Mexico, it's not difficult to find them. On the other hand, here in Texas, almost anyone could be a Zeta. Various law enforcement groups are constantly working to ferret them out, but as for apprehending the gang members who might be gunning for you, as you might put it…"

"I think I see," Mark said. "You're fighting an uphill battle already. I guess you're saying my life and that of my colleagues could be in danger indefinitely."

"Not necessarily indefinitely, but I can't say when it will end. If we can cut off the head of the monster, the tentacles curl up and die. There's one man in this area that is the chief, or *Jefe*, of the local Zetas. Believe me, he's the target of a number of law enforcement agencies, not just the Drayton

Police. We're all working to find and arrest him. Until we do..."

Mark felt his heart sink. "I understand."

"I wish we had enough men to provide security for all of you, but you can see our problem. This isn't our only case. Because of the Zeta aspect of it, I imagine you'll hear from one of the federal agencies fairly soon."

And in the meantime, I'm walking around with a bull's-eye on my back. Mark felt his stomach revolt, threatening to bring up what he'd just consumed. Then he realized that, once more, his first thought had been for his own safety, not Kelly's. What was wrong with him?

———

The shooter wondered how long the police investigation would last, and how intensive the manhunt would be. It had been almost too easy to kill Buddy Cane. And there should be nothing to connect the shooter with the incident. Soon the gun would be safely stowed where no one could possibly find it. Right now it had to be accessible for more killing if it was necessary. No, make that when it was necessary. There was definitely more to do.

Of course, the police would spread a wide net looking for the perpetrator, but the shooter wasn't afraid of discovery. All that remained was to stay calm and do nothing that would arouse the suspicions of the police. Meanwhile, there were other tasks to finalize and carry out.

———

Mark checked his watch and did some quick mental calculations. If he went back home, he'd literally arrive in time to turn around and head for work. On the other hand, if he drove to the hospital now he'd arrive more than an hour before his shift in the ER began. Maybe he could—

His cell phone buzzed. As Mark answered, he started walking toward his car. He could sit inside it, out of the sun and away from the buzz of traffic that had begun to pick up, while he talked.

The caller ID showed Memorial Hospital. Could Eric need something? No, Eric would call on his personal cell phone. Whoever was calling, Mark knew he needed to answer.

"Dr. Baker."

"Doctor, this is Diane, in Dr. Goodrich's office. He would like to know if you can meet with him . . . as soon as possible."

Mark thumbed the remote to open his car and climbed inside. He started the engine and let the air conditioner begin to overcome the effect of the summer sun on the interior of his vehicle, all the while wondering why the hospital administrator would want to see him—and why "as soon as possible"?

"I can be there in fifteen minutes," Mark said. "Any idea what this is about?"

"I'm sorry. He didn't say."

Mark ended the call and headed for the hospital. Well, that answered his question about what to do with the extra time before his shift started.

While he drove, Mark remembered that he hadn't yet notified Eric McCray of the possible malpractice suit. He pulled his cell phone from his pocket and dialed Eric. When his call rolled to voicemail, Mark ended it. *No problem. I'll let him know later.* As he stowed his phone, Mark wondered what Goodrich wanted from him. Oh, well. He'd see soon enough.

Kelly hurried out her front door to the curb, looking all around for suspicious activity. Everything seemed quiet, and she wondered if she wasn't being a bit paranoid.

She climbed into Tracy's little red Hyundai, tossed her purse and backpack into the rear seat alongside her friend's, and buckled her seat belt. "Thanks again for letting me ride with you."

Tracy pulled away from the curb. "Glad to do it. Matter of fact, you may recall that I asked you about doing this several months ago, but you wanted to have your own wheels."

"I know," Kelly said. "Usually I run errands on the way to work—stuff like picking up or dropping off dry cleaning. And I've found a 24-hour grocery where there's almost no one in the store around midnight when I'm on my way home. But with this scare about the Zetas..."

"No problem. And if we need to detour sometime to let you do an errand, I guess we can do that." She changed lanes. "But how long are you going to be looking over your shoulder? Surely the police can do something to neutralize this threat."

"I'm not sure." Kelly said. "Mark called me earlier about this. He talked with one of the detectives and apparently it's not as simple as finding one or two people and putting them behind bars. He offered to drive me, but I don't want a bodyguard or a babysitter." She sighed. "I just want this to be over."

"Speaking of Mark—"

"Before you ask, no, I didn't tell him I was falling in love with him. I was going to, but he beat me to it by saying he was disappointed in himself for thinking about escaping the gunman instead of rescuing everyone else. He wondered if he'd been guilty of making things revolve around him. So, until he gets his head straight, he doesn't think he should date anyone."

Tracy turned her eyes briefly on her friend. "Actually, in the end he took a big chance, put himself at risk, to save you."

"I told him we all fail at times. Even cited Scripture. It's how we do in the end that counts."

Tracy came to a stop sign. She applied the brakes and looked both ways before proceeding. "I heard a great comeback to the argument that people who fail God couldn't ever be used by Him."

"I'd love to hear it. Maybe it will come in handy."

"Let me see if I can get it right." She signaled for a right turn. "Oh, yes. 'If God doesn't use people who've failed, who's left for Him to use?'"

⸻

Mark parked his car in its usual spot and tossed his blazer into the back seat. He had a clean white coat in his locker in the ER. Maybe he'd pick it up and put it on before going to Goodrich's office. Wearing it might help remind the hospital administrator that Mark was a real doctor and Goodrich was not. On a few occasions in the past when the two of them engaged in dialogue, that distinction seemed to have been lost on Allen Goodrich.

Just a few minutes past the fifteen minutes he'd predicted on the phone, Mark arrived in the hospital administration suite. Diane, Goodrich's administrative assistant, looked up, smiled, and said, "Dr. Baker. Thanks for coming in. I'll let Dr. Goodrich know you're here."

It was well known among the staff that Allen Goodrich had flunked out of medical school in his freshman year. He'd gone on to get an MBA, and something—rumor was it was a large donation—prompted his alma mater, a small college in the Midwest, to confer an honorary PhD on Goodrich. Honorary or not, he clung to the title and used it at every opportunity.

Mark took a seat and wondered how long Goodrich would keep him waiting. He was betting on not less than five or more than fifteen minutes. Surprisingly enough, only three minutes later Diane emerged from the inner office and said, "Go right in. He's waiting for you."

Being called to meet with Goodrich wasn't totally unusual. Having to wait less than five minutes to gain entrance to the inner sanctum, on the other hand, was practically unheard of.

"Dr. Baker," Goodrich said. "Have a seat."

Goodrich didn't look like a hospital administrator so much as he resembled a college professor, down to the tweed sport coat with leather elbow patches. He was tall, thin, and wore reading glasses that repeatedly slipped down on his nose, giving rise to a Goodrich imitation that was the life of many staff parties... when the administrator wasn't present.

The man half-rose from behind his desk and nodded his head, making an unruly lock of straw-colored hair bob below his eyebrows for a moment. He didn't extend a hand, but simply pointed to the chair across from him. Mark nodded and sat, but decided to remain silent. Goodrich had called the meeting. Let him start.

"Quite an episode on Saturday night in the ER," Goodrich said.

"Yes," Mark replied. "It's a tragedy that we couldn't save Sergeant Purvis, but none of our people were injured by the gunman."

"I suppose the police have questioned you."

"Extensively and repeatedly," Mark said. "Is that what this is about? Because I've told them everything I could recall about the incident. It was too bad we couldn't save the sergeant, but—"

Goodrich held up his hand, palm out. "I've heard nothing from the police. But we were contacted first thing this morning by an attorney who mentioned more than once that a malpractice claim might be in the offing."

"By whom? What malpractice? There's—"

Goodrich turned to the computer monitor on a side table beside his desk. He tapped a few keys. "This is the electronic medical record for Hector Garcia. Apparently his family has engaged an attorney, who feels he has a strong case against you and the hospital for the treatment rendered to Mr. Garcia." Goodrich swiveled back to face Mark. "They claim you not only were guilty of malpractice, but violated his civil rights by not administering proper treatment in a timely fashion."

"May I see that record?"

Goodrich turned the monitor so Mark could see it. The chart, or what passed for one, was a brief narrative. Eric had volunteered to dictate it while Mark was tied up with the police. Mark read: "The subject was brought to the ER by his brother, who threatened the staff at gunpoint, telling them to save the subject's life..."

Mark looked up from the screen. He'd seen enough. "This man was DOA...dead on arrival. We didn't tell his brother, because he would have started shooting everyone. There was no malpractice. There was no treatment involved."

"Notice that this narrative was Dr. McCray's, not yours. You have nothing on the record. That, of course, calls the account of the incident into question."

"But what Dr. McCray said was accurate. I'll attest to that."

"How do you know?"

"I felt his carotid pulse—he had none. I put a stethoscope on his chest—there was no heartbeat. The man had expired."

"Did you try cardiopulmonary resuscitation? Can you swear that he was beyond saving with CPR?" Goodrich leaned back in his chair. "Think about those questions, because they're the ones you'll be answering under oath if this case moves forward. In the meantime, I think it would be best if Dr. McCray suspends you from your work in the ER until the matter of the lawsuit is settled."

8

KELLY REACHED INTO THE REAR SEAT OF TRACY'S CAR TO reclaim her purse and backpack. "Where do you want to meet after our shifts end?"

Tracy grabbed her stuff and used the remote to lock the car. "I guess the first question is what time we'll get away. If there's an emergency case going and I'm scrubbed in, it might be after midnight."

"And if things are crazy in the ER, the same with me," Kelly said. "Why don't we contact each other if we see that happening? Otherwise, I'll meet you in the food court. I think I'll be safe there."

The two women went through the sliding glass doors of the ER, and before they could go their separate ways, Kelly's cell phone rang. She looked at the display. *Why is Mark calling me?*

Tracy raised her eyebrows, but didn't speak.

"It's Mark," Kelly said. "I think we've spoken more often after he told me we shouldn't see each other than before."

"Are you going to see what he wants?"

"I think I have to." Kelly turned toward an unoccupied corner of the ER waiting area. "I'll talk with you later." She answered the call.

"Kelly, where are you right now?"

Kelly wasn't sure what there was in Mark's voice that made the hairs on her arms stand at attention, but whatever it was, she didn't like it. "I'm right outside the ER, headed for work."

"I'm leaving the administration suite right now. Do you know the benches in the lobby next to the admitting desk? Can you meet me there? This won't take long, but I've been given some news that might affect both of us... actually, I already know that it affects me. Matter of fact, it could be a death blow for my job here."

<hr />

Mark collapsed on the bench near the mural that was the centerpiece of the hospital's lobby and pondered the effect of the news he'd just received. It was ridiculous, of course. Any decent lawyer would turn down such a suit. And the results of the autopsy would confirm that Garcia's injuries were enough to kill him, no matter how heroic Mark's treatment might have been.

While he waited for Kelly, Mark wondered about getting a cup of coffee, but after what he'd heard from Allen Goodrich, he didn't think he could keep down even a couple of swallows.

When he saw Kelly, he rose from his seat and waved.

She hurried over, a frown on her face. "Mark, what this about?" She dumped her purse and backpack on the bench and sat.

"I've just come from the administrator's office," he began.

"That's what you said when you called." She looked at her watch. "Look, Mark. I have to get to the ER, so why don't you tell me why it's so important we talk...again."

Mark swallowed, but the cotton ball in his throat didn't move. "It seems I could be the target of a malpractice suit by the family of Hector Garcia."

"Who?" It was obvious from her expression that Kelly didn't recognize the name.

"That's the man you wheeled into the ER Saturday night—the one his brother wanted us to save."

Kelly shook her head. "That's ridiculous. He was dead when he reached the ER."

Mark shook his head. "That's the catch—was he? Did we consider CPR? No, we just pretended to start resuscitation until the police rescued us from his brother."

"But...But there was a man holding a gun to my head, threatening both of us. We couldn't be expected to—"

"Makes no difference," Mark said. "Anyone can sue anybody for anything. And our administrator is apparently so afraid of the publicity that might come of this, he's checking with my boss right now to see about getting me suspended."

Kelly sat, tight-lipped and silent, but Mark could imagine what was going through her mind. She'd undoubtedly be included in any malpractice suit. What would this do to her professionally?

"Don't worry, the doctor is still 'captain of the ship' in situations like this. If there's a malpractice action, I'd be the primary one named. They might include the hospital, because that's where the deep pockets are, but you're unlikely to be harmed by this. At most, you'd be called to testify. I just thought you should know what's going on."

"I don't—"

Mark looked at his watch. "You need to get to work, and I have to call Eric McCray and see if I still have a job. If I do, then it's time for me to get to the ER, too." He rose. "Kelly, I'm sorry you're involved in this. Believe me, I'll do everything I can to protect you."

Kelly nodded dumbly, retrieved her things, and hurried away. Mark sat down and scrolled through the numbers on his cell phone. He'd better see if Eric had talked with Dr. Goodrich. As he waited for his call to go through, he realized that, for a few minutes at least, his thoughts had been of protecting Kelly rather than saving his own skin. Maybe there was hope for him yet.

Dr. Eric McCray felt as though people were converging on him from all sides. He was at the end of his seven A.M. to three P.M. shift in the emergency room of Memorial Hospital when his cell phone rang. Unlike most of the doctors and nurses who worked there, he didn't leave his phone in his locker. As the person in charge of the ER physicians group, he had to be available 24/7.

Fortunately, he had a bit of breathing room, so Eric moved toward the staff lounge as he pulled his cell phone from the pocket of his scrub pants. "Dr. McCray."

"Eric, this is Dr. Goodrich. I think we should talk."

"I'm sort of busy. Why don't you give me the short version?"

The staff lounge was empty at the moment. Eric dropped into a chair and listened without comment as Goodrich told him of the threatened malpractice suit against Dr. Mark Baker.

"Don't you think it would be prudent to suspend Dr. Baker until this issue blows over?"

"No," Eric said.

Goodrich launched into an explanation of why it would be best for the reputation of Drayton Memorial Hospital to relieve Mark of his duties. "We simply must minimize any negative publicity," he concluded.

Eric shook his head. "We've had suits threatened, we've had suits filed, we even had one suit initially go against us, although it was reversed on appeal. What's so different about this one? You need to have a good reason to order Mark out of the ER."

Goodrich hemmed and hawed and began repeating his arguments.

Eric heard a noise and looked down at his cell phone. "Look, I have another call coming in. So far as I'm concerned the decision is made. Mark Baker stays unless you can come up with a better reason."

He ended that call and answered the next. The caller ID had already told Eric who was calling, and he knew why. Without preamble, he said, "Mark, I've just talked with Goodrich and essentially told him to stuff it. Now hurry on down here and get to work."

Kelly saw Mark when he came in and wanted badly to talk with him, but before she had that chance the EMTs brought in an elderly man who coded almost as soon as he came through the doors.

She saw the situation developing at the same time that the lead EMT, Mason, did. "Put him in there," she called.

Mason started external cardiac massage while his partner pushed the gurney into the curtained cubicle to which Kelly pointed.

As she followed the patient, Kelly caught Mark's eye. "Code," she mouthed and saw Mark speak softly into the ear of the nursing assistant who was holding out a clipboard toward him. The assistant nodded and hurried to a phone.

"What do we have?" Mark asked as he parted the curtains and edged in beside Kelly.

Mason didn't interrupt his external cardiac compressions, giving the salient facts without missing a beat. "Eighty-eight year old man, lives with his daughter, who found him unresponsive in the living room this afternoon. History of two prior infarctions, both managed with a stent. Moderate hypertension, controlled with a beta blocker and diuretic. Daughter was calling his internist as we left. EKG in the ambulance showed a large, evolving anterior infarction."

"Stop a second and let's see what his vital signs are."

Kelly bent over the patient and in a moment said, "No pressure. No pulse."

"Resume compressions," Mark said.

Another nurse had joined the group and was fitting an oxygen mask to the old man's face. "You going to intubate him?" she asked.

"Not yet," Mark said. "See if you can get an IV going."

"Switch?" the second EMT said.

Mason nodded, and the second man took over chest compressions.

Kelly finished applying the leads for the cardiogram. "Mark, the EKG is ready," she said.

"Stop chest compressions," he said. Everyone stared at the screen as though by their efforts alone they could produce a normal set of complexes. Instead, when the compressions stopped, the tracing became a flat line.

Kelly moved on automatic pilot, preparing and handing Mark the necessary drugs: epinephrine, vasopressin, amiodarone.

When there was no response, everyone in the room knew that the outlook was bleak, but they moved through the whole sequence. "We'll shock," Mark said.

Kelly moved the machine forward, and Mark applied conductive gel to the paddles. "Set to three hundred joules," he said. "Clear!"

Everyone stepped back. He pushed the button on the paddle, the patient jumped like a marionette whose strings had been jerked, then settled back.

Finally, after all measures had been exhausted, Mark stepped away and looked at the clock. "Time of death is 1600 hours."

Kelly began removing the IV and EKG electrodes. "I'll get the body ready."

"And I'll see if the family is in the waiting room," Mark said.

Their eyes met, but only for a second. Kelly knew that Mark was as anxious as she to talk, but that wasn't going to happen for a while. Right now, both of them had something to do—something that wasn't pleasant, but was part of their profession. How long either would be able to continue practicing that profession, of course, remained to be seen.

⸺ ∞ ⸺

It was almost ten P.M. before things were slow enough for Mark to snatch a moment to speak with Kelly. "How are you doing?" he asked.

"If you mean after we lost that man with the heart attack, I've learned to live with things like that. If you mean with the thought of a malpractice suit hanging over my head, I guess I've learned to accept that as part of the practice of my profession."

"But how about—"

She continued as though he hadn't spoken. "If you mean how do I feel, knowing that at any minute someone may make an attempt on my life? Well, let's just say that tonight every time someone dropped something, every time the outer door burst open, every time there was a raised voice here in the ER—my heart almost jumped out of my chest."

"We need to talk," Mark said. "I don't think the malpractice suit—"

"Please, Mark." She looked over her shoulder. "Let's find someplace quieter and more private for our conversation."

"Can you meet me in the food court after our shift ends?"

Kelly shrugged her shoulders. "I agreed to meet my ride there, but…sure. I'll see you then."

Things had quieted down by the time Mark did a handoff to the colleague relieving him. "Any questions, Gary?"

"No, I'm good." Gary Matthews grinned and pushed his brown waves back up onto his forehead in what Mark had observed was a perpetual battle. "I presume you didn't leave me any gunmen, threatening to shoot everyone in the ER."

Mark realized Gary was trying to lighten the moment, but he still had to take a couple of deep breaths before answering. "No, other than the man we lost with a heart attack earlier, it's been pretty quiet."

His scrubs covered with a fresh white coat, Mark slung his backpack over one shoulder and hurried to the food court. He'd seen Kelly giving her report and figured she'd be along soon. Mark sought out a table in a quiet corner, as far away as possible from the corridor along which a stream of hospital personnel flowed, some coming to work, others leaving.

Mark closed his eyes and took deep breaths. He tried a calming yoga exercise, but found himself drifting off to sleep as soon as he closed his eyes. The third time it happened, he surrendered and leaned back in his chair.

"Shall I let you sleep, or do you want to talk?"

Mark looked up and saw Kelly standing over him. Her neutral expression gave him no clue as to whether she was serious or playful. Given the circumstances, he decided that playful was unlikely. "Sorry. I was trying to relax. As you know, it was a busy night."

Kelly lowered herself into the chair across from Mark. "You wanted to talk."

"I didn't want you worrying about the threat of a malpractice suit by the Garcia family."

"Is there more to this than what you told me earlier?" Kelly asked.

"No, except that I talked with Eric after I left Goodrich's office. Eric doesn't think there's anything to it, and now that I think about it, neither do I." Mark stretched and heard the bones in his neck crack. "I'm going to call my malpractice insurance carrier in the morning and bring them up to date on this latest development, but I didn't want you worrying about it."

Kelly shook her head. "I'll try not to. Both you and I did what we could to save our own lives and those of the people around us. I'm at peace about everything."

"I wish I could feel that way—"

Despite her hurt feelings, Kelly decided to give it one more try. "You mean peace? We could talk about that if you'd like." Kelly's voice softened. "Just say the word."

"I don't think I'm ready quite yet," Mark said. He paused. "But thank you."

"Let me know if you change your mind," Kelly said.

"Ready to go?" Tracy Orton detached herself from the stream of people going by and approached the table where Mark and Kelly sat.

Mark stood, an automatic gesture from his early years, thanks to his mother. "Tracy," he said, and inclined his head.

"Am I interrupting something?" Tracy asked.

Kelly shook her head. "No, I think Mark and I were through talking."

A middle-aged Hispanic man wearing scrubs trailed Tracy to the table. She nodded toward him and said, "Carl, these are my two friends, Dr. Mark Baker and Kelly Atkinson." Turning back to Mark and Kelly, she said, "Carl is our new scrub tech. He's been working with me on the three to eleven shift."

Carl shook first Mark's hand and then Kelly's.

Kelly smiled. "Carl, I'm glad we've finally met. Tracy said I might be able to ride to the hospital with you sometime if our schedules don't mesh."

"It would be my pleasure," Carl said, with only a trace of accent in his words. "I've wanted to meet you—actually, to meet you both—since the episode in the ER Saturday night. I've heard so much about what you did."

Mark frowned. There was something about Carl, something that made the hairs on the back of Mark's neck prickle and come to attention.

Tracy consulted her watch. "Well, we should go."

Carl fixed Mark with a look that wasn't quite a stare. "I'll look forward to seeing you again, Dr. Baker." He started away, then halfway to the door, glanced back over his shoulder. The look on his face was fleeting, but it still made Mark shiver. He thought he knew what that look meant . . . and he didn't like it.

9

MARK PONDERED WHAT HE'D JUST SEEN AND HEARD AS HE watched Kelly, Tracy, and Carl exit the food court. He rose and was about to head for his car when he decided to check his cell phone for messages. He frowned when he thumbed the button and saw that he had one missed call and one voice-mail message...from Anna King.

Had something changed since his lunch with Anna only a few hours ago? The proof she'd furnished that she was sober during the operation on Ed Purvis would undoubtedly clear her in any action Purvis's family brought, although in so doing she made it more likely that Mark's inexperience as a surgical assistant could be called into question in a lawsuit.

Mark listened to the message. It was brief and to the point: "Mark, I guess you're at work with your phone turned off. It's important that I speak with you. Please call me."

The tone of voice, Anna's inflection, the words themselves gave no clue about her reason for wanting to talk with him. He checked the time the call came in: nine P.M. It was approaching midnight now. Surely Anna didn't want a call back this late. Tomorrow was Tuesday, one of Anna's scheduled days to operate, so calling her office in the morning was out. Maybe if he tried the OR he could make contact with her between cases. In the meantime, he'd try not to worry— something he was having no success with thus far.

He knew he wasn't going to drink—the death of Joe, Jr. at the hands of a drunk driver had seen to that more effectively than a lifetime of AA meetings. Mark's yoga meditation exercises hadn't been successful thus far. Nothing was working for him, and he felt sometimes as though he was going to jump out of his skin. Maybe he should take Kelly up on her offer. She'd mentioned being at peace. He certainly wasn't having any success finding peace on his own. Maybe that was another call he'd make tomorrow. First, he needed to think about it some more.

Tracy's red Hyundai hummed along through the quiet streets, moving from dark to light to dark again as it passed by streetlights and an occasional lit billboard. Kelly listened with one ear and murmured responses as Tracy rattled on about her evening's work. Normally, she'd be engaged in a spirited dialogue with her friend, trading stories and making comments, but tonight her mind was elsewhere.

It was unfair for the family of the man she'd wheeled into the emergency room to consider a malpractice suit because Mark failed to save his life. There was no question in her mind that the man was essentially DOA when his brother brought him through the doors. And for the hospital administrator to try to suspend Mark until the incident blew over? Absolute madness.

"What did you think of Carl?" Tracy asked.

Kelly roused long enough to consider her answer. "He seemed nice," she said.

"Carl's only worked in the OR for a short time, but he's trying to fit in. I mean, he's doing a good job learning procedures, but that's not all. He's always asking about the people who work in the operating room. And he was interested in the incident in the ER on Saturday night. That's why I was glad he got to meet both you and Mark tonight."

Kelly thought back to the brief encounter. Frankly, Carl hadn't made much of an impression, either positive or negative, but she was willing to accept her friend's judgment. "You know, until I'm sure I'm no longer at risk from the Zetas, I'm afraid to be in the car alone. I'd ask to ride with you again, but I worry about putting you at risk."

"Don't give it another thought," Tracy said. "Since I started working this shift, driving home late at night, I've made it a habit to watch my rearview mirror and drive with the doors locked. Actually, it's kind of nice to have someone I can talk to. So, no problem."

"Then can I ride with you tomorrow night?"

Tracy thought for a moment. "You know, I think I'm supposed to be off tomorrow night. I guess it was fortuitous, your getting to meet Carl tonight. When I get home, I'll give him a call. I'm sure he'll be happy to let you ride with him."

"I appreciate your doing that," Kelly said. "But you've never told me where he lives. Maybe it would be too much out of his way for Carl to pick me up."

"Don't you worry about that. He's a nice guy. I'm sure he'll be happy to swing by and get you. I'll just need to give him your address. Everything else will take care of itself."

The driver of the black SUV looked straight ahead as the red Hyundai stopped at the curb and the nurse exited. She'd ridden with a friend tonight, which might make it more difficult to eliminate her. It would be better to catch her alone, possibly in her own car. To encounter a situation where she was with the doctor and they could both be targets would be too much to ask for, but sometimes things change. It would require a bit more observation before it was time for action. But that was all right. Orders had been given—eliminate them—but there was no time constraint. And as the saying goes, "La venganza es un plato que se sirve frío." *Revenge is a dish best served cold.*

Mark wasn't really hungry, but he decided he should eat something before going to bed. He heated a Lean Cuisine dinner in the microwave and ate it standing at the kitchen sink, accompanied by the last few sips of a quart of milk consumed directly from the carton. The package he tossed in the trash told him he'd just consumed "Five Cheese Rigatoni." Frankly, it could have been powdered sawdust sprinkled with catsup for all he could recall tasting—not that the dinner was bad, but he was eating only because he knew he needed to fuel his inner engine. Ever since the shooting, his appetite had dropped to zero.

He stood under the shower, hoping the spray would clear his head, but found his thoughts returning again and again to the two malpractice suits with which he'd been threatened. When he tried to force himself away from that subject, his feelings for Kelly Atkinson and Anna King took center stage. He'd dated them both—Kelly because she was fun and genuinely seemed to enjoy their time together, Anna because...well, because she was interested in him and was available. Matter of fact, as he recalled, Anna had been the one who'd asked him out the first time, not vice versa.

He dried himself, climbed into the fresh scrub suit he favored over pajamas, and crawled into bed. Maybe he should follow Kelly's lead and read the Bible tonight before turning off the light. He knew sleep wasn't going to come easily anyway. Didn't he have a Bible around here somewhere?

Mark tumbled out of bed and looked through his bookshelves, scanning the titles of medical texts and paperback novels before pulling out a large volume bound in black imitation leather. When he and Joe had left for medical school and college respectively, their parents had presented each of them with a Bible. The books weren't expensive, although they probably were as nice as Joe Sr. and Erma Baker could afford. Mark pulled the purple ribbon that served as a bookmark, and when the Bible opened his eyes fell on the first words of Psalm 27. "The Lord is my light and my salvation—so why should I be afraid? The Lord is my fortress, protecting me from danger, so why should I tremble?"

Why should I be afraid? Mark decided he was afraid of everyone and everything: of revenge by the Zetas, of malpractice claims against him, of being alone instead of in a relationship. Maybe this promise was part of the peace Kelly mentioned.

Was it too late to call her? She'd only been off work...he looked at his watch and discovered it was after one A.M. If Kelly had gone straight to bed, she'd be asleep by now. No, he'd phone her in the morning. He'd make it his first call.

⸙

The shooter had dressed carefully—black jeans, black long-sleeved tee shirt, black driving gloves, black athletic shoes. A black ski mask completed the outfit, both providing anonymity and allowing the shooter to blend into the shadows. There was no moon tonight—not simply by happenstance. No, the date had been carefully chosen. There was no light from the sky, and since a well placed shot from an air rifle had taken out the street lamps on either side of the subject's house, none from ground level either.

All the houses around were dark. The shooter's car rolled to a stop half a block from the target's house. When the door opened, no light illuminated the interior of the car, since the bulb from that lamp was stowed safely in the glove compartment. The shooter placed the car keys above the sun visor. Everything was in place for a quick exit.

Do it. Sprint to the car. Drive away slowly and quietly. Leave the headlights off for a block or two, then turn on the lights, pull off the ski mask, and blend into the stream of traffic that would be present on the nearby freeway even at three A.M. Ten minutes, start to finish. Meticulous planning, leading to proper execution... in more ways than one.

Mark's dream was a montage of images and scenes involving the emergency room and men with guns. As police streamed through the double doors, they set off an alarm, producing a strident noise, a noise that eventually cut through Matt's sleep-deprived brain and woke him. It took a moment for him to realize what he heard was his cell phone. He rolled onto his side and reached for the bedside lamp.

He didn't bother to check the caller ID. Wrong number or emergency, either way he knew he had to answer it, if only to still the ringing. "Dr. Baker."

"Mark, this is Anna."

Mark swung his feet around and sat on the side of the bed. "Anna, what's—"

"I know it's late. You didn't return my call, and I had to talk to someone. My AA sponsor is out of town. Mr. Tanner's wife answered his cell phone and said they were on their way to the hospital. He may be having a heart attack. I'm sorry to bother you, but I need someone to help me...to talk me down."

Mark dry-washed his face, feeling the rough stubble of a day's unshaven beard. "I don't understand."

"I want a drink. I need a drink. But I have over fifty days of sobriety, and one of the things AA preaches is that before we take a drink we call someone." She laughed, with no mirth in it. "Tag. You're it."

Mark's brain was churning. "Anna, when we had lunch..." He looked at the bedside clock. "When I was with you about fourteen hours ago you were fine. You didn't drink then. You didn't even seem to want one. What's changed?"

"When I got home tonight, I ignored the mail. I never get anything worthwhile anyway—just bills and junk. I made some decaf coffee, heated some leftovers, and watched TV while I ate. Then I showered and got ready for bed. But before I turned out the light, I remembered seeing an envelope that reminded me of the stationery my ex-husband uses. It was cream-colored, with a raised blue return address in the corner. He's a lawyer, and...Mark, this is so hard."

"You can tell me." Mark stifled a yawn. "So you found the letter and opened it. What was in it that's making you want to drink?"

"My ex-husband is...he said he's going to fight my efforts to get visitation rights to Hannah, our daughter. Right now, I can only see her in a neutral location, a supervised visitation center. I'd told him I'd been sober for two months, that I was getting help and attending AA meetings. I'd even told him I was wearing the SCRAM monitor, but he doesn't care. He says I'm not a fit mother, and he's going to fight me." She sobbed, ending in a hiccup. "He's a lawyer, and the attorney who handled our divorce ripped me to shreds at that hearing.

That's why Carter has custody of Hannah. I don't stand a chance. It's not worth the effort anymore. I can't—"

"Stop it, Anna. You're letting this get to you. Think about it rationally. You're a professional. You're getting help for your drinking. You have proof that you've been sober for more than two months. That's not a guarantee, but it's a start."

There was silence on the other end of the line, broken occasionally by muffled sobs. Mark didn't know what else to say. Maybe Anna should see a counselor. Maybe someone at AA could help. Wasn't there some sort of twenty-four hour hotline for alcoholics? Would Anna know about that? How could he find out?

"Anna, isn't there—"

"Mark, there's one more thing that's bothering me. I haven't shared this with you because…"

"Because we were dating?"

"Well, actually, our dating was sort of a smokescreen," Anna said. "You see—"

Mark frowned, wondering what their dating could be screening. He waited for Anna to finish. Instead, he heard breaking glass, a muffled thud, and then silence. "Anna. Anna!"

He kept calling for Anna to answer, but there was only silence on the other end of the line. Had she dropped a glass? And if so, why? Did Anna faint, have a seizure, what? Finally, Mark took a deep breath, broke the connection, and dialed 911.

10

KELLY CAME AWAKE SLOWLY, LIKE A SWIMMER EMERGING from a deep dive, struggling up from the depths and reaching for wakefulness like pushing for the surface and air. Finally, she opened one eye and looked at her bedside clock, where red numbers showed 6:26. What had awakened her? Then she heard it again—pounding at her front door, interspersed with the ringing of her doorbell.

She slid her feet into slippers and wrapped her robe around her. When she reached the door, she looked through the peephole and saw two uniformed police officers, a black man and a Caucasian woman. The man had his fist raised, obviously ready to knock again. Since he was roughly the size of Mount Everest, Kelly decided she'd better open up before he knocked down the door.

"Just a second. Let me get the door unlocked," Kelly called. When she swung the door open she asked, "Yes, officers?"

The female officer, a petite blonde, took the lead. She pointed to her nametag. "I'm Officer Carter." Nodding at her partner, she continued, "That's Officer Mercer. We have a couple of questions for you." Carter smiled in what was probably her attempt at a non-threatening expression. "May we come in?"

Kelly stepped aside and gestured the two officers toward the living room. She closed the door and followed them. "Please, sit down." She yawned. "Sorry. I got home about midnight, and you woke me." She eased into an armchair. "What's going on?"

Carter leaned forward from her seat beside Mercer on he couch. "Where were you between midnight and four this morning?"

Kelly wished she'd excused herself to brew coffee. She could certainly use some to clear the cobwebs of sleep from her brain. "I was here...at home...in bed. Why?"

Mercer spoke. His voice was deep and surprisingly soft. "Is there anyone who can corroborate that?"

Kelly felt a blush rise on her cheeks. "No. I live alone. And I sleep alone, if that's your next question." She raised her voice slightly. "Again, why are you asking?"

Carter ignored the question. "Do you know Dr. Mark Baker and Dr. Anna King?"

Should she stop answering questions and call a lawyer? No, she was certain she had nothing to fear. Maybe this was still part of the investigation of the shooting Saturday night, although she wished the police hadn't awakened her to ask the questions. "I work with Dr. Baker in the emergency room of Memorial Hospital. I believe Dr. King is one of the surgeons at the hospital."

"Haven't you dated Dr. Baker?" Mercer asked.

Kelly thought for a moment about telling these two that Mark had broken off their relationship, but decided to keep her answers short and to the point. "Yes, in the past."

Mercer went on. "And didn't he also date Dr. King?"

"I...I think he did."

Carter stood and leaned forward toward Kelly. "And because you were jealous, did you slip away from your home about three this morning, go to Dr. King's home, and shoot her through the window?"

Mark yawned and wished he had some coffee—about a gallon should do it. He was still in the scrub suit he was wearing for pajamas when Anna called. He closed his eyes for a moment, but quickly opened them again because his eyelids felt as though they were lined with sandpaper. He'd experienced nights like this before, but they'd been spent in the emergency room, not in his own living room answering question after question from a detective he was learning to dislike more each minute.

"Take us through it one more time, please, doctor." T. R. Jackson's navy suit was pressed and wrinkle free, his pale blue shirt looked to be fresh from the laundry, his patterned gold tie was perfectly knotted, and—in contrast with Mark—he was freshly shaved and smelled of a good cologne. His hairless dome glinted in the overhead lights as though it had been polished. In short, Jackson was the antithesis of the way Mark felt and undoubtedly looked.

Jackson's partner, Detective Ames, sat quietly on Mark's sofa, his notebook open in his lap, apparently ready to pounce on any change in the story Mark had told the detectives twice already. Unlike Jackson, Ames showed evidence of being rousted out of bed and dressing hurriedly. Even at that, though, he was a veritable fashion plate compared with what Mark imagined his own appearance to be.

"Okay," Mark said. "I was awakened from a sound sleep by a call on my cell phone."

"Not your landline?" Ames asked, glancing at his notes.

"I have one, mainly because the hospital requires it, but most of my friends call on my cell." Mark started to say, "It's a generational thing," but decided not to antagonize the detective, who seemed about his age anyway.

"So you were awakened by the call," Jackson said. "Go on."

Mark told the two detectives what Anna had said. She'd received a letter from her ex-husband that said he would contest her efforts to see her daughter more often. She was about ready to take a drink. Mark had determined that she'd called him as sort of a last resort. As he tried to offer support, Anna said there was one more thing. She'd been dating him as…he searched his memory for the exact words. "She said dating me had been a 'smokescreen.'"

"What did she mean by that?" Jackson asked.

"I don't know. That was when I heard glass shattering and a thud as though something had hit the floor. I thought maybe she'd dropped a glass or something. Perhaps she'd fainted. I kept saying, 'Anna, Anna,' but there was no answer. Finally I called 911."

Jackson looked at Mark and shook his head. "Nice little story, and you've apparently got it down pat." He looked at Ames who closed his notebook and nodded. "But maybe that's not the way it went down."

Mark frowned. How many more times was he going to have to tell this? And why weren't the detectives out there trying to locate the person who'd shot Anna? "Look, you can check my cell phone records, or Dr. King's calls, or whatever you people do. But that's the truth."

Jackson shook his head. "We've already found out you had lunch with her today. We know you'd dated her a few times before that. Maybe she called you last night to break off your relationship. When you saw you couldn't change her mind, maybe while you were talking with her, you got in your car and drove to her house. I don't know if she hung up or if you two were still on the phone with each other when you did it—maybe she said something that was the last straw, but I think you were so angry or hurt or both that you walked up to her bedroom window and shot her."

⸺⸺

Kelly was on the verge of telling the police to either arrest her or leave when Carter rose, pulled a card from the pocket of her uniform shirt, and held it out. "One of the detectives on the case will be in touch. Don't leave town for the next couple of days. And if you think of anything else you'd like to tell us, give me a call."

"Do I need a lawyer?"

"That's up to you," Mercer said. He followed his partner to the door. At the threshold, he turned and looked Kelly in the eye. "But if you want one, the time to make that call is before the detectives interview you."

Kelly slumped in her chair and stared at the door where the two police officers had exited. Anna had been shot. And, judging from the tone of the interview just concluded, Kelly was a suspect. What should she do now? Then it hit her. The police never mentioned whether Anna was dead, was wounded, or if the bullet missed her. Surely she wouldn't be questioned this quickly and this thoroughly if it were a case of malicious mischief. No, if Anna wasn't dead, she was at least severely injured.

Kelly searched her brain for the name of a lawyer, but came up empty. Maybe there was someone in her church.... It was too early to call her pastor. Perhaps Mark knew someone. Besides, if the police had come to her doorstep, they undoubtedly had interviewed Mark as well. Interviewed? More like the third degree. Did they really think she'd shot Anna King because she was jealous? Then again, she had to admit that there had been times, as her feelings for Mark grew, that she did resent his dating Anna. It was a good thing she'd kept those feelings to herself.

Still in her robe, Kelly went into the kitchen to get some coffee started before calling Mark. She had things to do, and she was pretty sure the effort would require some coffee...a lot of coffee.

<hr />

Mark double-locked the front door, leaned against it, and exhaled. Jackson and Ames had just left, after voicing the warning he'd heard so many times on TV but never had directed at him: Don't leave town, we'll be in touch. His heart was still thumping from his experience. Certainly his adrenaline level had rocketed higher each moment the police were grilling him. And Anna's shooting added to the stress he already felt from being targeted by the Zetas. And— oh, yes—he could be in the crosshairs of a couple of lawyers poised to include him in malpractice actions. If he ever needed the peace Kelly had talked about, now was the time.

He strode into the bedroom long enough to pick up his cell phone, then carried it into the kitchen and checked the coffeemaker. Sure enough, the machine was bubbling along, a dark and aromatic brew flowing into the carafe. He looked at the kitchen clock and discovered it was seven thirty in the morning. Normally, he'd enjoy waking up to the smell of his favorite beverage. But he hadn't just awakened...he'd been up for several hours, and it didn't look like he'd be going back to sleep this morning.

Cup in hand, Mark eased into a kitchen chair and dialed Kelly's number. She needed to know about these latest developments. He took a sip of coffee, winced at the burn on his tongue he always got because he couldn't wait, and listened to the ring of the phone.

When Kelly answered, Mark asked, "Did I wake you?"

"No, two police officers did, pounding on my door earlier. Have you heard about Anna King?"

"Probably more than you have," Mark replied. He brought her up to speed, starting with the three A.M. call from Anna. "After I called 911, I started to go to Anna's home to see what was going on, but the police had told me they'd go there to do what they called a 'welfare check,' and I'd probably get caught up in the process. So I waited around for about an hour, then tried to call Anna's cell phone. Guess who answered?"

"Mark, I'm not in the mood for guessing games," Kelly said.

He noted the exasperation in her voice, so he went on. "Our friend, Detective Jackson answered. It seems that the police officers that arrived found the doors locked. They walked around the house, saw what appeared to be a bullet hole in the window of one of the rooms, then looked in and saw Anna on the floor with blood all around her."

Mark waited for Kelly to respond, but all he heard was a sharp intake of breath. He continued, "Detective Jackson and his partner were there when I tried to call Anna. Jackson had taken possession of her cell phone, and he answered. He told me to stay put, and after they finished their preliminary investigation at Anna's house, they showed up at my front door." He sighed. "They put me through the wringer, accused me of shooting Anna, and in general scared me to death. They just left, and I was about to call an attorney, but thought I should talk with you first."

"I'm glad you did," Kelly said. "The two policemen who were here—or, I guess you'd call one of them a police-woman—anyway, they talked about me being the shooter."

"Why?"

"Because I was jealous of Anna's relationship with you."

"That's—" Mark stopped. He'd never thought of get-ting serious with Anna, but he had to admit he'd had those thoughts about Kelly. Could she— No, that was preposter-ous. "Sounds like we need to get together. Maybe we can find an attorney who'll represent us both."

"I'm due to be at work at three," Kelly said. "And I need to contact Tracy about a ride again. How about lunch?"

"I don't think we should wait that long," Mark said. "I'll need some time to shower, shave, and get dressed. Why don't I come by your house about nine? We can go to the Daily Grind or somewhere for coffee."

"I guess that will work. Do you know any lawyers?"

"I'll check with some people. And don't worry about get-ting a ride to work. At first I thought it was a good idea for us to be separate, but I'm beginning to think there's safety in numbers. Why don't you ride with me tonight? In the mean-time, I'll see what I can do to help us both feel safer."

Kelly felt like a spy sneaking around behind enemy lines, facing capture or death at every turn. Her head swiveled right and left, her eyes flickered between the side mirror and the road ahead as Mark drove. Every car contained a Zeta, every pedestrian carried a concealed handgun, every drawn shade or blind along the route shielded a man with a rifle.

"We're almost there," Mark said. "You can stop cringing every five seconds. I think we're safe here at ten in the morning in the middle of Drayton. If someone's coming after us, it would be in a more secluded location than this."

Kelly considered Mark's words before she leaned back and took a deep breath. "You said there was something you were going to do to make us feel safer. I don't feel safer yet. What did you have in mind?"

Mark stopped at a red light, looked both ways, and turned right. "I had several ideas. At first I thought of buying a gun—"

"Please don't!"

"I said I thought about it. I decided that I was more likely to shoot myself in the foot than use a pistol against someone else. Besides, my carrying a gun wouldn't help you if we were separated. I even thought about trying to hire a bodyguard of some sort, but that would be terribly expensive. Actually, unless we had a Secret Service detail surrounding us every minute we were away from our homes, I figured that if someone wants to kill a person..."

Kelly could fill in that blank quite well. She'd seen enough movies and TV programs to know how difficult it was to protect someone from a killer. "Well, you're certainly making me feel more secure," she said, inching away from the window to the limit of her seat belt.

"For now, the best I can offer are those." Mark pointed over his shoulder to a bulky package in the back seat of the car. "I got them on my way over to pick you up. They're Kevlar vests. I figure that if we wear them when we're out, we're protected against—"

"Stop right there. It's June in Texas. Wearing one of those would be worse than getting shot. Besides, if a shooter thought we were wearing a bulletproof vest, why not go for a head shot? And there's no guarantee even Kevlar would stop a high-powered round anyway. I think—"

Mark took one hand off the wheel long enough to hold it toward Kelly, palm out, a gesture of surrender. "I see your point. Maybe you're right."

"While you were concocting all those schemes, I was doing the one thing that made me feel a bit better about this whole mess."

The look Mark gave her was equal parts puzzlement and disbelief. "And that is…"

"I read the Bible and prayed."

She expected to hear Mark pooh-pooh her actions, but was surprised by his next words. "Is this part of that peace you were telling me about?"

"It is. I read one of the Psalms, one where King David was being pursued, and it made me realize God knows when we're in danger. So I prayed for protection…for both of us."

Mark wheeled into the parking lot of the Daily Grind. "Maybe it would be good if we talked about this some more. But can we do it inside, where we're not so much of a target?"

As Kelly exited the car, she realized that a lot of things had changed since her conversation with her pastor, but the bottom line remained the same. She needed to have this conversation with Mark.

Then, as they walked toward the door, Mark did something that told her things were already changing: he reached down and took her hand.

<hr />

Mark got two cups of coffee and brought them to the table. For Kelly's sake, he hoped the coffee was good. He hardly tasted it. He kept looking around the coffee shop, silently assessing each person who came and went as a potential threat.

"So what did you want to discuss?" Kelly asked.

"You keep talking about peace—the peace your faith brings you." He shook his head. "I have faith in God...at least, I thought I did. But if that brings peace, maybe I don't."

Kelly stirred her coffee. "Why don't we start with this? What do you mean by faith in God?"

"I was raised in a Christian home. When I was thirteen, I heard a preacher talk about what it meant to be a Christian, and I accepted that...did it publicly. Not a lot changed after that, though, except maybe I hung out with a different crowd."

"Then what happened?"

"When I left home for college, I sort of decided that I didn't have to do things just because my parents expected me to. And the busier I got—first with college, then with med school—the less I thought about God. And eventually, I guess I stopped thinking about Him at all."

"You're a believer, but you got too busy for God," Kelly said.

Mark flinched. It was hard to hear, but Kelly was right. "Yes."

"I'm not saying that being a Christian guarantees an easy life—far from it. In fact, generally it's not easy at all," she said. "Look at where we are right now. What I'm saying is there's peace in knowing God's in charge."

Mark slowly nodded. He realized he, like most doctors, wanted to be in control. That was the way he was wired. Maybe he couldn't give control of his life to God. Not right now—maybe not ever.

He looked at his watch. Mark decided he needed to think about all this—not just what Kelly had said, but how it could affect their relationship. In the meantime there was something else he had to do. "I need to see Anna."

Kelly seemed to recoil at this pronouncement. "Mark, I don't want to go to the morgue. Besides, what would we learn there?"

"Who said anything about the morgue?" Mark shoved his coffee cup away. "The police wanted me to think she was dead. After questioning me over and over, they finally admitted that Anna was shot in the head, but she's still alive. I need to go see her."

11

IT TOOK A MOMENT FOR KELLY TO WRAP HER MIND AROUND this news. Anna wasn't dead! Why had she jumped to the conclusion that she was? Had the police said it? No, they said that she'd been shot. Kelly's imagination supplied all the rest.

Even though she knew she had nothing to do with Anna's shooting, the visit of the police had unnerved her. After all, their mention of a possible murder charge was hard to ignore. Now she could relax a bit, although she still might consult an attorney.

Mark seemed to read the expression crossing Kelly's face correctly. "You didn't know she was still alive? Didn't the police tell you that?"

"No."

"I guess they thought that, if you really were the shooter, they'd save that little tidbit of information for later—put a bit more pressure on you." He stood up. "Well, I need to see Anna. Shall I drop you at your house?" He paused. "Would you like to go to the hospital with me?"

"Why do you need to see her?" Kelly asked.

"She was going to tell me something just before she was shot. I have the feeling it was important, so I want to ask her." He paused a moment. "Besides, she's lying there in the hospital by herself. I want her to know there's someone who wants her to pull through."

Kelly shook her head. "There's a police officer outside her door. Do you think you have a chance of seeing Anna?"

"If we went up to the guard outside her room and asked for permission, probably not," Mark said. "But what if a doctor and nurse, both wearing scrubs covered by white coats, both with their hospital ID badges prominently displayed, went straight to her door? Do you think he's going to stop them?"

"Maybe."

"Well, I'm willing to take my chances. What about you?"

Kelly wasn't sure why she was agreeing with his idea, but she reached for her purse. "I guess so." She rose. "Is one reason you want to see Anna because you care for her?"

"Yes," Mark said. "But not the way I care for you." *There. He'd said it.*

"We need to explore what you mean, but I don't think we should do it while your mind is still on Anna," Kelly said. She turned and started toward the door.

Mark followed a step behind her. *I probably didn't handle that very well. Matter of fact, I know I didn't.*

At first, Allen Goodrich didn't recognize the noise. Then he realized that the buzzing from his desk drawer indicated an incoming call on his personal cell phone. Only a few people had the number: his wife, his son who was away at college, a few key people on the hospital staff. He pulled out the phone and consulted the screen, only to find that the incoming number was blocked. It was probably a robo-dialing telephone solicitor. He'd answer it and give the person on the other end an earful.

"This is Dr. Goodrich. Who's this?"

The answer came in Spanish, a language in which Goodrich had worked to become fluent. "Who do you think? We still have unfinished business," the voice said.

Goodrich felt the hairs on the back of his neck bristle. He answered in the same language. "I thought we were through."

"We're through when I say we're through. I told you there's a situation that needs your attention. You said you'd handle it, but you didn't make it go away. I don't like that."

Suddenly the button-down collar of Goodrich's blue Oxford cloth shirt felt too tight. He ran his finger around the neck band. "I tried to take care of it, but—"

"I don't care how you do it, but this has to end, right here, right now. After you do that, you won't hear from me again."

You mean I won't hear from you until the next time you need something. "Do you have any suggestions?"

"Yes. Here's what you should do..."

Goodrich pulled a pad toward him and actually had his pen in his hand when he realized that he couldn't commit any of this to paper. If anyone found out about this... no, he could remember. He wasn't sure how he'd make this work, but somehow he'd find a way. He had to. If he didn't, the consequences didn't bear thinking about.

Mark returned his cell phone to his pocket and grimaced. He looked at Kelly, seated beside him in the front seat of his car, and shook his head.

"What?" she asked.

"I guess it was a good thing I called the neurosurgeon taking care of Anna King before we trekked off to the hospital to see her."

"Problems?"

He shrugged. "I had no idea how bad the gunshot wound was. All the police told me was that they found her on the floor in her bedroom, her cell phone beside her, obviously shot in the head. Somehow, I imagined the bullet creasing her skull, plowing a furrow in her scalp, the force of the gunshot causing a concussion." He shook his head again.

"Worse than that? She's not dead, is she? I'd resigned myself once to her being killed. I don't know if I can go through that again."

"No, she's alive, but she may not wake up anytime soon."

Kelly scooted a bit closer to Mark and turned so she was facing him. "What do you mean?"

"She's in serious condition. They did bore holes to relieve the epidural hematoma that formed, but her condition was too rocky for them to do more until she stabilizes. The bullet is still in her brain."

Mark felt Kelly's hand touch his. He covered it with his other hand. "I talked with Troy Michaels, who's taking care of her. He thinks it's too dangerous to go after the bullet until she stabilizes. They've drained the blood that was pressing on the surface of the brain. They have her on steroids and mannitol to reduce the swelling. Now we wait."

"And pray," Kelly said quietly.

A flippant remark danced on the tip of Mark's tongue, but he swallowed it. "Yeah. And pray," he echoed.

Kelly looked around. Most of the people in the hospital food court were at tables near the service area: McDonald's,

Burger King, Seattle's Best Coffee, Subway, Taco Bell, and Hunan Palace. She'd found a spot in the far corner, far enough away from anyone else to ensure privacy.

While Mark got coffee for both of them, Kelly decided to make the phone call she'd been putting off.

"Tracy, this is Kelly. I need to tell you something."

"Sure. What's up?"

"I won't need a ride to work today. I'm already at the hospital."

"How did you manage that?" Tracy said.

"I . . . I rode with Mark."

"I thought you said the two of you together made too good a target. What changed?"

"Mark thought that we might be safer if we watch each other's backs. Some things have happened since I last saw you." Kelly told it all to Tracy—the police at her door, the news that Anna King had been shot, meeting Mark to discuss the situation. "After we got together and talked, Mark took me back home, waited while I changed, then brought me here to the hospital. I'll ride home with him after our shifts end."

"I'm not sure I understand all of this," Tracy said, "but I'll keep you in my prayers. Meanwhile, I'd better call Carl. I'm off tonight, and he was going to give you a ride to and from the hospital."

"Enjoy your night off," Kelly said. "And I appreciate your arranging my transportation with Carl. Please thank him for me."

"I'll be fine. And as for Carl, he was happy to offer. As soon as I gave him your address, he said he'd take care of everything."

Mark stretched and heard the bones in his neck pop. He caught Kelly's eye as she hurried by and gave her a reassuring nod. One might think they were safe here in the ER, in the midst of so many people. Then again, he'd felt safe Saturday night until the Garcia brothers showed up, with Nacho holding a pistol to Kelly's head. Now, he wasn't certain anyplace was safe.

He parted the curtains and entered the next cubicle, where a mother held a crying toddler, trying without success to quiet him. Mark glanced at the clipboard. "Mrs. Ames, how can I help you?"

The woman freed one arm for a brief moment and swiped at a lock of dark auburn hair. She wore a red tank top that stopped short of her low-rider jeans, exposing a band of pasty white skin. "I...I wanted you to look at my son. He's been crying for over an hour. I think he must have fallen down and hurt himself."

Mark looked up as Kelly eased into the cubicle. "I figured you might need some help examining the child."

He nodded his thanks. "Mrs. Ames, will you let the nurse hold..." He looked at the papers in his hand. "May she hold Junior? You can stand right there, so he'll be able to see you."

Junior was a chubby, red-cheeked little boy who looked to be about two. His hair, like his mother's, was light brown bordering on red. His crying had slowly subsided, but he still sniffled and sobbed intermittently. Kelly held out her arms and Junior grudgingly gave up his death grip on his mother and allowed the transfer.

It didn't take Mark long to see that Junior was holding his right arm against his chest, resisting any attempt to move it. There were old bruises on both arms at the wrists and one on Junior's forehead. Mark did the usual exam—head, eyes, ears, nose, throat, chest, abdomen, extremities—and found nothing particularly wrong. Other than the bruises, the only abnormality evident was an apparently tender right shoulder. Finally, with patience and reassurance, Mark was able to move the affected limb, noting no crepitus—the crunching sensation that marked a fracture—and a full range of motion.

"Mrs. Ames, you say you think your child might have fallen down and hurt himself. Did you see it?"

"No, I . . . I just guessed that's what must have happened."

"Where were you at the time? Were you in the house, out in the park, shopping?"

She took a moment to answer, raising one more red flag in Mark's mind. "We were in the house."

"Anyone else there with you? Is there someone who might have seen the incident?"

"My . . . my husband was at home. He was in the living room, trying to watch TV. I'm sure he didn't see anything."

Mark nodded. "It appears that Junior has a tender shoulder. I don't think it's worth sedating him to get X-rays this evening, but I want you to follow up with your pediatrician. Do you have one?"

Mrs. Ames nodded. "Yes, Dr. Krempin."

"I'll see that he gets a copy of our note," Mark said. "Some ibuprofen should be enough to relieve Junior's discomfort tonight, but call Dr. Krempin's office first thing in the morning. And if anything changes tonight, come right back here."

After a few moments' silence, Mrs. Ames said, "So he's okay?"

"I don't find any evidence that anything's broken or dislocated," Mark said. "But I think a follow-up visit would be a good idea."

The shooter picked up the pistol and examined it carefully in the light of a bedside lamp. The clip of the Smith & Wesson semi-automatic normally held ten .22 caliber bullets, another in the chamber. Now the chamber was empty and eight rounds remained in the clip. The others had done their job, dispatching two people. Well, one was dead. The other was clinging to life, but there was no doubt in the mind of the shooter that the job would ultimately be finished.

Now it was time to dispose of the weapon. The piece retailed for about $800 and, bought in a dark alley for cash, it might have cost almost twice that. In this case, though, no money had changed hands. There was probably no need for the gun in the future, and if there were, all it took to acquire a replacement was money, if you knew the right place to go. It was a beautiful piece—walnut grips and a blue carbon steel finish, a six-inch barrel unmarred by a single scratch. It seemed a shame to get rid of it, but it had served its purpose.

Tomorrow, the pistol would disappear, hidden away where no one would ever find it... would never even think to look for it. And the shooter would move on.

After Kelly gave Junior a dose of pediatric ibuprofen and the toddler quieted down, Mrs. Ames left the ER with a promise to call the pediatrician's office in the morning. It was almost an hour later before Mark and Kelly had a chance to talk, and when they did, they both voiced the same suspicion.

"I think we've got a case of child abuse," Kelly said. "Why didn't you notify the authorities?"

"I'm not sure we have enough to go on right now," Mark said. "I'll call Dr. Krempin's office in the morning. If he's Junior's pediatrician, he's probably had the same suspicions we did. I'll tell him about what we saw tonight and encourage him to report it to the authorities."

"So you're punting the responsibility to him?"

"No, I'm gathering corroborative evidence. If he thinks everything is on the up-and-up and declines to make the report, I may contact Child Protective Services myself. But I'd prefer that the first move come from him."

"Why not make the call now? You won't be subject to any action so long as you make the report in good faith."

Mark took a deep breath and let it out slowly. "I guess I'm trying to stay out of this because of the possible repercussions."

"But I just said you're safe from any suit against you."

"I'm not worried about a lawsuit," Mark said. "Think about this. In the situation we saw tonight, what is the most likely scenario?"

"The father is trying to watch TV. The child wants to play. Daddy gets angry, loses his temper. He grabs the child by one arm and flings him to one side. This probably isn't the first time this has happened, which explains the old bruises. This time he yanks too hard, stretching the shoulder muscles and ligaments. Sometimes this can even dislocate the arm, although that's unlikely in kids this young. But to answer your question—the father is most likely the aggressor."

"Did you notice the first name of the father...and his employer?"

Kelly shook her head. "No. But I've heard you say that you treat everyone the same way. What's different about this one?"

"The father is Addison Ames. Employer is City of Drayton." He paused a moment until he saw Kelly's expression change. She'd connected the dots.

"So, he's—"

"Right. He's one of the two detectives working the shooting of Anna King. In case you've forgotten," he said with a wry smile, "that's the one in which we're both apparently suspected of attempted murder."

12

When Mark walked with Kelly to his car, it was almost midnight. Although they were only two of the dozens of people moving through the well-lit parking area after their shift, he kept his eyes open and his senses on high alert. He had one hand on Kelly's arm, and he felt her shiver despite the warm, muggy night.

"Want something to eat?" he asked as he buckled his seat belt.

Kelly shook her head. "No, I just want to go home, lock all the doors, and try to forget the mess we're in." She reached into her purse and pulled out her cell phone. She punched a couple of buttons, and the face of the instrument lit up.

"Making a call?" Mark asked.

"No, just checking for text messages." She shoved the phone back into her purse. "Nothing."

Mark pulled out his own phone, the process made more difficult by the seat belt stretching across him and blocking the pocket of the white coat that covered his scrubs. Unlike many of his friends, he preferred to communicate by making a call, rather than sending a text. As a result he sometimes forgot to check for them. His phone had been locked away in the pocket of his white coat while he was in the ER, so he hadn't looked at it for over eight hours. He took his eyes off the road long enough to see the number 1 superimposed on the message icon.

"Got a message?"

"Yeah." Mark said, "I'll have a look at it after I drop you off and head home."

"Don't you think it might be important?"

He shrugged. "I doubt it." Mark handed the phone to Kelly. "Here, you can read it to me."

At first she protested about invading his privacy, but eventually she punched the right buttons. "It says, 'Call me ASAP, no matter how late. Leo Murphy.' And there's a number—not a local area code, though." She handed the phone back to Mark. "Who's Leo Murphy?"

Mark shook his head. "I have no idea. Probably got a wrong number."

"Aren't you going to call?"

Mark sighed. "Ordinarily, I'd ignore a text from somebody I don't know, but...Yeah, I guess I should. I'll do it after I get home."

Kelly turned her face toward the passenger window and rode in silence for a moment before she spoke again. "You can call him from my house."

"Okay, I give up. You're curious, and you'd like to know what this is about."

"No comment," Kelly said. Mark couldn't see her expression in the darkness of the car interior, but he was willing to bet he was right.

Mark looked at his watch. It was well after midnight. He should head home.

Kelly pointed Mark to the sofa, and said. "Have a seat. Would you like some coffee? Or would it keep you awake?"

"There's no danger of that," Mark said. "I drink this stuff all day, but it never keeps me from sleeping."

"Let me put some on, while you make that phone call." And she disappeared through the door into the kitchen.

Well, it seemed that Kelly wasn't going to let this rest, so he might as well call the mysterious Mr. Murphy. Mark pulled out his phone, noted the number from the message, and punched it in. After three rings, a sleepy voice answered. "Leo Murphy."

"Mr. Murphy, this is Dr. Mark Baker. You sent me a text this evening, but—"

"Thanks for calling back. We haven't met, but I'm Buddy Cane's half-brother. Buddy's death has hit Marge pretty hard, and it's been left to me to make most of the arrangements for his funeral tomorrow. I received word tonight that one of the men we'd asked to serve as a pallbearer was taken to the hospital with appendicitis, and I wonder if you'd fill in."

Mark had made a deliberate decision not to go to the services for Ed Purvis. He'd paid his respects to the widow and the son and gotten only a withering look from the younger Purvis for his trouble. Buddy Cane's funeral was scheduled for Wednesday afternoon—just hours away. He was still struggling with his conscience about attending that service. Now it appeared the decision was going to be made for him.

"I know you didn't know Buddy very well," Murphy said, as though he sensed Mark's hesitation, "but I was hoping you'd consent to serve. I know Margaret would appreciate it."

Mark ran through possible excuses. Work? No, actually he was scheduled to be off tomorrow. A conflict? He couldn't think of one. How about not liking funerals? That was true enough, but he didn't think that would fly.

He knew he should do the right thing. And he knew what his answer should be. "I'll be honored to serve," Mark said. "Just give me the details."

Mark's sleep that night was filled with wild dreams. Interspersed with scenes where he was a mourner at a funeral were others where he lay in a casket. Then came the dreams in which faceless detectives pummeled him with clubs and fists. He awoke in a cold sweat amid tangled sheets. The bedside clock told him he'd been asleep for only a few hours, but he couldn't stand the thought of returning to those dreams. He stumbled out of bed, splashed some water on his face, and headed for the kitchen and coffee.

An hour later, fresh from a shower and shave, dressed in clean jeans and a golf shirt, Mark sat at the breakfast table, hunched over the morning paper. He forced himself to eat a piece of buttered toast, washed down with his third cup of coffee.

Mark had a few hours before he needed to be at the funeral home where Buddy's memorial service was scheduled. He hoped it would be a small ceremony, mercifully brief, and that he could get away quickly afterward. When his brother's funeral was over, Mark had vowed never to attend another. But here he was.

Why did he say yes? He knew it was the right thing to do, of course. Besides, it would be a nice gesture for Buddy's family. Mark tried to picture Buddy Cane's wife. Initially he drew a blank before he finally remembered that he'd met her once, at some kind of hospital function—a plain woman with muddy brown hair. Did they have children? He didn't recall any mention of them.

Mark realized he barely knew Buddy Cane, yet here he was, about to carry the man's casket to its last resting place. And how, exactly, was he going to do that? Murphy had told him that the funeral director would guide Mark and the other pallbearers through the accomplishment of their duties today. How hard could it be?

In a few hours, all this would be over and Mark could concentrate on his other problems: he was the target of a drug cartel, there was no doubt he was a suspect in a murder, and he'd obviously acquired the enmity of his hospital administrator, who wanted him removed from duty. And he had no idea how he might resolve any of those situations.

In the meantime, he had to help bury a colleague.

———————

Mark paced the length of his living room, cell phone in hand, one eye on the clock. According to Dr. Troy Michaels's office, the neurosurgeon was scheduled to be in the operating room most of the day. The nurse who answered in the OR was pleasant. Yes, Dr. Michaels was between cases. She'd offered to call him to the phone, but if Troy didn't hurry—

"Mark, what's up?" Troy's voice was upbeat. For the life of him, Mark couldn't figure out how someone who dealt day after day with life and death surgical situations could be so chipper. But he was, each time the two men talked and today was no exception.

"Troy, I'm sorry to bother you. I know you've just finished a long case—"

"And another one to follow, but I'm happy for the break. How can I help you?"

"You're taking care of Anna King. What can you tell me about her situation?"

There was a pause, and Mark knew what caused it. Troy was figuring how much he could legally share without violating HIPAA. The Health Insurance Portability and Accounting Act was designed to protect patient privacy, but the restrictions sometimes made communication with a colleague—even a so-called "curbstone consultation"—difficult.

"What do you need to know?" Troy said.

"Is Anna waking up any?"

"She reacts to pain now, but there are no voluntary movements," Troy said. "If she wakes up more, I may need to sedate her."

"I guess you know about her alcoholism," Mark said. "But she's been dry for about six weeks."

"We found the SCRAM unit strapped to her ankle, but I haven't heard back from the people whose phone number was on it."

"That's because Anna told me she'd tried to call him the night she was shot, and he was on his way to the hospital with a possible heart attack. I'm guessing his was pretty much a one-man operation."

"If she gets any lighter, I'll give her Toradol," Troy said. "That should be safe for an alcoholic. But I think we're going to be taking her back to the OR before she wakes up very much."

"So she's stabilized?"

"She's as stable as she's going to get. And we can't leave that bullet in there. If it shifts the least bit, she'll die. Of course, she may die with the surgery. Or it may leave her paralyzed or unable to speak or—"

"I get the picture," Mark said, his heart sinking. He tugged at his collar, vowing to get out of the tie he was wearing as soon as the service was over.

"Anything else?" Troy asked.

"No. I guess we both need to get on with it." Mark sighed. "I've got to leave for Buddy Cane's funeral—I have to go be a pallbearer. Would you mind—"

"I know what you're going to ask. Yeah, I'll call your cell after we come out of surgery."

"Is there anything else I can do?" Mark asked.

"Just pray," Troy said and ended the call.

<hr>

Kelly had wondered about driving alone to the funeral, but finally decided it was a risk she was willing to take. At the funeral home, she beeped her car locked and joined the people filing into the chapel. It looked to be a small crowd, and what she could see so far confirmed her guess that the attendees would be mainly doctors, some with their wives, some unaccompanied. To her left, Mark, dressed in a dark suit, white shirt, and maroon-and-gold striped tie, stood under the porte cochere of the building, partially hidden by a black hearse. Around him were five other men, similarly dressed. A couple of them were smoking, puffing as though this were their last cigarette before the blindfold and firing squad. One was talking on a cell phone. Mark stood gazing out at the parking lot, and when he saw her, he strode in her direction.

He grabbed her hand in both of his. "Thanks for coming."

"This isn't just for you. This is for a coworker and his family." She scanned the people walking into the chapel. "How's it looking?"

"Pretty small crowd. Margaret and Buddy's half-brother, the one I talked with on the phone, are the only family. Both parents are dead. No other living relatives."

"What about Margaret's parents?"

"Apparently she's estranged from them. They're retired and live in Mexico somewhere. So basically…" He turned and indicated the few people entering the chapel. "What you see is what you get."

"How's Margaret taking all this?"

Mark shrugged. "Hard to read her. The pallbearers were in the room where they had Buddy's body in an open coffin when Margaret came in to thank us for what we're doing. Then she asked us all to step out and give her a few minutes alone with her husband before the funeral directors closed the casket for the final time." He pointed to the other men around him. "That's why we're out here."

Kelly looked at her watch. "Isn't it time for you to be in the chapel?"

"They'll call when they're ready for us. One of the funeral directors told us what we do. We ride in a limo to the cemetery and carry the casket to the graveside. When it's over, we throw our boutonnieres into the grave, extend our sympathies to the widow, and we're done."

"You should be able to handle that. I'll be at the cemetery, and you can ride back with me," Kelly said.

Mark took a deep breath, and she could see that he wanted to say something. "What's on your mind?" she asked.

"I'll be sitting in the front of the church, with my back to everyone else. Would you take a seat in the rear and keep an eye out for someone with a gun?"

Kelly's first impulse was to laugh, but Mark appeared to be dead serious. She started to argue, but realized that she, too, had been more attentive than usual to her surroundings. Maybe they both were paranoid. And it was certainly possible that a Zeta gunman would use this occasion to exact revenge on one or both of them. She nodded. "Sure."

A man appeared in the doorway and motioned to the group of pallbearers. "Looks like it's time for me to go," Mark said. He turned, but before he had taken two steps he stopped and reached into his coat pocket for his cell phone. Kelly saw him start to hit a button to send the call to voicemail, then do a double take as he saw the caller ID.

He answered. The conversation was short and one-sided. As Mark returned the phone to the inside pocket of his coat, he grimaced at Kelly. "That was Eric McCray. The hospital administrator is threatening to fire the whole ER physician group if Eric doesn't suspend me until the Garcia malpractice suit is settled."

13

MARK FELT THE MUSCLES IN HIS NECK RELAX AS KELLY pulled away from the cemetery. He felt better, now that the funeral was behind him. He'd carried out the unfamiliar duty without incident, so he no longer was troubled by visions of dropping Buddy's coffin or doing something equally embarrassing. He was still alive—no one had taken a shot at him as he sat, vulnerable and unprotected, at the front of the chapel. Now it was time to turn his attention to his other problems.

"What was your reaction to the service?" Kelly asked as she turned onto the main road.

"What do you mean?"

"Was it the kind of funeral you'd want for yourself?"

"I'm no expert on funerals. The last one I attended was for my brother, and I've sort of blocked out that memory." Mark furrowed his brow, trying to recall the service that just ended. "Honestly, I guess this one was sort of generic. I think the clergyman—at least, I suppose he was a clergyman—the man who did most of the talking was someone the funeral home brought in. He apparently didn't know Buddy, didn't know Margaret. Then again, maybe there wasn't much to be said about Buddy Cane's life."

Mark turned toward the window and watched the scenery pass. If his funeral were held tomorrow, what could be said about him? Sure, he was a good doctor. He would readily admit that. But surely there was more to life than one's profession. Aside from his medical practice, had he contributed to the lives of others? Would there be anecdotes at his funeral, stories of how he'd changed the lives of those with whom he came in contact? Sadly, he didn't think so. Well, now was the time to change all that.

Kelly stopped the car and shifted into park. "Here's the funeral home, and there's your car. What's next for you?"

"I'm going to the hospital."

"To talk with Goodrich? I thought Eric was going to do that."

"I may eventually try to talk with the hospital administrator, but not now." Mark paused with his hand on the door handle. "Troy Michaels was going to take Anna King back to surgery this afternoon. I want to see her first, to tell her someone cares."

Kelly frowned. "What are you trying to accomplish?"

"Don't get the wrong idea," Mark said. "Anna was a friend, nothing more. But before she goes to surgery she deserves to know there's someone who cares about her." He climbed out and spoke through the open door. "You talked about changing my life. Well, that's what I'm going to do, and this is where I'll start."

"You mean, by praying for her while she's in surgery?"

"I mean by finding out who shot her."

"Isn't that the job of the police?" Kelly said.

"I don't know if they're looking at anyone else but me." He opened his car door. "Anna deserves for the person who shot her to be brought to justice. I don't want this to be like everything else in my life—all about me—but if I uncover the real shooter it would clear me."

"Mark, if they see you hanging around Dr. King's bedside, what's to stop them from thinking you're trying to finish the job so she can't identify you?"

Mark hadn't thought of that. If he went ahead with his plan, it might very well tighten the noose the police had already tried on him for size. The smart thing to do would be to hold off. But he'd been doing that most of his life. It was time to change.

He looked directly at Kelly. "Whether it puts me in a bad light or not, I'm going to go ahead." He closed the car door behind him and headed toward the hospital.

Kelly rinsed her dishes and stowed them in the dishwasher. Buddy's funeral and her discussion with Mark had blunted any appetite she might have had. But she knew she had to eat, so she managed an early supper of most of a sandwich washed down with half a glass of iced tea.

The subject of the hospital made Kelly think about tomorrow's shift in the ER. She considered the pros and cons of driving herself to work. The trip to the hospital in broad daylight didn't worry her. It was coming back late at night that presented the greatest danger. *Don't be silly. Just lock the car doors. You'll be safe.*

As she thought about it, though, Kelly could picture half a dozen scenarios in which a Zeta assassin could get to her, all of them more likely if she were alone. No, for now she was better off being with someone else, especially late at night. She'd see if she could ride once more with Tracy.

She punched in Tracy's number, but when her friend answered, Kelly knew the answer to her question before she asked it. Tracy's "hello" was preceded by several dry coughs and followed by a series of sneezes.

"You sound terrible," Kelly said.

"Unfortunately, I feel pretty much the way I sound," Tracy replied. "Are you at work? And how did you get there?"

"I took the day off to attend Dr. Cane's funeral. But I have to work tomorrow and I was wondering—"

Another paroxysm of coughs from Tracy stopped the conversation for a moment. "Sorry. I think this is more than a simple cold," Tracy said. "I've already told my supervisor I'd be out the rest of the week. And I'll bet you're going to need a ride tomorrow."

Kelly was already rethinking her decision. Maybe she could go alone. After all—

"Stop trying to think up excuses," Tracy said, as though reading Kelly's mind. "I'll call Carl. He has your address, and he'll be happy to do this. How does two o'clock tomorrow sound?"

"But—"

"Don't argue with Auntie Tracy." Another round of coughing followed. "Sorry. I shouldn't talk. But don't worry. Carl is glad to help. I think he's looking forward to it."

<hr>

At the hospital, Mark traded his suit coat for the white coat hanging in his locker, made sure his hospital ID badge was clipped onto his lapel, and headed for the ICU.

Outside Anna King's room were three people, one whom he wanted to see, the other two he definitely didn't.

"Mark, I'm about to take Anna to the OR," Troy Michaels said. "Her vital signs are deteriorating. The catheter we left in her brain to drain blood accumulation isn't putting out much, and her brain swelling seems to be stable. If we're going to get that bullet out, now's the time."

"Doctor, if you'll wait here, as soon as I've finished talking with Dr. Michaels I need some time with you." Detective Jackson said.

"Sorry, but I need a couple of minutes with Anna before she goes to the OR," Mark said, turning away from Jackson and his partner, Ames.

Jackson put a hand on Mark's sleeve. "I don't think Dr. King can hear you," he said. "Let me finish with Dr. Michaels and I'll get to you."

Mark very deliberately moved the hand. "For your information, detective, it's quite possible that people in coma can hear. If you'll excuse me, I want to pray with my friend before she goes to surgery."

If Troy Michaels was surprised at Mark's words, he didn't show it. Instead, he moved aside and gestured Mark into the room, then turned back to Jackson and said, "Now what else can I tell you? I need to get Dr. King to the OR."

The Anna who lay in the bed looked nothing like the woman with whom Mark had lunch just twenty-four hours earlier. Her head was swathed in bandages from which a clear plastic tube issued, a scant amount of bloody fluid within it. This was the EVD, the external ventricular drain to which Troy had referred. The apparatus to which it led showed a fairly stable intracranial pressure. This was critical in patients such as Anna. If the pressure went up, there was a danger the spinal fluid would push the brain downward against the bony bottom limit of the skull, causing vital functions to cease.

A larger plastic tube, securely taped to the corner of her mouth, connected her to a respirator that maintained her breathing at a uniform level. Occasionally Anna would take a deep breath, overbreathing the setting, but most of the time her respirations were mechanically driven.

Mark scanned the machines that monitored Anna's blood pressure, pulse, and oxygen saturation. As Troy had said, the readings were truly "all over the place." None were critical, but they could go in that direction at any moment. If the neurosurgeon was going to remove the bullet still lodged in her brain, this was the time.

Mark put his lips close to Anna's ear. "Anna," he whispered, "It's Mark. I don't know if you can hear me, but I want you to know I'm here. Troy Michaels is going to take you to surgery and remove the bullet from your brain. When you wake up—and you are going to wake up—I want you to tell us who shot you. And I swear I'll do everything in my power to see that they're brought to justice."

He moved back and watched for some movement, some outward sign Anna heard, but there was none. Once more he whispered in her ear. "I'll be here when you come back to the recovery room. You need to know there's someone here who cares. I'll be praying for you while you're in the OR."

Mark straightened up, thought a minute, then bent over and kissed Anna's cheek. *Dear God, bring her through. Please.*

⸺∞⸺

Mark stood outside Anna King's ICU room, ignoring the two detectives who stood on either side of him. His eyes were focused on Anna, still in her ICU bed and attached to various tubes and wires, as she was wheeled away toward the OR.

"I'll call you when she's in recovery," Troy Michaels said to Mark before turning to join the procession.

Detective Jackson gripped Mark's arm lightly—not so firmly as to imply restraint, but certainly with enough force to get his attention. "Doctor, we need a few minutes of your time."

Mark started to resist. He was tempted to tell the detective that he had more important things to do than talk with him, but then he realized that for the next few hours he'd be waiting for a call from Troy. He might as well get this over with while he waited.

Other than talking with the detectives, his next objective would be talking with the administrator. He'd confront Goodrich face to face and see why the man was dead set on getting rid of him.

He pulled his arm away from Jackson's grip and said, "Okay, let's talk."

Ames spoke. "Is there somewhere we can have a little privacy?"

This, from the other detective, reminded Mark that he still needed to call the pediatrician caring for Ames's son. Until he did that, although he still had a strong suspicion that Ames was abusing the child, maybe taking out his frustrations on the toddler, Mark decided to keep his opinions to himself.

"Let's see if we can find a table in a quiet corner of the food court," Mark said. "I could use some coffee."

Jackson gestured for Mark to lead the way. "I guess you doctors drink about as much coffee as we do at the police station."

"And I suspect the coffee's equally as bad there as here," Mark replied, surprised at the spark of humanity Jackson showed. "But it keeps us running."

Ames trailed silently behind the other two men. When they reached the food court, he said, "That table in the corner looks like it would be good. I'll get the coffee. Doctor, how do you take yours?"

As they sat waiting for Ames, Jackson said, "I didn't see you at Ed Purvis's funeral, doctor."

Mark wondered if he'd hear about that decision, and here it was already. He could have attended the Purvis funeral, but at the last minute, he decided...no, to be honest, he chickened out. "I...I had already paid my respects to the family," Mark said. "I don't like funerals."

"But you were at Dr. Cane's service today," Jackson said. He paused a beat to let that sink in.

"How did you—?"

"We had someone there. Surely you've read enough mysteries to know the police always cover funeral services for people who were murdered. You'd be surprised how often the person we're looking for actually shows up."

"If you know I was there, you know I was serving as a pallbearer. I wasn't planning to attend this one, either. I—"

Mark stopped when he saw Ames approaching. The detective held three Styrofoam cups clustered in his two hands. He set them on the table, dealt them out, and eased into the chair between Jackson and Mark.

Jackson looked at his partner. "I guess it's time to let the doctor in on our news." He turned toward Mark. "We have a couple of things for you. First of all, let me remind you that you're still a suspect in the shooting of Dr. King."

"I told you, I was at home when that happened. She called me. We were talking when she was shot."

"That's not an alibi. I've already explained what we think could have happened, doctor. If I were you, I'd start looking for a very good lawyer. Then I'd put them on notice, so that when you make that one phone call you're allowed after your arrest you'll have the number handy."

Mark decided it was wasted effort to argue. "You said you had two things to tell me. What's the other?"

"Oh, it's another heads-up. The Purvis family is going to consult an attorney. They're thinking about suing you for being complicit in Ed's death. There's some concern that you deliberately put Sergeant Purvis in harm's way and then failed to save his life after he was shot." He pushed his untouched coffee away and stood. "Have a good day, doctor."

14

Dr. Goodrich, Dr. Mark Baker is here to see you."

Allen Goodrich hit the "talk" button on the intercom. "Ask him to wait for a moment, please."

He rose slowly, walked to his closed office door, and retrieved his suit coat from a wooden hanger on the hook there. Normally, he preferred the comfort of working in his shirtsleeves, but since he was about to face Baker, who didn't seem impressed with the power a hospital administrator could wield, Goodrich wanted everything possible in his favor.

Goodrich kept the doctor waiting for fifteen minutes by his watch before he punched the intercom. "You can show Dr. Baker in."

The office door opened, and Baker came through. He nodded once, took a chair without being asked, and crossed his legs. "I can't believe you'd go this far just to get me out of the way."

It's almost like he heard my earlier conversation. No, he's simply using that as a figure of speech. Goodrich looked down his nose over the top of his reading glasses. "I don't know what you mean. I suppose you mean my desire to keep you out of the emergency room until this situation blows over."

"Exactly."

Goodrich leaned back in his specially designed desk chair. He knew the chair across his desk where Baker sat wasn't particularly comfortable. It had been chosen for that very reason. "I simply think that the less attention that's directed toward this hospital, either by the police or during malpractice litigation, the better off we'll be." He pulled a folder toward him. "As you may know, we're in the midst of a building campaign. In this folder are pledges from a number of sources, pledges that will help defray most of the cost of adding to our maternity and emergency departments. Can you imagine how many of them would be withdrawn if Memorial Hospital becomes the favorite subject of some investigative reporter who's trying to win a Pulitzer?"

Baker made a wry face. "First of all, I'm betting that the autopsy results on Hector Garcia will confirm a mortal injury, one that would have caused his death long before he reached the emergency room. Second, there's no doubt in my mind that any talk of a malpractice suit against me or the hospital centered on this case is merely a ploy by some lawyer looking for a quick settlement."

"Are you willing to stake your reputation on that?"

"If necessary, yes. I've notified my malpractice carrier, I've talked with Dr. McCray, and so far as I'm concerned, I'm now ready to move on with my professional life," Baker said.

Goodrich took a deep breath. *Time to play the other card.* "What about the fact that you and Dr. King may be the subject of a malpractice suit filed by the family of the policeman who died on the operating table under your care?"

There was silence for a moment, and when Baker answered, his voice was softer. "I'm not sure where you heard that, but again, I don't think there's any merit to such a suit. If it were filed, and I'm not saying it will be, it would simply be the first step toward negotiating some kind of settlement."

"But how do you think it would play out if the case came to court. Dr. King has been shot. She may never recover. The anesthesiologist, Dr. Cane, is dead. The nurses in the OR can't give expert testimony about your medical decisions. It would come down to your word against whatever witnesses the Purvis family's lawyer engages. Have you discussed this one with your insurer?"

Baker shook his head. "No, I just heard about it less than an hour ago. But Anna King might recover. And even if she doesn't..." He closed his eyes for a moment. "If she doesn't, I'm confident that I'd prevail."

Goodrich was acutely aware of the phone call he'd received. *Make it happen.* He had one more arrow in his quiver, and this one had to find its mark. "As I understand it, you're the prime suspect in the shooting of Dr. King. If she doesn't recover, that means a charge of murder. You'd be arrested, probably denied bond. Do you think you'd be able to work in the emergency room while you were in police custody?"

He could see by the expression on the doctor's face that these points were beginning to hit home. Maybe, if he continued to hammer Baker... no, to tell him repeatedly that it would be best for him to step away from his job, the stubborn doctor would eventually give in.

"Let me talk with Dr. McCray and my insurance carrier... and with a lawyer," Baker said. "I'll get back to you tomorrow."

As the door closed behind the doctor, Goodrich leaned back in his chair, closed his eyes, and took a deep breath for the first time since he received the phone call with his orders. He thought that, with that last argument, he'd broken through Baker's defenses. If he hadn't— No, better not to consider that. This had to work.

Mark sat in his car in the physician's parking lot, his cell phone pressed to his ear, as Troy Michaels brought him up to date on Anna King's surgery. "It was touch and go, but I got the bullet out. She's in the recovery room now."

"Can I see her?" Mark asked. "She may not seem to hear me, but—"

"Mark, think about this as a doctor, not a friend. She's not conscious. Her condition is rocky at best. Let us do our work. If she wakes up—and mind you, I said if, not when—I'll call you immediately. In the meantime, at least give us a day."

"Thinking of a medically induced coma?"

"Not necessary. I plan to let her wake up on her own—if she will."

"Thanks," Mark said. "I'll drop by tomorrow and look in on her, if that's okay."

After Mark ended that conversation, he dialed another number. He'd been putting this one off, but he needed to make the call in time for Eric McCray to arrange coverage for Mark's shift tomorrow in the ER.

Eric was surprised at Mark's call. "Hey, Mark. Want to come in tonight and work alongside me?"

"Eric, I'm afraid you're going to need to arrange coverage for my shifts starting tomorrow."

"I—" Mark heard a faint murmur. "Sorry. I'm working, and I had to tell the nurse something. Now what's this about your not coming in tomorrow."

Mark explained his most recent conversation with Goodrich.

"I told you not to let Goodrich worry you," Eric said. "I've got your back on this, buddy. Don't back down now."

"Eric, maybe he's right. Maybe it would be better if I took a leave of absence from my ER duties."

"This is quite a reversal since we talked last," Eric McCray said. "What happened to change your mind?"

"The malpractice threats are bogus. We both know that," Mark said. "And I didn't shoot Anna. I hope you believe me."

"Sure."

"But the police have made it pretty clear that I'm high on their list of suspects for the shooting. I don't know if Jackson and Ames are just toying with me like a cat playing with a mouse, or if they're serious. Either way, I'm going to engage the services of a lawyer and prepare to defend myself. And it might be best not to try that while working full-time."

There was silence on the other end of the line for a long minute. Then Eric said, "Tell you what. You have some vacation time coming. Why don't you take a week off? I can rearrange the schedule to handle that. Then we'll look at the situation again."

"I think that's a good idea," Mark said.

"And Mark—I believe you're innocent. If there's anything else I can do…"

Mark hesitated for a second. Then he took the plunge. "Eric, are you a man of faith?"

If Eric was surprised, his voice didn't reflect it. "Of course I am. If it hadn't been for my faith, I don't know how I'd have made it when Cynthia died. Is there a reason you're asking?"

"Yes," Mark said. "Can I see you this evening after you finish your shift? We need to talk."

Kelly sat in front of the TV set, although she was sure that ten minutes from now she wouldn't be able to name the program, the actors, or the plot. Her thoughts ranged back and forth like rabbits running through a field with neither pattern nor destination. A gunshot from the TV followed by the ring of her cell phone made her jump. She thumbed the remote to silence the TV. "Hello?"

"Did I catch you at a bad time? Did I call too late?"

"No, just sitting in front of the TV. Don't even know what I was watching." She tucked her feet under her. "Want to bring me up to date on your adventures at the hospital?"

"I talked with Goodrich. He wants me off duty until all the dust settles." He told her about the malpractice suits, then hit her with the clincher—the possibility that he might be arrested for Anna King's murder.

"That's ridiculous. I hope you told him—"

"I've decided to take a week's vacation. After that...it depends on what happens, I guess."

"Do you need the name of a lawyer?"

"Actually, I know one, someone from my hometown who practices in Drayton now."

"I hope you'll call him in the morning."

Mark was quiet for a beat. "Probably. I'm still trying to decide."

"If you're going to be off work..."

"I can still take you to the hospital and pick you up tomorrow," he said.

"No, no. You'll have other things to do. I'll arrange a ride." Kelly wondered why she was avoiding telling Mark about Carl—probably because she knew he would worry, and he had enough on his plate without adding that to it.

"How's Dr. King?"

"She's out of surgery and in the ICU. She probably won't wake up for a day or two...if she wakes up."

Kelly started to say, "I'll pray for her." But she knew she was going to do that, and Mark might think she was getting pushy.

After ending the call, Kelly sat with the phone in her hand. She had mixed feelings about riding to the hospital tomorrow with Carl. Despite Tracy's expressed opinion that the surgery tech would be a good person to protect her, she still had a bad feeling about the man. She didn't want to be racist about it, but he was Hispanic, and the members of a Hispanic drug cartel were apparently out to kill her and Mark.

Maybe she should bite the bullet—bad choice of words— maybe she should drive her own car. After all, going to the hospital in the afternoon should be safe enough. When she left, she'd ask a security guard to walk her to her car. Then she could lock the vehicle's doors, go straight home, and not get out until the garage door was safely closed behind her.

She had her hand on the phone to call Carl and tell him not to come by when it dawned on her—she didn't have his phone number. *I'll call Tracy and get it from her.* Kelly was about to push the speed dial number for her friend when her cell phone showed an incoming call. The number was unfamiliar, and at first she was tempted to let it go to voicemail, but she decided she'd better answer. "Hello?"

"Is this Kelly?" The voice, like the number, wasn't one she recognized.

Fearing an obscene call, Kelly started to hang up, but decided to ask, "Who's calling?"

"This is Carlos Ortiz. Remember, Tracy introduced us at the hospital."

"Oh," Kelly said. "Yes. I'm sorry, I didn't recognize the number or the voice."

"I wanted to confirm that you're riding with me tomorrow. I'll pick you up at about two. Okay?"

Tell him you've changed your mind. This is your chance. "I...I'm—"

"Don't tell me you're having second thoughts. Tracy told me about your situation. Believe me, I'm the right person to protect you." His voice grew softer, and a bit of an accent crept in. "All you have to do is get in my car, sit back, and relax. After that, I'll take care of everything."

⸎

"Thanks for staying around to talk," Mark said.

"No problem." Eric looked around to make sure there was no one near their table in the almost empty food court. "What's on your mind?"

"I guess it started with my brush with death last Saturday night when the gunman held us hostage. After that there was the constant sense that the Zetas might kill me anytime. I couldn't stop thinking about it. I was worried sick. Apparently Kelly was, too, at least at first. But later she told me she had peace with the situation. I want...no, I need that peace."

"And you think that because I'm, as you called it, 'a man of faith,' I can help you?"

Mark nodded. "I hope you can."

"What do you think Kelly has that you're missing?" Eric asked.

"I'm not sure," Mark said. "I thought her being a Christian had something to do with it, but I became a Christian when I was a teenager. I'll admit that I let my focus slip away during college and medical school." He ducked his head. "I'm not making excuses—a lot of my classmates did."

"So you got busy with other things and, the more time they took, the less you even thought about God. And eventually, you forgot about Him altogether."

Mark swallowed hard. That was hard to take, mainly because it was true. "Yeah, I guess so."

"And now you're trying to find your way back. Is that right?"

"Yes, but I'm not making much progress," Mark said.

"What have you tried?"

"I guess...I guess mainly I've tried to...to be a better person," Mark said. "But I can't see any change. I don't feel anything—certainly not the peace Kelly talked about." He spread his hands in a gesture of frustration. "What have I missed? What's missing from my life?"

"God." Eric looked Mark in the eye. "Every action, every decision in your adult life has been made with one person in mind—you. That's human...but it's not right."

Mark opened his mouth to reply, but once he thought about it, he realized Eric was right. "Go on."

"Once you put God in control of your life, once you make up your mind to surrender to His will, some of those decisions will be different. Your life will change."

"And I'll see a difference?"

"No," Eric said. "You'll feel a difference. That's when you'll begin to experience the peace you're so desperately seeking."

⸎

Mark slept fitfully that night. Maybe it was because of his conversation with Eric, a conversation that had left him vaguely uneasy. Then again, perhaps it was because of something he had to do this morning. He needed to call a lawyer.

Mark's mother had given him the number almost a year ago when Gwen moved to Drayton, along with some strong hints that Mark should call her. The two had been high school sweethearts. Apparently Mrs. Baker hadn't given up hope that Mark would get married and give her grandchildren before she was too old to play with them, and she seemed to think that Gwen Woodruff was her best hope.

Mark scrolled through the list on his cell phone until he found what he was seeking, both an office and home number for Gwen. Was this a bad idea? Well, the detective had warned him that he should engage an attorney, bring them up to speed on the situation, put them on standby because Mark could be arrested at any moment. Right now the possible charge was attempted murder. If Anna died...no, he didn't want to think about that right now. He dialed the number.

The phone rang twice before it was answered. Mark fully expected a disembodied voice telling him to press 1 or 2 or star or whatever. Instead, a soft alto voice said, "Gwen Woodruff." It was a voice he recognized instantly, one that brought memories flooding back.

Get a grip. This is serious, not a scene from a romantic movie. "Is this the law office?"

"Yes. May I help you?"

"Gwen, it's Mark Baker. I didn't expect you to be answering your own phone."

The laugh that followed was full-throated and deep. Gwen's laugh had always been...Well, face it. It had been sexy. "What's funny?" he asked.

"My secretary called in sick this morning, and I thought this was the temp agency phoning to tell me the replacement was on her way. Instead I get an old boyfriend with whom I haven't spoken in years. I was just thinking that life is full of surprises."

"Unfortunately, I have another one for you," Mark said. As succinctly as he could, he told Gwen about his situation. "The detective said I should have a lawyer on standby. My first thought was that I didn't know any lawyers in Drayton. Then your name popped into my mind." He swallowed twice before he could get the words out. "Can you help me? Will you?"

The silence that followed was broken by a rhythmic noise. He guessed Gwen still had the habit of tapping a pencil on the desk in front of her as she thought. Some things never seem to change.

At last, Gwen said, "Of course I'll help in any way I can. I'm in solo practice, and I do a little of everything, but I don't have a lot of experience in criminal defense. If you like, I could put you in touch—"

Mark broke in. "Gwen, if you'll take the case, I want you."

"Even if—"

"Even if you're not an experienced criminal defense attorney. I know I can trust you." He took a deep breath. "And that's important for me right now. Probably because I'm not sure who else I can trust."

"We need to talk more about this." He heard papers rustle, then a deep sigh. "I'm tied up for the rest of the day. Can you come by about five?"

"Of course." He wrote down the address. Almost before he ended the call, Mark was questioning his decision to call Gwen. Well, time would tell.

<hr>

That afternoon Kelly paced the front room of her house, wondering again and again why she had been unable to turn down Carl's offer of a ride. Was it because her friend Tracy had vouched so strongly for the man, had actually arranged for this? Could it be simply that Kelly had been afraid she couldn't do it without hurting Carl's feelings? Or did she harbor the hope that Mark would call, offering to drive her to work and protect her from the faceless shooters she was imagining lurked around every corner?

A light tap on her front door made Kelly stop in her tracks. She hurried to the door and looked out the peephole. She searched her memory to match the bronze-skinned face smiling back at her with the man she'd met briefly at the hospital. Yes, this was Carl. The white Ford Focus at the curb must be his car.

She took a deep breath and opened the door widely. "I...I expected you to honk or something. You didn't have to get out and come to the door."

Carl shook his head. "In my country, as I suspect in yours, that would be discourteous. I recall a television program I saw years ago—I believe you call them 'sitcoms'—in which the father of a teenage daughter tells a suitor, 'If you sit in your car in front of my house and honk, you'd better be delivering a pizza.'" He smiled, showing even white teeth. "I would never show such disrespect for a friend of Tracy's."

Kelly nodded her understanding. "Well, it's nice of you to give me a ride. I suppose Tracy explained to you why I don't like to be in my car alone at night."

"I understand very well," Carl said. "And your fear isn't unreasonable. In my home country, the mere name of the Zetas is enough to frighten anyone. But don't worry. I will be delighted not only to escort you but furnish protection as well."

"Thank you." She gestured to the couch. "Please have a seat while I get my things. Would you like something to drink?"

"No, thank you." He looked at his watch. "And don't hurry. We have plenty of time."

Kelly felt a tingling between her shoulder blades when she turned her back on Carl and left the room. *Get over it, Kelly. The man's harmless. Just because he's Hispanic you've imagined he's a Zeta.* Yet she had to force herself to walk slowly until she'd turned the corner in the hall and closed the door of her bedroom behind her.

In her bedroom, Kelly pulled out her cell phone and called Mark. It rang six times before it rolled over to voicemail. "Mark, this is Kelly. Call me back ASAP. It's urgent."

Mark was never without his cell phone. He kept it at his bedside at night, in his pocket during the day. His failure to answer must mean that he was talking with someone. If she could delay—

The ring of her own cell phone made her jump. This would be Mark. "Hello?"

"Hey, girl. Did Carl make it by to pick you up?"

Kelly felt her shoulders slump. Ordinarily, she'd be pleased that Tracy would call to check on her, but right now Kelly wanted the phone line clear. "Yes, he's here right now. I'm just doing a few last-minute things before we leave."

Apparently Tracy was recovering quickly from her illness, because it seemed to take forever for Kelly to wind down the conversation. No sooner had she cleared the line than the phone rang again. Kelly looked at the display and felt a rush of relief. Mark was calling back.

"Mark, I need your help," Kelly said without preamble.

"Sure," he said. "What's going on?"

"I know it's silly, but Tracy's sick and couldn't give me a ride to work. She called Carl to fill in, and he's already here. I was about ready to send him away and drive myself, but the more I thought about it…"

"No, you're probably right," Mark said. "This afternoon I imagine you'd be safe. But leaving the hospital by yourself near midnight you'd make a good target for anyone who wanted to pick you off. I'd feel better if I were with you."

"I was hoping that maybe you could come by when my shift ends tonight. That way I could tell Carl my plans had changed. I know you're not working tonight, but if you could—"

"I'll do better than that," Mark said. "Thank Carl, tell him I just called and insisted on handling this, and send him on his way. I'll be there in ten minutes to pick you up and take you to the hospital. And I'll come get you tonight after work. I imagine that by that time I'll need to bring you up to speed on some things anyway. The ride will give me an opportunity."

Kelly blew out a breath she didn't realize she'd been holding. "Thanks, Mark." She smoothed her hair, which had fallen into her eyes during the conversation. "I'm sorry—"

"No need to be sorry about anything. We're both in danger, and it's best that we recognize it, not try to ignore it."

In the living room, Carl was still sitting on the sofa, apparently absorbed in his own thoughts. Kelly felt guilty thinking that he represented a threat. Then again, Mark was on his way, so she might as well proceed. "Carl, while I was in my bedroom getting my things, I got a phone call. Another one of my friends is going to pick me up and escort me to and from the hospital. I'm grateful for your willingness to step in, but I guess it won't be necessary."

She thought she saw a faint frown flit across his face, but it was gone as quickly as it came. "Are you certain? I'm happy to help."

"Thanks, and I'll feel free to call you if this comes up again. But for now, you can go on to the hospital." She forced a smile. "Maybe I'll see you there."

Carl nodded noncommittally. He eased himself off the couch, and in so doing the leg of his khaki pants momentarily hung on something. He quickly shook the pants leg to settle it, but not before Kelly caught a glimpse of something strapped to Carl's right lower leg. She was no expert, but she was pretty sure she'd had a fleeting view of an ankle holster—and the small black automatic pistol it held.

15

Mark told Kelly he'd be there in ten minutes. Actually, it only took eight before he was knocking on her door. He sensed movement behind the peephole, then the door opened.

Kelly stood there smiling, her backpack and purse slung over one shoulder. "Thanks for coming by."

"No problem." He looked at his watch. "We'd better hurry, though. I don't want you to be late."

While Kelly fastened her seat belt, Mark hit the button to lock all the doors. "I'll walk you to the hospital entrance. Tonight, when you get off, wait inside the sliding glass doors of the ER while you call me on your cell phone. I'll come in and walk you to the car."

"Why don't I ask one of the security guards to escort me?" she said.

"I'm afraid that if you cry 'wolf' often enough, the security people will relax. I won't make that mistake. Besides, I'm thinking about getting a pistol for protection."

"I thought we discussed that and you decided against it."

Mark shook his head. "I've had time to give it some thought, and I decided that maybe it wasn't such a bad idea."

"Does someone taking a shot at Anna King have anything to do with this?"

"Yeah, that sort of brought things home to me—especially since I was talking with her on my phone when it happened."

Kelly shifted in her seat to turn toward Mark. "Well, I'm not going to argue with you. I saw something this afternoon that made me think the Zetas are a lot closer to us—actually, to me I guess—than I thought."

Mark listened to Kelly's account of seeing Carl with a pistol. "And you're sure that's what you saw?" he asked when she'd finished.

"I'm no expert on pistols, and I don't think I've ever seen an ankle holster before, but...yes, I'm pretty sure."

"If that's true, I think I'd better have a talk with whoever's in charge of personnel for the operating room. Better yet, why don't I let the police know?"

"What are you going to tell them? Your friend thought she saw Carl carrying a concealed weapon? What if he has a permit? What if he's one of the thousands of Texans who say they're exercising their Second Amendment rights by carrying a gun? Unless he brings it into the hospital, it doesn't create a problem." Kelly sighed. "No, I think that for now I just need to be extra careful when Carl's around."

"Are you going to mention this to Tracy? She works with him every day."

"I don't know. Tracy and I have been friends ever since nursing school, but what if she's a part of this? Maybe the Zetas have their hooks into her, or maybe she's an unwitting pawn in their scheme to kill me."

Mark slowed as he approached the emergency entrance of the hospital. "I'm going to see you safely inside. Don't forget to call me tonight when you get off work."

"You're off today. What are you going to do this afternoon?"

Mark decided it would be best not to get into the Gwen Woodruff thing—at least, not yet. "Oh, I'm going to see a friend from high school."

Gwen Woodruff's office was located on the ground floor of an unpretentious red brick building in downtown Drayton. The building was within easy walking distance of the courthouse, which Mark figured must be convenient for a lawyer. Inside, he consulted the building directory and easily found her office. The door on one side of hers was half-glass on which black letters spelled out the name of a CPA. On the other side were the two elevators that served the four-story building.

When he opened Gwen's door, Mark expected to be greeted by a secretary sitting behind a magnificent mahogany desk, guarding a huge waiting room filled with men in thousand dollar suits, holding briefcases in their laps as they awaited their appointments. Instead, the desk, which was small and looked to be an Office Depot special, was unoccupied. A half-dozen upholstered chairs scattered around the walls were empty at the moment. A single door at the back of the room stood open, and through it he could see Gwen, bent over her desk typing on a computer keyboard.

In high school, he thought he was in love with Gwen Woodruff. Then again, every boy in their class had some of those feelings. She had long auburn hair, gray eyes that sparkled with a hint of mischief behind wire-rimmed glasses, a body that made anything she wore look like a million dollars.

He figured that the years of college and law school would have taken their toll. Instead, Mark saw that time had not only been kind to Gwen, if anything it had enhanced her beauty. The glasses were gone, either replaced by contact lenses or made unnecessary by Lasik surgery. The auburn hair was shorter, but styled flawlessly. She wore a simple green suit, and judging by what he could see above the desk, either good genes or diet and exercise appeared to be keeping her figure trim.

Suddenly, Mark was acutely aware that he was a few days overdue for a haircut. He wore a blue blazer, an open-neck sports shirt, khakis, and scuffed loafers, all of which seemed much too informal for the occasion. He ran his hand over his chin and decided that at least his shave from that morning was holding up.

He tapped on the frame of the open door. "Gwen?"

She looked up and brief puzzlement gave way to genuine pleasure. "Mark, is that you?" She hurried out from behind her desk and embraced him. "It's so good to see you again."

At least she hadn't thrown something at him. That was promising. Mark approached the desk and took the chair to which she gestured.

Gwen apologized that her secretary was out sick, and offered coffee, water, or a soft drink, all of which Mark declined with thanks. He figured they'd spend some time catching up, and he dreaded the question to which he had no good answer. Instead he was spared, as Gwen leaned back, pulled out a fresh legal pad, and said, "You told me on the phone you might need a criminal defense attorney. I'll warn you again that I don't do much of that—truthfully, I avoid it whenever possible. But if you're determined to have me represent you, I need to know what's going on."

Mark sketched the details of his situation, beginning with the night that Ignacio Garcia brought his brother, Hector, into the emergency room of Memorial Hospital. He told her about the threatened lawsuits from the Garcia family and Ed Purvis's survivors. He described the shooting death of Buddy Cane and the attempt on Anna King's life. "And I'm here because Detective Jackson essentially told me I was their number one suspect in that shooting."

Gwen tapped the pencil on the desk. "I suspect that was designed to scare you. Sometimes a guilty person can be goaded into making a mistake when they feel the pressure is on them." She looked up at the corner of the room with an unfocused gaze. The moment seemed to last forever. Finally, she looked Mark in the eye. "Do you really want me to represent you? If you're not sure, I can give you the names of two other lawyers here in Drayton with a lot more experience in criminal defense."

Mark didn't hesitate. "I told you—I don't know them. I know you. I trust you. I'm innocent, so how hard could it be to protect my rights?"

"Harder than you think," Gwen said. "You read every day about people who are sent to jail, even executed, only to have it shown later they were innocent. This could possibly end with a murder charge, a capital offense. This is literally life or death, Mark. Think before you give me your answer."

Mark wondered if he was making the biggest mistake of his life. He'd chosen Gwen to defend him because he knew and trusted her, but was there some hope deep in his mind of rekindling their romance from years ago? He formed a prayer for guidance in his mind. No disembodied voice replied. He looked around but didn't see the answer written in fiery letters on the wall. Finally, with a bit more certainty than he felt, he said, "Yes. I want you to represent me."

Kelly had been on duty for a couple of hours when it happened. Up to that point, she'd managed to forget her own dangerous situation and lose herself in ministering to others with more acute (although in most cases less deadly) problems. Then she saw the EMTs wheel in a stretcher bearing a toddler. The little boy's head was immobilized with a long loop of tape that ran to both sides of the stretcher. The EMT at the front was bent over, whispering words of comfort, doing his best to keep the child calm. Behind the stretcher came a man with his arm draped over the shoulder of a crying woman. Both looked familiar to Kelly, although she couldn't place them.

"What do we have?" she asked the lead EMT.

"Climbed up on a coffee table at home and fell, hitting his head. Either dazed or unconscious for less than a minute, as best we can tell. When we got there he was crying and moving all extremities. Vital signs were okay. Parents—" He nodded to the man and woman who hovered at the foot of the stretcher. "Parents initially apologized for calling us unnecessarily. They wanted to ignore the problem. When we told them about the possible consequences, maybe a head injury or broken neck, they agreed to come here."

By this time they were in a cubicle, and the ER doctor was moving the curtain aside to enter. It was Eric McCray, and Kelly gave silent thanks. Eric was experienced, but more than that, he exuded an aura of calm, even in the most difficult situation.

He looked at the record of the child's vital signs, shone a penlight into the little boy's eyes, tested his reflexes, all the while speaking to the toddler in a calm voice. The child's crying had subsided to a whimper, and he'd managed to get his thumb up to his mouth so he could suck it.

"We're going to do some X-rays of his head and neck," Eric said. "This may be a simple concussion, but we don't want to miss a fractured spine or an early collection of blood pressing on the brain," Eric indicated Kelly. "The nurse will take him to the radiology department and stay with him there. You can go along if you wish."

The mother was still sobbing. The man spoke up. "I'd better stay here and try to calm my wife."

The lead EMT turned to Kelly. "I'll go with you. If the lateral X-ray shows no C-spine problems, we'll transfer the little guy to a hospital gurney. While I'm gone, my partner can clean up the back of our vehicle and get ready for the next run."

Kelly nodded and moved to the head of the stretcher, where she began to speak soothingly to the child. He was whimpering only occasionally now, still had his thumb firmly in his mouth, and seemed about to go to sleep. "What's his name?" she asked the parents.

The father spoke. "We call him Junior, but his real name is Addison. Addison Ames, Jr."

Gwen Woodruff pushed the legal pad away from her and leaned back in her chair. Mark had given her a detailed account of everything, starting with the gunman in the ER and ending with Anna lying in the hospital near death. She couldn't believe the police would proceed with such a flimsy case, but if they did, she'd be ready.

She and Mark had hammered out most of the details of her representation. He now had her cell number programmed into his own phone. They'd established a fee, and to give him credit, he didn't flinch when she named the figure. Apparently, he'd been expecting to pay, which was a refreshing change from distant acquaintances who some-how seemed to expect a "friends and family discount" for her services.

"So what do I do now?" Mark asked.

"You let me do what you retained me to do. I'll find out what the detectives have, how serious they are about mak-ing you a suspect. In the meantime, you go on about your business."

"And if they arrest me?"

She leaned forward to face him across the desk. "You punch in my number on your cell phone. Even if they make you hang up, I'll see the missed call and know what it's about. You go with them, don't fight or balk. You can say you understand the Miranda warning, but after that your only response is 'I want my attorney.'"

"If they take me to jail—"

"If you're arrested, you'll be taken to jail. You may be questioned, you may be booked, but whatever they do, just clam up until I get there." She shoved the legal pad away. "In the meantime, try not to worry."

"Easy for you to say," Mark muttered.

"Yes, the same way it's easy for a surgeon to tell someone not to worry about a procedure. The surgeon knows what he's doing, and the patient has to trust him. Now you have to put your trust in me." She paused, considering her words, then plunged on. "That is why came to me, isn't it?"

Now that he was face-to-face with her, should she ask him why, although they'd been in the same town for over two years, he'd never called, never made an effort to see her? She knew this wasn't the setting for such a conversation. But now that he was here, it was definitely a conversation she intended to have.

"Do you have plans for this evening?" she asked. "Maybe we could go out for dinner. Not as lawyer and client, but as two friends who haven't seen each other in years." When he was silent, she added, "I'm inviting you, so it would be on me. Or we could split the check if it would make you less uncomfortable."

Mark frowned, and she could see him pondering the decision.

"I know what you're thinking," Gwen said. "Maybe it would open old wounds. But I'd like to find out what happened between us. I know we went to different colleges, but sometimes long-distance relationships work out. I'd like to know why ours didn't. Actually, it seemed that you were glad of the excuse to break off all contact with me. I guess I want to know why."

Mark spoke while looking somewhere above her head, apparently afraid or ashamed to meet her gaze. "I like you a lot, Gwen. Maybe I even loved you. But when I got to college, so many things came at me at all at once—I guess I couldn't handle them all. I sort of pushed some things aside, and our relationship was one of them."

Gwen looked him in the eye. "Mark, I think there are some unresolved issues between us. I'll say it again. Let's have dinner together tonight—not as former high school sweethearts, looking to get back together again, but as two friends who want to reconnect. We'll talk—see if we can clear the air. That's all. What do you say?"

Kelly stood behind the Ames family as Dr. McCray talked with them. So far, Ames had made no mention of their meeting on Saturday night after the gunman terrorized the ER. Perhaps he'd forgotten her. After all, Mark was the focus of the drama that played out that night. Maybe Ames hadn't considered her important enough to remember.

"The CT scan of Junior's head and his neck X-rays were negative," McCray said. "My exam doesn't indicate any active problem, but it takes the brain a couple of weeks to fully heal after a concussion, so Kelly will give you a list of things to watch for—incoordination, headaches, vomiting, things like that."

"But we can take him home?" Ames said, one arm tightly gripping his wife's shoulder.

"Yes," McCray said, "but be sure to check with your pediatrician tomorrow. We'll send him a copy of this record, but he may not see it immediately."

After the doctor left, Kelly went over the checklist with the Ames family. The father seemed to focus on the instructions, while the mother's attention was on Junior, whom she cradled in her arms as he slept.

"Do you have any questions?" Kelly asked, handing the instruction sheet to Ames.

"No, but thank you." He folded the sheet and put it in his pocket.

"Don't forget to call the pediatrician," she cautioned. "And come back here if he has a convulsion or a severe headache or—"

"I know what you said. We have the instructions. We'll take it from here," Ames snapped.

Her mention of the pediatrician triggered a question in Kelly's mind. Had Mark called the Ameses' doctor? To her knowledge, this was the second instance of the child being treated in the ER because of trauma. Everything about the situation pointed to child abuse. If Mark hadn't reported it, someone needed to.

As the family turned to leave, Ames fixed Kelly with a glacial stare. "I hope you're taking steps to protect yourself after what happened here Saturday night. The people you encountered can be quite dangerous—in so many ways. If I were you, I'd be very careful."

16

Mark let Gwen pick the restaurant. It was an early dinner, but as they sat down the smells of Italian food wafting out of the kitchen made him remember he'd skipped lunch.

"Have you been here before?" he asked Gwen, as he held her chair for her.

"I occasionally bring clients here," she said. "It's relatively quiet, and I thought that would be a good thing for us tonight."

Mark buried his nose in the menu as he wondered exactly what agenda Gwen might have in mind for their time together. It didn't take long for her to make it clear.

"You didn't write, you know. Not a single letter. Not even a postcard." He looked up and saw her eyes steady on him, her hands folded on the unopened menu in front of her. "Even when you were home from college for the holidays, you seemed to go out of your way to avoid me. Why? What happened?"

The necktie Mark had put on for tonight's dinner felt like a noose, gradually tightening around his neck. He resisted the urge to tug at it. "I think it's pretty much what I told you. Things changed."

"What changed?" Her voice was flat, almost emotionless. But her expression told a different story.

"My parents were very happy when we started going out together," Mark said. "I think they hoped you'd be a good influence on me. I'd taken the first step—become a Christian—but I wasn't very active when we were dating. On the other hand, you were a preacher's daughter. Some of that was bound to rub off on me." He reached for his water glass and drank deeply. "Then, my first night at college, my roommate and I had a long talk about almost everything—including religion. His contention was there was no need to go to church. The church was full of hypocrites anyway. Why go to church? God didn't check roll."

"And you listened to him." Gwen fixed him with those deep gray eyes.

He looked down, avoiding her gaze. "It was easy to believe him. Now I was away from home. I could do what I wanted."

"That doesn't explain why you broke off contact with me."

"No, I guess it doesn't." Mark began to doubt the wisdom of making contact with Gwen again today. But he needed her help. Might as well get it all out in the open. "My roommate discovered I'd never dated anyone but you. He kept telling me now was my chance to shop around. You know, date other girls, see if what you and I had was something beyond puppy love."

"And what did you find out?" she asked, her eyes boring into his.

He picked up his water glass and discovered he'd drained it. Where was the waiter? He needed a break more than he needed water. Mark took a deep breath. "Just to shut up my roommate, I started dating. He helped—it seemed that he knew half the girls on campus. The ones I went out with were nice. And it did help to have a standard for comparison."

"You mean to compare with me?" Gwen's voice fairly dripped with sarcasm.

Mark chose to ignore that. "My dating didn't last long. Once my premed classes got started, I discovered there wasn't a lot of time for socializing. I had to work hard to keep from flunking out. So I buckled down. I didn't date, and I didn't write you. Then, by the time I came back home for Christmas vacation, I was too embarrassed to face you. So I let our relationship slide."

The waiter appeared and took their order. Mark hoped that the interruption would refocus their conversation, but obviously Gwen had other ideas.

"You know I had scholarship offers from any number of colleges for my pre-law work," she said. "I chose Harvard, mainly because it wasn't too far from where our folks lived. I figured that when you came back for a weekend I could make the trip as well, and we could get together." She grimaced. "That didn't work too well, though."

"I'm sorry. I—"

"After the first semester, I knew something was wrong. That's when I decided I wanted to be as far away from you as possible. So I transferred the next year to Stanford in California. It's almost impossible to get into, but I made it. And when you still didn't contact me, I decided to stay there for law school."

At that point the waiter appeared with their salads. As soon as the server left the table, Mark jumped in to make certain the subject stayed changed—anything to avoid talking about his breakup with Gwen, which was still embarrassing after all these years. "So how did you end up in Drayton, Texas?"

"I had a lot of job offers, but the one I accepted was with a large law firm in Dallas: Gilmore, Chrisman, and Rutledge. I worked there for a year, sort of a probationary time. I did well, impressed everyone, but I discovered pretty quickly that I'd rather be a solo practitioner. I chose Drayton because it was close enough to Dallas to offer the things I wanted, but still small enough for me to be comfortable." Now it was her turn to drink deeply from her water glass. She put it down and continued. "I didn't know you were here. If I'd known…"

"I'm glad you're here. I'm glad we could reconnect. And I need to tell you something. I know I told you that during college and medical school I drifted further away from God, but that's changed. I'm trying…for lack of a better word, I guess you could say I'm trying to be a follower—not just an observer."

Gwen grimaced and took a deep breath. "That's just too funny. Sort of like something by O. Henry."

"What do you mean?"

"I'm where you were ten years ago," Gwen said. "I haven't set foot inside a church since I started law school."

⸙

Kelly gathered her things from her locker and sank into a chair in the ER break room. She pulled her cell phone from her purse and called Mark. It was late—almost midnight—but he'd insisted that she call him for a ride home.

He answered on the first ring. "Mark, are you sure—"

"Don't give it another thought," he said. "I'm sitting in the ER parking lot right now, in a slot marked for patients."

There was a pause and the sound of a slamming car door. "I'm heading for the double glass doors. I'll meet you there."

Once they were safely in the car, Mark asked, "Do you want to go somewhere for coffee? I know that when I get off around midnight I'm generally too wired to sleep."

He paused, and she could tell he was trying to decide whether to say more. Maybe if they stopped for coffee...

"Sure," she said. "Do you have someplace in mind?"

As it turned out, he did. In a bit, they were seated in the back booth of a diner with cups in front of them. "Anything interesting happen on your shift?" Mark asked.

Okay, I'll go first. Maybe he'll open up after that. "Actually, I wanted to talk with you about what happened tonight. Detective Ames and his wife came in with their son, Junior." She tried to relate the story objectively, but when she repeated Ames's final words, the menace that had been in them came through in her voice.

Mark put down the cup he was holding. "So do you plan to keep this to yourself... and me, of course?"

Kelly shook her head. "No, I think we should follow through." She looked at Mark. "You were going to call the Ames's pediatrician. I guess that's the next step."

"I still haven't done that," he said. "I'll go by the hospital tomorrow, get the doc's name off the ER record, and make the call."

"And if he agrees that there's probably some abuse?"

"If he hasn't already done something about it, I'll call Child Protective Services myself," Mark said. "I'm not going to let the child suffer because I'm afraid of his father."

Kelly wanted to tell Mark to be cautious, but she could see there was no use. When it came to the well-being of patients, Mark wasn't one to be deterred. That was one of the many reasons she'd been fond of him. Now there was more than fondness there. And she sensed that Mark had the same feelings for her.

"What about you?" she asked. "How did your dinner with your friend go?"

Mark stared down at his virtually untouched cup of coffee as though it were a crystal ball. "I...I guess I should level with you. The person I went to see this afternoon really was a high school classmate, but she's also an attorney. The detectives warned me that I'm still a prime suspect in Anna King's shooting. They told me I should get a lawyer."

"I don't see anything wrong with that," Kelly said. "If anything, I'd think your knowing her in high school might be a good thing. The question is how good a lawyer is she? Does she do a lot of criminal cases?"

"Not really." Mark sipped from his cup. "Cold." He put it down and frowned. "No, Gwen does general law, and she offered to refer me to another attorney, but I insisted on her."

"Why?" Kelly asked.

"Because I know her. I figure that would mean something when it came to defending me."

"You make it sound like she was more than an acquaintance," Kelly said.

"True, we were something of an item in high school," Mark said, his eyes fixed on the tabletop. "I didn't choose her for that reason, and since I broke off our relationship I was afraid she might tell me to take a hike. But at least there was some connection there."

Kelly pushed her cup away. First Anna King, then this woman from Mark's past. The phrase "fear of commitment" came to mind. This wasn't what she wanted to hear—not at all.

The man sat in his dark SUV outside the diner, slouched so low behind the wheel that his head was barely visible. This opportunity was too good—both of the people involved in the deaths of the Garcia brothers, together in a car after midnight. The streets of Drayton weren't exactly deserted, but traffic was light enough that often two or three minutes passed with no cars, no pedestrian traffic. This was the perfect time for the Zetas to exact revenge.

He had already pulled his pistol from the holster he wore strapped to his calf. There were times he chose something with stopping power, such as a Glock, but for this assignment he had selected a Beretta Bobcat. The pistol was small and light, but, in the hands of a marksman, the seven .25 caliber bullets in the chamber could be just as deadly as the .357 Magnum loads from a larger gun. And he was certainly a marksman. That's why he'd been chosen for this assignment.

Had a casual observer seen him slumped in the driver's seat of the vehicle, they might have thought he was asleep. However, he was wide-awake and attentive. He was used to being up for long hours at a stretch and was prepared to watch as long as—

Here they came. The door of the diner opened, and the two emerged. She had pushed through ahead of him, despite his apparent efforts to open the door for her. The woman hurried around the car and stood there until he unlocked her door using his key fob, then clambered in before he could get around the car to open the door. The man shrugged, climbed behind the wheel, and drove away.

He started his car and fell in behind them, careful to stay back far enough to avoid raising the driver's suspicions. The perfect spot for an ambush would be coming up quickly. He'd be ready.

"Kelly, I didn't mean to hurt you when I told you about Gwen. I wanted to be open about our past, but believe me, there's no spark left of my past relationship with her."

There was silence from beside him. "I certainly didn't mean to make you angry," Mark said, his eyes glued on the road ahead. "Let's talk about it."

"There's nothing to talk about," she said and turned to face the passenger-side window.

Mark slowed the car and turned in to a strip shopping center. He brought the car to a stop and turned off the motor. "I can't drive and talk, and this is important. Will you at least look at me?"

She half-turned her head so she could see him. "Go ahead. I'm listening."

Mark realized he wasn't the world's best extemporaneous speaker, but he needed to get this right. "When the detective told me I needed a lawyer, I remembered my folks had sent me Gwen's information when she moved to Drayton. They were disappointed that I broke up with her when I went to college, and I think they hoped our being in the same town would eventually get us together again."

He waited for a reply, but was met with only silence.

"Anyway, I wanted a lawyer who knew me, whom I could trust, so I chose her. She doesn't normally take criminal cases, but I insisted."

"That explains the professional component of your visit with her," Kelly said. "What about the rest of it?"

Mark hesitated, trying to frame his response. His words were halting at first, but as he talked they poured out faster and faster. "As I talked with her I realized I used the distance between us when we went to college as an excuse to break up with her. I promise, there's nothing between us now except the lawyer-client relationship." He reached out and covered her hand with his.

"So what you had years ago—"

"Gone. One twist I discovered was this. We've even switched viewpoints about the role of God in our lives. I'm trying to find Him again, but she's ignored Him since our breakup. "

Kelly's failure to respond told Mark he'd better stop his narrative. He put his hand back on the wheel, started the car, and pulled out onto the street. "I'm sorry to have to tell you all this, but I thought you deserved to hear it. I'll be quiet now. I should have you home soon."

They rode in silence for a few minutes before Kelly spoke. "There's something I guess I should tell you, since we're being painfully honest with each other. And maybe it explains why what you've told me is especially painful."

Mark glanced at her but decided he'd better just listen.

"I know we've only dated for a few months, but when we were being held at gunpoint the other night, I realized how important you were to me, and how devastated I'd be if you were hurt or killed. Afterward, I decided to share my feelings with you, but at that time it was obvious you were in no mood to hear them."

"What exactly were you going to tell me?" he asked.

The silence seemed to last forever. Finally, Kelly said, "I guess I'd better get it out in the open. Mark, I'm—"

Gunshots and the sounds of shattering glass overrode Kelly's voice, and she slumped forward in her seat.

17

KELLY FELT AS THOUGH SHE'D BEEN HIT IN THE BACK BY A three-hundred-pound linebacker. She couldn't breathe. Her chest was on fire. She was driven forward, and although her brain sent a warning to her hands to reach out, she was unable to complete the move. Her head hit the dashboard. She was fleetingly aware of tiny shards of glass scattered on the plastic before everything faded into blackness.

She didn't know how long she was out—maybe only a few seconds, maybe longer—but when consciousness returned, the car was speeding through the streets, Mark hunched over the steering wheel as though by posture alone he could make the vehicle go faster.

"What...what happened?" she asked, her voice barely above a whisper. She continued to gasp for air.

"Sit back. Don't move. I'm on my way to the ER."

Mark turned a corner. Tires squealed, the car rocked and settled, and Kelly wondered if a couple of wheels didn't momentarily leave the ground.

"What happened?" she croaked again.

"Someone shot at us. Several times. The bullets came in the back window and exited the windshield, but at least one of them got you in the back." He braked for a second, whipped the car around another corner, and accelerated again. "You need medical attention fast. I don't have anything in the car to even give first aid, and I decided it was quicker for me to drive you to the ER than wait for EMTs to arrive."

Kelly had trouble thinking coherently. Who could have shot at them? She vaguely recalled they were in danger, but the specifics fled her brain. She looked up in time to see the illuminated red letters, EMERGENCY, just ahead. As she watched, they became fuzzy, then faded, and finally dissolved into a silent blackness.

⸎

Mark screeched to a stop right outside the sliding glass doors to the emergency room. He could run inside and get help, but maybe it would be faster to lean on the horn until someone responded. He did that, counting the seconds. If no one came within thirty seconds— No, there was someone now. A security guard, one Mark had seen but whose name he didn't know, came through the door, one hand on his gun, frowning at the car with the blaring horn.

Mark lowered his window and yelled, "Gunshot wound. We need help."

The guard didn't waste time with questions, but ducked back inside, yelling as he went. In less than a minute, Dr. Eric McCray came running, followed closely by an orderly pushing a gurney. "Mark?" he yelled when he was close enough to see the situation.

By then, Mark had vaulted from the car and run around to open the passenger door. He unfastened Kelly's seat belt as he talked. "Someone shot through the back window of the car. Kelly was hit. I don't know how many bullets got her, but—"

Eric shoved Mark aside. "Let me handle this." He motioned to the orderly, and together they moved Kelly onto the gurney and took off for the ER at a half-run.

Mark started to follow, but the security guard said, "Doctor, why don't you move your car? Then come inside. I'm sure Miss Atkinson is in capable hands. Meanwhile, I'm going to call the police. I'm sure they'll want to talk with you."

"But—"

"What's going on? Can I help?"

Mark whirled and saw Carl, the scrub tech, climbing out of his auto and hurrying toward them.

"Who are you?" the guard asked.

Carl had reached the group by now. He held up his hospital ID card. "Carl Ortiz. I work in surgery," he told the guard. Carl put one hand on Mark's shoulder. "I was driving home and saw your car speed by. I sensed that something was wrong, so I decided to follow. What happened?"

"Doctor, I'm going to have to ask you to move this car. You're blocking the ambulance entrance," the security guard said. "Then you can bring Mr. Ortiz up to speed while we wait for the police to arrive."

"But, Kelly—" Mark protested.

"Let Dr. McCray do his job," the guard said. "When you've moved your car, go to the ER break room. You can wait there."

Mark shrugged a half-apology to Carl. "I guess I'd better do as he says. I'll see you inside."

———

Carl looked around him and marveled at how much this break room in the ER resembled the one in the surgical suite. Maybe all such rooms in US hospitals looked like this. He was more familiar with the ones he'd seen in Mexico. But that was a subject for another time, one to be explored in his own head but not shared with anyone. Especially Dr. Mark Baker.

He put his hand on Baker's shoulder. "I'm sorry I couldn't help," he said.

"No, but I appreciate your turning around and following me to the hospital. If I'd done something stupid like sideswiping a car or blowing out a tire, we could have loaded Kelly into your car. I'm glad you were there."

"I'm afraid that you and Miss Atkinson are still in danger from the Mexican drug cartel—what was the name again?"

"Zetas," Mark answered, his mind obviously elsewhere. He continued to peer through the open door of the break room. After a moment of silence, he turned and faced Carl. "Look, I'm distracted here. You've done what you could, and if you give me your phone number I'll call you with an update later. But right now, I'd like to be alone."

"Of course," Carl said. "As you say, I've done what I can."

Outside, as Carl made his way toward his car, he thought, *Actually, I didn't do enough. But maybe I'll be able to remedy that soon . . . very soon.*

Mark couldn't sit still. He paced the length of the ER break room, occasionally looking out the door, his attention focused on trauma room 1 where Eric and several other doctors were working on Kelly.

When Mark looked out the door the next time, he saw Eric, another surgeon whom he recognized but couldn't fully identify, and a nurse wheeling Kelly toward the elevator. She had two IV lines in place, one delivering blood and the other connected to a bag of IV solution that he figured had medications added. An anesthesiologist walked at the head of the gurney, squeezing and releasing a bag that delivered air to the tube now in Kelly's windpipe.

Mark stepped outside, but Eric saw the action and shook his head. "Later," he mouthed as the procession disappeared into the staff elevator, undoubtedly on its way to the operating room on the second floor.

"Later." How could Mark wait until "later?" He was a physician, used to being in the thick of the action, not a non-combatant standing by worrying, waiting, helpless. And that wasn't just a patient on the gurney. That was…Mark retreated to the sofa and dropped onto it. What exactly was Kelly to him?

He and Kelly had worked together for the best part of a year, but he hadn't gained a sense of her until the past few months, when they'd gone out for dinners, movies, sporting events, and the occasional concert. And the more he knew about her, the more he was attracted to her.

There'd been a few dates with Anna King, but as he thought back on them, he realized that Anna had asked him out on most of those occasions, not vice versa. If he was interpreting some of the things she'd recently told him, dating him had been a smokescreen to mask…what? She'd never finished that conversation. Did he have feelings for Anna? Yes, but feelings related to her situation, the same kind of feelings he would have for anyone else who lay in a coma in the ICU, fighting for her life.

Then there was Gwen Woodruff. In high school, he'd had visions of spending the rest of his life with her. She'd get her law degree, he'd graduate from medical school, and then they'd marry and live a perfect life as two professionals, with a family of two children and a dog. But that dream gradually was replaced by reality, and he realized Gwen wasn't "the one."

Now that they'd been thrown together again, Mark discovered another twist: while he was in the process of reconnecting with God, Gwen had disconnected from Him. That might change—he hoped it would, for Gwen's sake—but he no longer felt what they shared when they were younger.

That brought him back to Kelly. Before the shooting in the ER on Saturday night, he'd felt close to her—closer than he'd ever been with anyone. He'd even wondered if this were the beginning of true love. His selfish actions that night had sunk him into despair about himself, but now he was trying to change…to get back on the right track in so many ways. Mark was starting to feel he was ready to be in a serious relationship. And Kelly would be "the one."

God, I haven't prayed—really prayed—in so long. I don't even know if I'm doing it the right way now. But please bring Kelly safely through this experience. And give me a chance to get right…with her…and with You.

⸺⸻⸺

As Mark sat in the break room, he wondered if there was someone he should call to let them know Kelly was in surgery. Only recently had she opened up to him about her family, and it made Mark think his own hadn't been so bad.

Kelly's parents divorced about the time she started college. Each had remarried and moved away, one now living in Montana and the other Maine, and Kelly saw her parents perhaps once a year. He remembered her confiding that since she was an only child with essentially absentee parents, she'd come to rely on God as the only constant in her life. Well, maybe that wasn't such a bad thing.

Mark was lost in his thoughts when Eric entered the break room and sat down next to him.

"How—"

"Kelly's on the operating table right now," Eric said. "One bullet entered the top third of her right lung and is lodged in the anterior chest wall. She has blood in the chest cavity on that side, as well as a pneumothorax. They'll stop any bleeding, put in a chest tube to re-expand the lung, remove the bullet. You know the drill."

"Blood loss?" Mark asked.

"Pretty significant. They're replacing it as we speak. Vital signs have stabilized." He looked at his watch. "She should be in the recovery room in another hour, maybe less. I'll be sure they let you know."

"Who—"

"Mel Johnson was in the house. He's a good trauma surgeon. He called Tom Sellers to deal with the chest wound." Eric patted Mark's shoulder. "She's in good hands. Just hang on."

Mark patted his friend on the shoulder. "Thanks, Eric." He shook his head. "Maybe I should have called 911 and let the EMTs handle it. But—"

"You may have saved her life by what you did. Don't beat yourself up." Eric rose and turned toward the door. "Hey, I know what you're going through. It's tough. If it hadn't been for my faith, when I lost Cynthia...Well, anyway, I'll be right out here if you need anything. And in the meantime—"

"I know. You'll be praying. Thanks, Eric."

Mark had no sooner collapsed back onto the sagging couch than two men appeared in the doorway. *I might have known.* "Detectives Jackson and Ames. Are you the ones I need to talk with about the shooting?"

After a perfunctory "Sorry about this," the two men got down to business. "While we get the information from you, we need to let a couple of people go over your car."

Mark told Jackson where he'd left his auto and handed over his keys. The detective stepped to the door, passed the keys to a uniformed officer and relayed the information. "They'll be a while," Jackson said to Mark, "But I suspect you're going to be around."

Mark moved to the coffeepot and poured a cup. When he gestured to the two policemen, Ames shook his head while Jackson accepted a Styrofoam cup and added creamer and sugar.

"I don't guess we need to ask who could be shooting at you," Jackson said. He sipped the coffee, made a wry face, but continued to drink.

"I suppose it was the Zetas," Mark said. "But there could be others."

While Ames maintained his poker face, this seemed to surprise Jackson. "Who?"

"Suppose the bullets that hit Kelly were meant for me." Mark paused to let that sink in. "Some police officers seem to still have the idea that I'm responsible for Ed Purvis's death," he said. "Matter of fact, you've told me his family may be filing suit against me for what I did." Mark tasted his coffee, then dropped the full cup into the trash. "I went to the Purvis home to express my sympathy, and on my way back I was almost run off the road by an SUV that looked a lot like the cruisers the Drayton police drive." He grimaced. "But you wouldn't know anything about that, would you?"

"Now wait a minute—" Jackson began.

"Then there's the matter of Anna King's shooting," Mark continued. "Apparently I'm the number one suspect, but suppose what I'm telling you is true, and I'm innocent. If someone kills me, I'm betting your investigation into the attack on Anna stops right there."

Neither Jackson nor Ames replied to that.

"So perhaps the person who fired those shots at my car was the person who really shot Anna King. You might think about that, as well."

Jackson flipped to a new page in his notebook. "Dr. Baker, we're in sort of a difficult position. You and Miss Atkinson are in danger from the Zeta cartel—we know that. And we're going to try to get them before they get to you. But because you're also a suspect in the shooting of Dr. Anna King, I'm walking through a legal minefield here. So before we ask any more questions about this attack that has Miss Atkinson in surgery, let me be certain you understand your rights." He pulled a laminated card from his shirt pocket. "Mind you, you're not under arrest. But this is simply to be sure. You have the right to remain silent. If you…"

Mark tuned out the rest of the Miranda warning. He'd heard it on TV enough times he could have recited it back to Jackson. Could this situation get any more complex?

A sharp pain in the right side of her chest aroused Kelly. She tried to take a deep breath and more pain shot through her. Where was she? What was happening? She tried to open her eyes, but it was as though they were glued shut. She could hear the murmur of voices, superimposed on a background of a mechanical to and fro sound. Kelly tried to cry out, but there was some sort of obstruction in her throat. She summoned up all her strength and finally managed to move her right arm.

"She's moving." The unfamiliar male voice seemed to come from directly above her.

Another voice from behind her head answered. "I've kept her light, but I guess she's coming around. Let me make an adjustment."

Kelly tried to move again, but now it was as though there was some sort of disconnect between her will and her muscles. She felt as though she were wrapped in plastic, unable to move even the tiniest bit. How could she breathe? Panic overcame her. Then she felt her chest move and air rushed into her lungs. In a few seconds, it moved out again with no conscious effort on her part. Weird.

Now the second voice said, "I've given her some Sux and ketamine." There was a brief pause. "That should keep her still until I can breathe her down."

Sux? Succinylcholine, a paralyzing agent used in surgery. Ketamine? That was an anesthetic agent. She was in surgery. But how? What?

"How's she doing?" the voice asked.

Kelly never heard the answer. Blackness enfolded her, and she slipped away.

<hr>

Eric McCray paused at the door to the ER break room. Mark was in earnest conversation with the two detectives, and Eric hated to interrupt. On the other hand, he knew that Mark needed to hear the news he brought. Eric had volunteered to break it to his friend, rather than letting someone else convey it. That was the least he could do.

The stocky black detective—Eric didn't recall his name—talked with Mark, while the other policeman, the tall, thin one, stood by and took notes. As soon as Eric stepped into the room, Mark stopped in midsentence. He moved away from the detectives until he stood face to face with Eric.

"What's the latest?" Mark asked.

Eric gestured to the sofa. "Let's sit down."

Mark shook his head. "I'm fine right here. What—" His voice broke and he started over. "What's the news?"

There was no easy way to say this. Eric decided to get it over with. "I'm sorry. She's dead."

18

Mark had played football in his youth, and in one of the games he'd been kicked in the gut. He remembered the sensation, curled up on the ground, unable to breathe, unsure if he would be able to get up. Although he remained upright this time, he had the same sensation. It was as though he'd been hit in the midsection by a pile driver.

"I'm sorry," Eric said again. "They thought she was going to recover. She wasn't fully lucid yet, but she could respond to commands, open her eyes, move her fingers. Then suddenly, she just...I'm really sorry."

Mark shook his head. He'd finally taken an honest look at the three women in his life and come to a decision about which one he truly loved. Now...

"Doctor." Jackson moved forward. "I think we'll wait to complete this interview. I'll contact you later." He took a deep breath. "I'm sorry for your loss."

The two detectives eased out of the room. Mark dropped onto the sofa, and Eric sat beside him.

Mark sat in silence for several minutes. Finally, he asked, "Did she say anything at all before she died?"

"Her surgeon was at her bedside, and he'd asked her if she saw who shot her."

"I don't see how she'd know that," Mark said.

"Well, apparently she did, because she said something. But I'm not sure you want to hear it."

"Of course I do," Mark said.

Eric shrugged. "Okay. When the surgeon said, 'Did you see who shot you?' she managed to choke out one syllable: 'Mar—'. Then she died."

"Are you going to stop questioning him?" Detective Ames asked.

Jackson didn't answer immediately. Instead, he jerked his head toward the exit from the emergency room. They walked outside, and Jackson stopped to stretch. The mercury lights around the entrance made the area bright as day. He yawned and turned to face his partner. "About the time that other doctor came into the break room, my cell phone buzzed. I'm expecting a text from Rodgers, the patrolman assigned to stay with the surgeon who got shot, Dr. King. I thought we'd give Dr. Baker a little time to grieve while I check on what Rodgers has for us."

"But we're going back."

Jackson grinned. "Oh, you bet. We're going to talk some more with Dr. Baker. His story is that someone took a shot at him and the nurse, and her injuries and the bullet holes in his car back him up on that. On the other hand, I don't want to lose sight that he's one of our prime suspects in the shooting of Dr. King." He moved toward a quiet area of the parking lot. "Let me call Rodgers and see what he has for us. After that, we can decide how we want to approach Baker."

Mark sat with his head in his hands. "I can't believe that Kelly is dead." He stifled a sob. "And apparently the last thing she did was try to call my name. I should have been there with her."

Eric pulled back and held up his hands. "Wait a minute. I think you have this all wrong. I don't mean that Kelly is dead." He looked at his watch. "She's probably out of surgery and in the recovery room by now. We can check in a few minutes to find out when you can see her."

Hope burned through the confusion in Mark's mind. "That's wonderful. But if Kelly isn't the one who died…" Mark thought for a second, and the obvious answer came to him. "You mean Anna King, don't you? Anna's dead."

Eric nodded. "Yes. I'm sorry."

"But you said the doctor asked her who shot her, and she said, 'Mar—.' Right?"

"I'm afraid so."

"And they had a police officer standing by in case Anna regained consciousness. So I guess either he heard or the doctor told him—"

"Right. So I suspect you'll see those two detectives again real soon."

<hr />

Mark stood by the bed and looked down at the body of Anna King. The nurses had removed the tubes and electrodes from the corpse, but still she looked anything but natural. Her head had been shaved and surgical staples outlined the craniotomy incision. Mark bent and brushed her cold forehead with his lips. *I'm going to find out who did this to you, Anna. You deserve that.*

"Do you need any information from me? I suppose her ex-husband will have the contact information for her parents and her brother," Mark said.

Dr. Troy Michaels put his hand on Mark's shoulder. "If there are any questions, I'll ask the chaplain to page you." He cleared his throat. "I wish we could have saved her. Actually, I thought we had. The surgery seemed to go well. We got the bullet out without a hiccup. I don't know if she threw a pulmonary embolus or had some kind of arrhythmia or—"

"It doesn't matter," Mark said. "She shouldn't have been here in the first place. Sure, Anna made some mistakes in her life, but why would anyone shoot her?"

"That's what we'd like to know."

Mark flinched at the voice. It was easy enough to recognize Detective Ames. It was just like him to intrude on this brief quiet time. "Please. Can you wait outside? I wanted a few moments alone with...." His voice gave way to a choked sob.

The detective didn't question whether Mark was talking about time with the body of Anna King or a chance to discuss the case with Dr. Michaels. He simply said, "Sure. We'll be right outside."

Troy looked around to be certain they were alone before he continued. "Look, Mark. I'm not sure the policeman stationed outside the ICU room heard what Anna said, but—"

"I know. You saw that she seemed to be regaining consciousness, so you asked her if she knew who shot her."

Troy nodded. "She said, 'Mar—', then she died."

"I didn't shoot her, Troy. Maybe she was calling for me. I don't know. But I didn't shoot her."

Troy yawned. "I wish I could stick around to support you, but I've got a leaking cerebral aneurysm I have to look in on. It may be a long night for me."

Mark nodded and followed Troy from the room. The detectives were waiting right outside, and fell in with Mark, one on either side. It looked like a long night for him, as well.

———

Kelly heard sounds. Some were mechanical—whooshes and clicks and beeps. Others were voices, mostly muted although occasionally raised a bit, but never to the level of a shout. She tried to open her eyes and was frustrated when they didn't respond. Kelly moved the fingers of her right hand and was pleased to note that they wiggled at her command. She got the same result on the left. But when she tried to raise her arms, the motion was restricted.

Gradually, struggling past a nightmare-like feeling of helplessness, she emerged into a hazy sort of consciousness. She was in a hospital. Her arms were restrained. Attempts at speaking resulted in only a strangled grunt, so she probably had a tube in her trachea.

She forced herself to relax. *Easy. Don't panic. You know this situation. You've been on the other end of it before.* Like a spider crawling over the sheets, she moved her right hand on the covers—down, back, right, left. There it was! She felt the familiar cold plastic of the control button.

Kelly tried to recall the configuration of the devices used in this hospital, but her memory came up blank. She punched one, and heard the click and thrum of the TV set at the foot of her bed turning on, followed by a disembodied voice saying "We'll be right back after these messages." She moved her finger to another button and the sound died.

Move your fingers downward. But which way was down and which was up? She fumbled until she found the largest button, located toward the center of the device. She pressed it and was rewarded with the sound of a faint buzzing in the distance. That was followed by the rapid squeak of rubber soles on vinyl tile, then a voice above her. "Are you awake?"

That seemed a silly question, but Kelly answered with a nod.

"Let me get a warm washcloth and wipe your eyes. Generally the anesthesiologists use sterile ointment to hold the lids closed and protect your corneas. Sometimes enough remains to make it difficult to open them."

Kelly heard water running. In a moment, she felt a wonderfully soothing sensation as the nurse wiped her eyes with the warm, moist cloth.

"Try that."

She opened her eyes, blinked twice, and as the haze cleared from her vision she could see that she appeared to be in a room in either ICU or recovery. Kelly had been in many of these before, but never as a patient. Nevertheless, the familiarity helped her relax a bit.

She moved her arms, and the nurse responded by removing Kelly's restraints. "Careful. You have IVs in both arms. And there's a chest tube on your right side."

Kelly nodded. She tried to speak, but again her efforts produced only the strangled grunt.

"Let me get the doctor. We'll see if he'll remove your endotracheal tube." The nurse, an older woman with steel-gray hair, patted Kelly's hand. "Hang on. You're doing fine."

Kelly forced herself to relax. She hoped the nurse was right. Bits and pieces of her shooting came back to her. Then she had a thought that sent her heart into free fall. What about Mark?

∞∞∞

"Do you want to find someplace that's quiet, where we can talk?" Mark asked.

The look that passed between Jackson and Ames was brief, but apparently they had been partners long enough for such silent communication to be effective.

"I think it would be better if we went down to the station," Jackson said.

Mark tried to keep his voice even. Don't make them mad—especially not now. "What if I don't want to go?" he asked.

"I'm afraid we're going to have to insist," Ames said, grabbing Mark's arm in a viselike grip. "You have the right—"

"Hold on," Mark said. "Am I under arrest?"

"Not at this point," Ames said. "But I just want to be sure you're familiar with your rights."

"You've already done that once. I'm pretty certain that I have two main rights at this point, and I want to invoke them both. I want to call my attorney, and I don't plan to say another word to you guys until she's here." He jerked his arm free from Ames's grip, and reached into his pocket for car keys, only to recall that the police had them.

"I'm afraid I'm going to have to ask you to ride with us," Jackson said. "Your car should be safe on the lot here. We'll see that you get a ride back to claim it when you leave the police station."

"*If* you leave the police station," Ames murmured under his breath.

∞∞∞

Gwen Woodruff scrabbled blindly for the cell phone on her bedside table. The red numerals on the clock there said 3:57. Her practice wasn't one that involved a lot of emergency calls. One coming this late meant a client was in trouble. Just how much trouble and what kind remained to be seen.

She clicked on the lamp beside her bed, cleared her throat, and answered the call. "Gwen Woodruff."

"It's Mark, Gwen. The police are taking me to the station." Sleepy as she was, Mark's voice was like a bucket of cold water in her face.

Gwen sat up on one elbow. "Tell me about it." She opened the drawer of the bedside table and removed a pen and notepad.

She listened, jotting notes in a shorthand only she could read and nodding her head, even though Mark couldn't see her. "So you're not under arrest? I want to be clear about that."

"No, I asked specifically. They said they were bringing me in for questioning. But I get the impression that nothing would please these guys more than tossing me behind bars and keeping me there."

"Where are you now?"

"I'm using my cell phone to call from the back of their police car." A rumble of voices in the background came through. "We're going to the police station. I think we're almost there. Can you come?"

"I'll be there soon. In the meantime, listen to me." Gwen didn't practice criminal law, but she figured she could give some decent advice. "When you get to the police station, ask them for some coffee or something to drink."

"Why?"

"So they don't have you thinking of yourself as a prisoner."

"Okay."

She continued. "Make sure the door to the interrogation room or wherever they put you isn't locked. If they give you any static, keep asking if you're under arrest. And, above all, don't answer any questions until I get there."

"How long will you be?" Mark asked, a note of desperation in his voice.

"Give me half an hour."

Gwen rolled out of bed, hurried to the kitchen, and turned on the coffee. As she applied makeup, her thoughts went back to what she and Mark had when they were younger. Why did he break off their relationship? Why did she react to his actions by putting a continent between them? And why had they been brought together now, in a situation that was probably the worst possible one for rekindling a relationship?

Gwen pulled a dress from the closet and slipped it on. She remembered her recent meeting with Mark. She'd insisted that she really didn't do criminal defense. He was equally insistent, saying, "I know you. I trust you. I'm innocent, so how hard could it be to protect my rights?"

Harder than you'd think, Mark. She remembered something one of her professors told her class in law school, something that had a lot to do with her choice of legal specialty. The hardest client to defend is an innocent man, because he has the most to lose. That was multiplied here, because in this case both she and Mark had a great deal at stake.

19

MARK WANTED TO LAY HIS HEAD ON THE SCARRED SURFACE of the interview room table and drop off to sleep, but knew that wasn't an option. He tried not to look at his watch every thirty seconds, but when he did he noticed the hands had hardly moved since his last glance. Where was Gwen?

Jackson stuck his head through the door. The overhead lights glinted on the sweat that dotted his shaved head. His shirt was wrinkled, his tie at half-mast. The detective had shed his coat and apparently stowed his automatic in his desk. Now the holster of his shoulder rig was empty, but its mere presence made Mark's pulse beat faster. Jackson frowned. "Your attorney still isn't here. Why don't you answer a few questions so we can wrap this up? We can have you back at the hospital in less than an hour."

Mark silently shook his head. He wasn't a lawyer, but he remembered Gwen's advice. Before Anna's death, the police had told him he was a suspect in her shooting. Now the possible charge had been upgraded to murder. No longer was just his freedom on the line, but his very life.

Ames came up behind Jackson. If anything, his appearance was worse than Jackson's. He was disheveled and his eyes were red-rimmed. When the light hit Ames's face just right, a healthy crop of blonde stubble was evident. The two men stood right outside the partially opened interview room door, and Mark could hear their conversation clearly.

"I say we lock him up as a material witness," Ames said. "Then we can go home, get some sleep, and do this interview later in the day."

"Why are you so anxious to get home?" Jackson asked. "I thought—"

Ames inclined his head toward Mark. "We don't need to discuss that in front of the suspect."

"His attorney is on the way. Let's wait a bit longer. I don't mind collecting a little more overtime, and I'm sure your wife—"

"We agreed not to talk about my wife," Ames said. He turned away, calling over his shoulder, "I'm going to get some more coffee. Want some?"

Neither Jackson nor Mark had a chance to respond, because at that moment Gwen hurried through the door. "Sorry, there was a wreck on the freeway, and I had to take the long way here."

She brushed past both Jackson and Ames into the interview room, where she took the chair beside Mark. The two detectives followed her in. Jackson introduced himself and his partner, but no one made any effort to shake hands. Gwen tossed two of her cards onto the table, gave her name, and said, "Let's do this. My client has already been held too long. Ask your questions so he and I can get out of here."

This Gwen was different from the one Mark knew. That one had been smiling and full of fun. This one was dead serious. She had taken control of the situation and served notice that she was here to protect Mark's interests. Maybe, despite her protestations that she wasn't a criminal defense attorney, he'd made the right choice.

⸻

"We've been at this for almost an hour," Gwen said. "And for the last fifteen minutes you've asked my client the same questions, and he's given the same answers. Let's wind this up."

Gwen removed her glasses—she hadn't taken the time to insert her contact lenses—and rubbed her eyes. Her eyelids felt like they were lined with sandpaper, and she could hardly keep them open. She'd pulled lots of all-nighters in law school, but being roused from a sound sleep and put into a stressful situation like this one wasn't helping her stay sharp.

"Counselor—" Jackson started.

Gwen held up her hand. "No. No more. Just answer one question. Is Dr. Baker under arrest?"

"No, but—"

Gwen rose and motioned to Mark to do the same. "If you need my client, feel free to contact him through me." She pointed to her business cards, which were still on the table. "Gentlemen, good night. Or rather, good morning."

She resisted the urge to turn and look over her shoulder to be certain Mark was following her. When they reached the outside door, he reached past her to open it for her.

"Thanks for coming," he said.

"It's what lawyers are supposed to do. I told you to call me if something like this happened. I just didn't know it would be this soon."

They reached the parking lot. Gwen looked at her watch. "It's six in the morning. Want to get some breakfast?" She wondered if he'd take her up on that last offer. He must be thinking about it, since he didn't answer immediately.

Finally, Mark said, "Thanks for the offer, but I didn't have a chance to see Kelly before those detectives rushed me off to the station. My car's at the hospital, and if you'd drop me off there, I'd appreciate it."

Gwen tried to hide her disappointment. "Sure. But you and I will need to talk later today. Why don't you give me a call?"

"Talk about what?"

Surely Mark couldn't be that dense. No, the Mark she knew was sharper than that. Admittedly, the fact that he'd been up all night didn't help, but surely he could see—never mind. "I'm your attorney. I need to sit down with you in private and get some answers. Can we do that?"

"Of course. I wasn't thinking. I'll call you later today, after I check in at the hospital."

And we'll just see where things go from there.

The feeling was akin to what Kelly experienced when she knew she was having a nightmare, but couldn't rouse herself from sleep. She could hear hospital sounds all around, mixed with voices—some distant, some near—and she wanted to join in, but couldn't wake up. She strained muscles that wouldn't respond, tried to struggle back to full consciousness, but felt as though she were encased in plastic, unable to move.

"I think she's waking up a bit."

The words were spoken by a familiar voice.

"After she came out of the anesthetic, I removed her endotracheal tube." Another man was speaking. This was a voice Kelly didn't recognize. "She's been breathing on her own since then, vital signs stable. But we had to give her some morphine for pain, and I think it hit her pretty hard."

With one final effort, Kelly opened her eyes. Her vision was blurred at first. Was that Mark leaning over her?

He brushed her forehead with his lips. Yes, it was Mark. She tried to smile.

"What...what happened?" she managed to whisper. Her voice was rough, her throat was raw and dry.

"Here," Mark said. "Take these ice chips and suck on them."

Kelly felt a spoon touch her lips. She opened, took the proffered ice, and sucked on it. "Tell me what happened. I know I'm in the hospital, but..."

"I was driving you home when someone took a shot at the car. You were hit in the chest. I got you to the hospital as fast as I could. You've had surgery—removal of a bullet that punctured the upper lobe of your right lung. They controlled the bleeding, inserted a chest tube to re-expand the lung."

That explained her pain and some of her difficulty taking a deep breath. "Are you okay?" she asked.

"Yes. I'm fine. And you will be. In a few days, they'll pull that chest tube and you can leave here."

"Who—"

"Dr. Baker." It was the recovery room nurse. "I'm afraid we can't let you stay in here any longer. We have a lot of patients, and there's just not—"

"I understand," Mark said. He looked down at Kelly. "Why don't you rest? We'll talk more later."

Kelly managed a feeble nod. Mark was safe. She was going to live. Someone had shot them, and she had the impression that it was critical to find out who did it, but that didn't seem important now. She closed her eyes and drifted off.

Kelly had left the recovery room and was now in the ICU, but when he started to enter the unit, Mark was told he'd have to wait. "But I saw her when she was in recovery. And I'm a doctor here. Why can't I see her now?"

"Yes, doctor," the nurse said. "As you know, we let you see her briefly, assure yourself that she'd come through the surgery. But now she's in ICU. We have work to do and she needs her rest."

Actually, Mark knew this. The staff had to check vital signs, deal with her chest tube, encourage coughing and deep breathing, and in general carry out the dozens of things necessary for her to recover. He just wasn't happy about it. "Okay. I'll be in the waiting room."

Finally, after thumbing through several well-worn magazines and not recalling a word he'd read, Mark—along with several other families—was allowed into the ICU for a ten-minute visit.

When he saw Kelly, he almost cried. Only hours before, Mark had been at the bedside of a colleague and friend, also lying pale and still, but in that case her pallor and stillness had been that of death. Mark realized how close he'd come to losing Kelly, and it was almost more than he could stand.

He bent and kissed her cheek. "I'm so glad you're okay," he whispered.

Kelly was more awake now, although her words were still occasionally slurred and her voice raspy. " I guess the cartel is still angry at you and me. But it's not your fault."

Mark recognized the truth of what Kelly said. And at least during this crisis he hadn't been thinking about himself. No, his only thought had been how to get medical aid for her as quickly as possible. If she'd died...he couldn't even think about it. If she'd died without his having the chance to tell her his true feelings, he would have wanted to die himself.

Was this the time? "Kelly, I've been thinking about what I said to you when all this started, about my not deserving to be involved with anyone." He swallowed hard. "I think you were about to tell me something before I dropped that bombshell. And I need to tell you how things have changed—how I've changed in those few days."

Kelly looked up at him as he leaned over her bed. Her lips parted, then closed again. She gave the briefest of nods.

"Kelly, I—" A buzz from his cell phone made him frown. He reached into his pocket. Whatever it was, it could wait. But as he started to push the button to send the call to voicemail, Mark saw that it was a text from his friend and colleague, Eric McCray. It was short, but it got his attention. "Call me STAT, 911."

The combination of "stat," the Latin abbreviation used by medical personnel to indicate "immediately," and "911," code among them for "emergency," meant that he really had no choice.

He sighed. "I'm sorry. I have to make this call." He squeezed Kelly's hand. "But I'll be back soon. And I plan to finish that story."

───※───

Mark realized he was gripping the phone so tightly he might shatter the plastic shell. He transferred it to his other hand, took a deep breath, and said, "What do you mean?"

Eric's voice was steady, but there was an edge to it. "I was trying to get some sleep this morning when I got a call from Goodrich. He said that Anna King's death has escalated the situation with you, and he's more adamant than ever—he doesn't want you associated with the hospital." Eric paused as though looking for the right words. "He told me to start looking for a replacement doctor for you."

The next words almost stuck in Mark's throat. "What... what did you tell him?"

"I told him that my recollection of the justice system in the US was that a person was innocent until proven guilty. I respect your decision to take a short leave of absence to deal with the charges, but anytime you're ready to come back to work it'll be fine with me."

Mark felt his shoulders relax. He took a deep breath. "Thanks, Eric. I appreciate your putting your job on the line for me."

"Hey, you'd do the same if the roles were reversed. Now I think I'll try to get back to sleep. I have another shift in the ER tonight."

Mark pulled the phone away from his ear, but before he could end the call he heard Eric say something else. "What was that?"

"How's Kelly?"

"I think she's going to be fine." *And I have some things to tell her. But first, maybe I'd better have a face-to-face with our hospital administrator.*

Allen Goodrich looked at his schedule, centered neatly on his cherry wood desk. Then he consulted his wristwatch, a gold Patek Philippe of which he was quite proud. He loosened the alligator band one notch and flexed his fingers. Maybe he should get an expansion bracelet for the watch. Then again, the leather band added to the prestige of the instrument. And prestige was high on his list of priorities.

The intercom in his desk buzzed, followed by his secretary's somewhat harried voice. "Dr. Goodrich, Dr. Baker is—"

At that moment, the door burst open and Mark Baker strode in. Over his shoulder, the physician called, "Don't bother announcing me. He'll see me, whether he wants to or not."

Baker closed the door behind him firmly, not quite slamming it, and moved to one of the two chairs in front of Goodrich's desk. He didn't sit, but looked down at the administrator. "I'm tired of this nonsense."

Goodrich took a moment to decide how to handle this. Be forceful? Be conciliatory? Have Baker thrown out of his office? No, he'd do this carefully. He had his orders, but there was a certain amount of leeway in them. At least, he hoped there was. "Please," he said with a smile. "Have a seat. Explain."

He could tell by the puzzled expression on Baker's face that he'd put him off balance already. Good.

Baker eased into a chair. "I've just gotten off the phone with Dr. McCray, who told me you called him and insisted that he fire me from my position with the emergency doctor group. Well, I have no intention of leaving. I told you I was willing to take a leave to try to get my status with the police straightened out, but that's as far as I'll go."

Goodrich patted the air in a conciliatory gesture. "Dr. McCray must have misunderstood me. I merely expressed my concern that—with the death of poor Dr. King and increased police suspicion falling on you—it was more important than ever to avoid any adverse publicity about the hospital." He leaned back in his chair. "Certainly, your being on leave until this is settled is a good idea. I simply wondered if it wouldn't be better for you to sever the relationship completely."

"Even if I'm innocent?" Baker's face was getting redder by the moment. *Perhaps he'd rupture an aneurysm. No, we can't have him dying in this office.*

"Calm down, Dr. Baker. I can see how important this is to you, so please forget that I brought it up." He consulted a leather-bound appointment book that lay on a corner of his desk. "Today is Friday. Suppose we meet again next Wednesday at noon and discuss this further."

"Okay. We'll leave it until Wednesday. But I don't want any more phone calls to Eric McCray trying to get rid of me. I've got enough on my mind without looking over my shoulder at you."

As the door closed behind Baker, Goodrich nodded to himself. *Oh, don't worry. You won't see it coming at all—until it's too late.*

20

As Mark approached the central desk in the ICU where the ward clerk sat, a nurse stopped him. "You're Dr. Baker, aren't you?"

Mark nodded, trying to ignore the hard, cold lump that had suddenly formed in his gut. "Yes. Is something wrong?"

"Not at all. But Miss Atkinson fell asleep shortly after you left, and her doctor thought it would be a good idea for her to rest undisturbed by visitors for a while. He suggested you might want to go home, shower and change clothes, maybe even get a nap." She paused, and when there was no reply she said, "I'll make sure we call you if there's any change... any change at all."

Mark had been too busy to pay much attention to his appearance. These were the same clothes he'd worn for twenty-four hours. He rubbed his hand over his chin and felt beard stubble that would have been right at home if he were the doctor on *House*. A discreet sniff convinced him that the suggestion about a shower was probably a good idea, as well.

"I guess you're right," he said. "Do you have—"

The nurse smiled. "We have your cell number here at the nurses' station. It's on a slip of paper you left at her bedside.

And if for some reason we can't find it, we can call the emergency room or the hospital operator." She made a shooing motion. "We'll see you in a few hours."

Mark stopped at the emergency room secretary's desk and retrieved his car keys the police had left for him. As much from force of habit as from any desire to go to work, he peeked inside the ER, which wasn't too busy in mid-morning. The children who'd gotten sick during the night had already been treated and taken home by their parents. The accident and trauma victims would come later in the day. One pregnant woman moaned softly as she lay on a gurney awaiting transportation to the obstetrics suite.

Mark turned back toward the exit door, but paused upon hearing a familiar voice. "I'm telling you, I don't care that I'm too young for a heart attack. I feel like an elephant is on my chest. It hurts, and I can't breathe."

He followed the sound to a treatment cubicle, pulled the curtains aside, and saw one of his fellow ER physicians bending over Jimmy, a boy whose facial lacerations he'd repaired just six days earlier.

"What do you have, Earl?" Mark asked.

The doctor, Earl Meador, looked at Mark and shook his head. "Sixteen-year-old male came in complaining of chest pain and dyspnea. His EKG doesn't show any cardiac damage. Of course, we'll check his enzymes, but if he's having a heart attack he'll be the youngest patient I've ever seen with one."

"I know this patient and a bit of his medical history," Mark said. "You'd get this eventually, but let me ask him something that may give us a shortcut." He bent over the teenager, who was writhing on the gurney. "Jimmy, did you have a migraine this morning?"

Jimmy nodded. "I used the shot, but when the headache didn't get better, I took a couple of the tablets. The headache's almost gone, but my chest is hurting and I can't breathe."

Mark turned to his colleague. "Imitrex injectable, followed by tablets, resulting in coronary vasospasm." He pointed to the EKG Earl held. "You were looking for ST segment sagging, like we see in a typical coronary. Look here—the ST segments are actually elevated. It's Prinzmetal's angina."

Jimmy moaned louder. "It's back. It comes in waves." He looked at the two doctors. "Can you do something?"

"I don't want to give him nitrates," Earl said. "They might bring back his migraine."

"How about a calcium channel blocker?" Mark suggested.

Thirty minutes later, Jimmy lay relaxed on the gurney, oxygen flowing from a plastic tube into his nostrils. "Good pickup," Earl said to Mark. "We'll watch him, check his cardiac enzymes for any heart damage. Then he'll need a follow-up appointment."

"Want me to talk with his parents?" Mark asked. He hoped he could convince Jimmy's family of the importance of a follow-up visit, both to make certain there was no underlying heart disease and to consider changing his migraine management. Besides, he'd need the stitches removed from that facial laceration.

"My parents didn't bring me. I drove myself," Jimmy said.

"Aren't you a bit young to have a license?" Earl asked.

"A license doesn't make any difference. If I need to get somewhere, I just take my mom's car keys and go."

Mark shook his head. He couldn't imagine a teenager whose parents cared so little for him that they wouldn't get him to the emergency room. If Jimmy were telling the truth, this might be a situation for him to talk with Child

Protective Services. And that, in turn, reminded him that he hadn't yet made contact with the pediatrician caring for Detective Ames's son. He'd add that to his list of things to do later today...if he finally made it home.

Mark's car was where he left it in the ER parking lot, still encircled by yellow crime scene tape. He hadn't seen the two detectives since Gwen rescued him from the interrogation room of the police station, but he figured that if the police left his keys with the secretary, it was okay for him to use the car.

He wadded the yellow tape and tossed it onto the floor of the car. In his concern for Kelly, Mark had forgotten the damage to his Camry. The back window was riddled by four bullet holes, and there were three more in the windshield on the passenger side, each surrounded by stellate cracks. However, the glass in front of the driver was clear enough for him to see the road. He'd need to keep his speed low unless he wanted to hear and feel the wind whistling through the holes. Given how sleepy he was, that was probably a good thing.

Mark tried to ignore the bloodstains on the passenger side of the car, but when he saw the track through the top of that seat made by the bullet that struck Kelly, he shivered. He'd come so close to losing her. He wished he could be back at her bedside now, wished he'd been able to tell her what was on his mind before the urgent phone call interrupted him. He knew that now it would be better if Kelly got some rest. He'd clean up, take a brief nap, and get back to the hospital as quickly as he could. And this time, he wouldn't let anything interrupt him as he shared his feelings with the woman he loved.

Mark was faintly aware of something demanding his attention. He struggled into semi-consciousness and realized that it was his cell phone ringing. He yawned and stretched out his hand to retrieve the instrument from his bedside table.

Without bothering to look at the caller ID, he answered the call. "Dr. Baker."

Gwen sounded worried. "Mark, are you all right?"

Mark frowned. Why wouldn't he be? His puzzlement was reflected in his voice as he said, "Sure."

"I asked you to call me this afternoon so we could talk about your case. It's five o'clock, and I haven't heard from you. Between the police and the Zetas, I was afraid something more had happened to you."

Five o'clock? When Mark got home, he'd been too tired to eat or shower or do anything except flop onto his bed. That had been almost seven hours ago. He still wore the same clothes, even more wrinkled than before. His beard was starting to make him resemble a porcupine. And his lack of a shower was now more evident than ever.

"I've got to get to the hospital. Kelly's going to wonder why I'm not there."

"Wait!" Gwen said. "When can we meet?"

Mark was already on his way to the bathroom, shedding clothing as he struggled to keep his phone to his ear. He turned on the shower. "Look, I've got to clean up and change clothes. Let me call you from my car. Maybe we can get together later tonight or tomorrow."

Fifteen minutes later, Mark was in his car, alternately speeding up in response to the sense of urgency he felt and slowing down when the wind whistling through the bullet holes in the windshield became too loud to tolerate.

He pulled his cell phone from his pocket and dialed the main number of the hospital; he had the direct number for the ER preprogrammed, but not the ICU. "Hello, this is Dr. Baker. Would you connect me with the ICU nurse's desk?"

A series of buzzes and clicks was followed by, "ICU. This is Ramona."

"Ramona, this is Dr. Mark Baker. I'm the one who brought in Kelly Atkinson, the patient in room six. I sneaked off to change clothes and fell asleep. Would you—"

"Oh, they told us about you, Dr. Baker. Miss Atkinson rested very well today. She asked about you once, and when the other nurse told her you'd gone home, she said, 'That's good. I hope he gets some rest.'"

Mark felt a bit better, although his conscience still troubled him for leaving Kelly's side. "Please tell her I'm on my way back, and I'll see her soon."

Gwen Woodruff was still in her office, shuffling through papers on her desk, one eye on her watch, when her cell phone rang. "Mark, where are you?"

Wind whistling in the background made it difficult to understand him. "I'm about five minutes away from the hospital," he said. "I'm sorry I didn't call you earlier."

She sighed. Apparently Mark wasn't going to be able to give her his attention until he'd been back to the hospital and seen the nurse who got shot while riding with him. "When will you be through?"

"I don't know. I guess it depends on how things go when I talk with Kelly. With ICU visiting limited to ten minutes every couple of hours, it's hard to carry on any kind of conversation. I may even stay there overnight. If I get sleepy, I can snatch a nap in one of the call rooms."

"Look, I'll bet you haven't eaten since last night. Why don't you give me a call when you can? I'll meet you somewhere, and we can talk while you eat."

"I'm almost at the hospital." The wind noise in the background diminished. "Let me see how things go when I see Kelly. Whatever happens, I'll call and let you know."

"But we really—" Gwen realized she was talking into a dead phone. She dropped the instrument onto the desk and buried her head in her hands. What a mess! She really did need some uninterrupted time with her client. Probably as important, she wanted a chance to possibly straighten things out between them. Sure, she was angry when he dumped her, but it seemed that now she had another chance to rekindle that flame. Gwen was determined not to waste it.

She thought about the irony of the situation. Once their relationship was so strong she was certain they'd spend the rest of their lives together. Now she had to practically beg him for a few minutes out of his crowded schedule...even though she was defending him against charges that could cost him years behind bars or possibly his life.

Gwen wasn't sure whether to laugh or cry. When she was younger, she would have prayed over the situation, while Mark rolled his eyes at the gesture. Now their positions were reversed. Perhaps it was true what they said. God really does have a sense of humor.

"You're looking better," Mark said.

Kelly smiled up wanly from her bed in the ICU. "I'm glad you think so. I don't feel so hot."

She tried to turn, and winced. Mark figured most of the discomfort was from the tube protruding from her right side midway below the armpit. Then again, the surgery to remove the bullets had involved stretching and cutting muscles. All things considered, he guessed her demeanor was pretty stoic. "Do you need something for pain?" he asked.

Kelly shook her head. "Not unless I have to. I feel like my head is just now clearing from all they've given me."

For a while they were silent, Mark sitting at her bedside with the fingers of one hand intertwined in Kelly's. Sometimes she'd open her eyes and look directly at him, but most of the time her gaze was unfocused or her eyes closed altogether. He didn't know why he expected her to be totally lucid. She was still hooked up to a patient-controlled morphine pump.

Kelly might have told him she wanted to avoid any more morphine, but he was willing to bet she was still under the influence of the drug. And that was good. *Don't let the pain get ahead of you.*

Although he wanted nothing more than to confess to her the changes in his feelings, changes that had come about when she was shot and afterward, Mark recognized this still wasn't the right time. The best thing he could do was to sit beside her when they'd let him, then wait outside until it was time to do it again.

The second time he was in Kelly's room, when the nurse came to tell Mark he had to go, Kelly roused enough to say, "Mark, it's late. Why don't you...get some rest? Come back in...in the morning." She barely got the words out before she closed her eyes, and by the time Mark was at the door, she was asleep.

Before Mark could say anything, the nurse was at his side. "Dr. Baker, this isn't a sprint, it's a marathon. We have your cell phone number. Go home and get some sleep."

Mark nodded. When he reached the hospital lobby, he pulled out his cell phone and dialed Gwen's number. He might as well get that out of the way since the opportunity had presented itself.

"I'm glad you agreed to come to my house and have dinner," Gwen said. She used a fork to flip the chicken breasts as they sizzled in the pan. "I'm sure that, after all you've gone through recently, a quiet, home-cooked meal is what you need."

Mark leaned back on the couch. It was nice to let someone else do the cooking. His meals, those that didn't consist of fast food consumed in his car, were generally what a bachelor would cook, frequently eaten standing at the kitchen counter.

He felt himself relax. Kelly's medical care was in good hands. She seemed to be out of danger, although he knew she wasn't yet ready for discharge, and it would probably be several weeks before she could return to work. That was okay with him. While she was in the hospital, she was safe from the Zetas or whoever had shot her in the first place. He hoped that by the time she was discharged, the police would have caught up with the shooter and both he and Kelly would no longer feel as though they had invisible targets on their backs.

"Okay, dinner's ready," Gwen said. She shed her apron and carried two plates to the dining room table.

"We could have eaten in the kitchen," Mark protested as he slipped his shoes back on and made his way to the table.

"Nonsense. I don't often have guests."

Gwen had argued that they needed both to discuss his case and to eat, so it made sense to combine the activities.

Then, since she was already home from the office, she maintained that it simply made sense for him to come over and let her throw something together.

She saw him surveying his plate. "I hope this is okay. It's just some sautéed skinless chicken breasts, a baked potato, and salad. Nothing fancy."

"It's perfect." The candles on the table, a nice tablecloth, and what he guessed was good china, told him this wasn't just a simple working dinner. Mark decided he'd better be on his guard.

He was about to ask if she wanted him to say grace, but she'd already unfolded the cloth napkin sitting by her plate and was reaching for her knife and fork. Mark did a mental shrug, said a brief, silent thanks, and followed suit.

The food was good, and Mark enjoyed it. When he paused to take a sip of ice water, he noticed that Gwen's wine glass was already half empty. So far the conversation had consisted of lawyer-type questions from her, with no mention of their past relationship. Maybe it was truly going to be just a working dinner.

Gwen emptied her wine glass, took a deep breath, and said, "Mark, I have to confess something. I don't think the police have anything but unfounded suspicions that you might be involved in the King shooting. And, unless you're hiding something from me, I have all the information I need to defend you."

"Then why did you—"

Gwen held up a hand. "Please. I need to get this out." She picked up her wine glass and found it empty. She reached for the bottle, then pulled back her hand. "When you called my office, I had visions of your coming back to me all apologetic for dropping me. Instead, you needed my professional help.

When I finally got up the nerve to ask why you dropped me, you told me you decided that what we had wasn't love—just extreme *like*."

Mark forced himself to remain silent, but he had to admit she was right. Once he discovered that there were other girls in the world, he realized he wasn't really in love with Gwen. She represented a high-school romance, but not the real thing.

Gwen continued in that same vein for a minute, then asked the question Mark knew was coming...and which he dreaded. "So here it is. Do you think there's a chance we can get back together? I don't mean immediately become engaged or anything. But do you want to date? Get reacquainted with each other?"

Mark thought about the women in his life. He and Gwen had a history, and he had to admit he'd wondered if that flame could be rekindled. Anna King had been fun—for a while—but he'd already given up any thoughts of getting serious with her before she was fatally shot.

Then there was Kelly. He'd enjoyed dating her, but it was only after he saw her with a gun to her head, recognized that he'd be devastated to lose her, that he realized he was falling in love with her. And the shooting in his car cemented his feelings. As soon as she was lucid enough to realize what he was saying, he intended to tell her of his love.

All this meant that Gwen wasn't going to like the answer he was about to give. Mark wished Gwen still had the faith at which he'd secretly scoffed years ago. It might make this easier for her to hear. *God, please give me the right words to say.*

The shooter was almost asleep behind the wheel of his car when the door to the house opened and the doctor emerged. The *dashboard clock showed ten P.M. The time and the circumstances were right for removing the next member of the medical team that let Hector Garcia die. If revenge were to be exacted, tonight would be the night.*

The doctor pulled slowly away from the curb. The shooter would let him get a bit ahead before sliding in behind the little Toyota. Since getting this assignment, he'd spent some time familiarizing himself with the territory. He had a pretty good idea of the ideal location for the hit, and he'd be ready.

Mark left Gwen's home still wishing he could have explained himself better. In one corner of his mind was the thought that the woman he'd left disappointed and a bit angry was still responsible for defending him against a possible charge of murder. *Don't obsess about it. You can't unsay the words.*

By and large, Mark had the road to himself. If his speed exceeded thirty miles an hour or so, the wind whistling through bullet holes in his windshield was a definite distraction. Not a problem. He'd drive slowly. He needed to think anyway. A few minutes difference in his travel time wouldn't matter.

As he turned to go through a less populated area, he noticed headlights behind him. He thought back and realized they'd been there for some time. Don't be paranoid. Nevertheless, he decided to take a few random turns. If the vehicle were following him, it would soon be evident.

After a series of right and left turns, sometimes doubling back the way he'd come, Mark was pretty certain he was being followed. Not only that, but his maneuvers had apparently tipped the driver of the other vehicle that Mark was onto them, because now the headlights were coming closer.

It was time to ignore the holes in the windshield and the partially shattered back window. Mark accelerated, but the headlights crept closer still. Should he take a detour toward an area where there would be people? There was an all-night café not far away, one where Mark had stopped from time to time. But what if there was shooting? Would he be putting innocent people at risk? The ethics of the situation bothered him, just as they had bothered him after the incident in the ER when he realized he'd initially placed his own welfare above that of others.

By now, the headlights were close enough for Mark to tell they were part of a dark SUV, a fairly large one. Mark jammed the steering wheel hard to the right and took a turn on two wheels. The SUV followed, but the driver had to hit the brakes to do so, and Mark gained a little bit of ground. The police station was probably the safest place to head, so he took the next turn that would take him in that direction.

The SUV was gaining ground again. Even though Mark plowed through stop signs and intersections without regard to traffic laws, the vehicle behind him closed the distance between them.

Now the dark SUV was almost on his tail. Mark had the accelerator to the floor at every opportunity. What else could he do? In a desperate attempt to escape, he jammed the wheel into a hard right turn and jumped the curb to drive into a park he was passing. Maybe he could lose himself in the trees. That's when he heard the shots.

Mark felt things whiz by his head like angry wasps. In front of him the windshield burst with multiple holes surrounded by cracks that made it difficult for him to see. He stamped on the brake, but it was too late. Mark saw the tree in his path and braced himself. He felt the jarring crash at the same time the air bag deployed in front of him, knocking him back and blinding him momentarily with a cloud of powder.

A car door slammed behind him. The gunman was coming to finish him off. Mark tried to open the car door, but it was jammed. He was trapped.

21

Gwen Woodruff stared at the ceiling above her bed. Her plans, plans that had slowly taken shape in her mind since Mark's first call, had been dashed tonight. When she first heard from him, she was angry, angry that a man who'd shed her like a bad habit would now be back asking for her help. But gradually she found herself wondering if it might be possible to rekindle the romance they'd had. And the more circumstances made Mark depend on her, the better she thought her chances were to make that happen.

But this evening had put an end to all that. What could she have done differently? Was it the doctor who'd been shot? If Mark was hiding something from her, if he'd been the one to kill Anna King, he was doing a great job of disguising it. He seemed genuinely broken up over her death. Had she been more than a friend?

What about the nurse who was in the hospital now? Was the attention Mark paid her just because he felt guilty she was shot while riding with him? Or did he, as he said, truly have feelings for her?

And, of course, wouldn't you know it, religion played a part in the change in Mark. When they were dating, Mark had attended services with her because it was expected, but she had the impression his Christianity had never taken root. Having grown up in a preacher's family, Gwen followed a path that wasn't unusual for a preacher's kid, drifting away from the church at the first opportunity. As it turned out, Mark did the same thing, but now he'd reversed his course. And just as before, they stood on either side of a chasm that divided them as surely as a wall.

As clearly as though she had spoken the words, she cried out. Whether it was an exclamation or a prayer, she wasn't sure. *God, I'm a mess.*

Mark turned to look through the rear window of his car, a hole now almost completely open to the warm night air. The vehicle stopped behind him had its lights on, and their reflection in the rearview mirror momentarily blinded Mark. He twisted the mirror so the light was no longer in his eyes. Backlit by the headlights was the silhouette of a man. He was approaching Mark's car, his hands hanging free with what looked like a pistol in the right one.

Mark's eyes stung from the powder on the air bag. His hands hurt because of the force with which they had been driven off the steering wheel. He fumbled for the release button on his seat belt. He knew he probably didn't have a chance, but at least he was going to try. Forming a quick prayer in his mind, Mark edged past the center console of his car, ready to exit on the passenger side, assuming that door would open.

The driver's side door opened slowly and a dark form filled the space. It was a man, his face still masked by darkness. His right hand held a short-barreled revolver. "Dr. Baker." The voice was unfamiliar, the words flat and unemotional.

They didn't form a question. Rather, it seemed to Mark as though his assailant was simply announcing the name of the next person to die at his hands.

Mark wondered if could spring across the seats and get the passenger-side door open before the man got off a shot. He was preparing to try it when that door opened, and he heard a familiar voice, one with a faint Hispanic accent. "Dr. Baker, are you all right?"

"Carl?"

"That's right," the second voice said. "Carlos. Or Carl, I guess, is how you know me."

Like the first man, Carl held a pistol. This one was a small, boxy gun. Carl saw Mark eye the gun, so he stooped, pulled up his right pants leg, and shoved the pistol into a holster concealed there.

"Don't be afraid," Carl said. "We're here to protect you. But let's get back to Abe's car before the shooter comes back."

Mark was halfway out the door when Carl said, "Turn off the lights and leave your key behind the sun visor for the tow truck driver. No one's going to drive this car away—not the way the front end's wrapped around that tree."

When all three men were walking toward the vehicle that sat behind them, its motor running, its headlights illuminating the scene, Carl said, "Dr. Mark Baker, this is Abe Nunez. He and I are special agents with the DEA. We've been tracking the Zetas since they moved into north Texas."

Abe was taller and stockier than Mark. His dark hair was neatly cut. He wore a sport coat and tie. He stowed his revolver in a shoulder holster and extended his hand. "Doctor. Sorry we couldn't prevent the shootings."

Carl explained. "Abe and I have been shadowing you and Miss Atkinson since we learned the Zetas were after you."

"Which explains why you seemed to be so willing—actually, so insistent—to offer Kelly a ride," Mark said.

Carl nodded toward the vehicle they were approaching, a dark blue four-door pickup of some sort. "Get in the front. Abe will drive you home when we're through talking. You can call a wrecker to pick up your car in the morning."

"What about you?" Mark asked, as he opened the passenger door.

"My car's parked on the street about fifty yards back. Abe was following you, and I was trailing behind the vehicle we suspected belonged to the Zeta shooter. After he shot at you, he accelerated away."

"So you lost him?"

"I didn't try to chase him. Instead, I radioed his plate number and vehicle description to the police, who had a couple of cars already in the area. They've been cooperating with us, and I imagine that by the time we're through here the shooter will be in a cell, waiting for Abe and me to question him."

Abe, silent behind the steering wheel during the conversation, turned to face Carl who was in the back seat leaning forward. "Might as well tell him the rest of it."

"The rest of what?" Mark asked.

"The reason I'm working at Memorial Hospital is that we have reason to believe it's a drug trafficking way station for the Zetas. When we learned they were probably going after you and Kelly Atkinson, it was a perfect opportunity to get a handle on some of the local people involved."

Mark couldn't believe what he was hearing. "You're saying that we were the goat you staked out to catch the lion."

Abe said, "You were never in danger. Either Carlos or I was always around."

"Well, you weren't close enough." Mark's words were forceful. He knew he shouldn't be angry with the two men. They'd probably saved his life this time. But..."If you'd really been shadowing us closely, Kelly wouldn't be in the hospital recovering from a gunshot wound. And I wouldn't be sitting here."

"When Miss Atkinson got shot, I was trying to catch up to your car. Unfortunately, I was a few seconds too late, although I did make him hurry his shots," Carl said.

"It seems to me that you all have been a couple of steps too late during all of this," Mark said, his words dripping with sarcasm.

"Maybe," Abe said. "But, if we hadn't been around at all, both of you would be dead by now."

<hr />

Kelly opened her eyes and scanned her surroundings. It took her a minute to adjust, to realize where she was and how she got there. Her dreams had been filled with images of men chasing her with guns. But now she realized she was in the ICU, recovering from surgery. She started to roll over, but pain in her right side and back stopped her. Kelly fumbled until she found the right button to call the nurse.

In a moment, a cheery brunette hurried in. She wore a short floral-print jacket over blue scrubs. Her nameplate read Rachelle. She smiled at Kelly. "What can I do for you?"

"I...I don't remember you," Kelly said.

"No wonder. Less than thirty-six hours ago, you were in surgery. When I first started taking care of you in the ICU, you were pretty well out of it. But it seems you're making some progress." She fussed with Kelly's covers. "What do you need?"

"I'm trying to turn, but it hurts to move."

"Let's try this."

After the nurse helped Kelly move into a more comfortable position, she said, "The doctor said when you're ready you could have a clear liquid diet. How does that sound?"

"I'd kill for a cup of coffee," Kelly said.

"Can't do that quite yet," Rachelle replied. "Would you settle for some bouillon and hot tea?"

"I guess that's a start. Thanks, Rachel."

"It's Rachelle...but don't worry. Most people get it wrong."

As Rachelle left, a visitor stuck his head through the door. "Knock, knock."

Kelly's eyes widened. "Pastor Steve. I'm glad to see you. But how—"

"I told you—just plain Steve is fine." Steve Farrington smiled as he moved into the room. "Your friend, Tracy, called me yesterday, but warned me you probably wouldn't be ready to have visitors right then. Now it looks as though you're starting to recover."

"I don't recall Tracy being here," Kelly said. "Then again, the past couple of days are sort of a blur." She pointed to a chair. "Please. Have a seat."

She and the pastor exchanged small talk for a minute before he looked at his watch and said, "You know, they're going to run me out of here soon. You and I had a pretty serious talk the night you were held hostage by that gunman in the ER. Want to tell me what's been going on since then?"

Kelly bit her lip. She hated to relive some of the things she'd been through in the past six days, but perhaps it would help to talk them out with her pastor. "I saw Mark after you and I talked, and he told me he was ashamed he'd considered trying to escape from the gunman, leaving the rest of us to fend for ourselves." She went on to explain Mark's spiritual struggle. "I think he's sincere in his commitment, but it's hard to tell."

"I'm glad he's trying to rethink his relationship with God," the pastor said. "What about his relationship with you?"

"I'm not sure. When he was here yesterday evening, I think he was going to discuss that with me, but I was so groggy from the meds that I sent him home. I'm sort of waiting for him now."

A nurse stuck her head into the room. "Reverend, it's time for you to leave."

The pastor nodded. "If you could give me a second to have a word of prayer with her..."

The nurse nodded and left.

The pastor put his hand over Kelly's. "What shall we pray for?" he asked her.

"For healing, I guess." Kelly thought for moment. "And maybe for God's will in Mark's life...and mine."

<hr>

Mark struggled slowly and unwillingly out of a deep sleep, awakened by sunlight outside his bedroom window. He was aware on some subliminal level that he had things to do, although at first he couldn't recall what they were. He wasn't working, but...oh, yes. Kelly was in the hospital, Anna was dead, and he was a suspect in her murder.

He stumbled to the kitchen more by instinct and muscle memory than by sight. There, Mark flipped on the coffee-maker, then noticed he hadn't filled the machine. He grumbled as he rectified his error, and by the time he emerged from the shower, the smell of the fresh brew filled his small home.

He poured a cup and sat down at the kitchen table to consider what he had to do next. At least he didn't have to report last night's shooting to the police. Carl and Alex would have taken care of that.

He guessed his first priority was his wrecked car. Mark figured his insurance agent probably wasn't thrilled to get a phone call this early on a Saturday morning. On the other hand, Mark was a good customer who paid on time, and this was the first claim he'd filed with the company. "I'll arrange for a flatbed wrecker to pick up your car," the agent said. "He can haul it to Drayton Toyota, and I'll have an adjustor look at it there. It will be Monday or Tuesday before we have an answer, though. I'll talk with someone at the dealership about a loan car."

"Thanks, Ronnie," Mark said. "I'll take a taxi over there as soon as I can shave, shower, and dress."

The next thing on the list was the hospital and Kelly. In the past twenty-four hours, Mark had been interrogated by police, bullied by the hospital administrator, had a difficult conversation with his attorney (who happened also to be a former girlfriend), and been shot at and almost killed. Yet the butterflies in his stomach seemed to be more active right now than during any of those situations. He had no idea how Kelly would react to his presence. Would she be angry because she had been shot? Would she recognize that perhaps Mark had saved her life? Well, there was only one way to tell.

By nine-thirty that morning, freshly shaved, dressed in clean jeans and a polo shirt, Mark was behind the wheel of a red Toyota Corolla rental, headed for Memorial Hospital. When he arrived, he realized that his parking sticker was on his wrecked car. Rather than go through the hassle of trying to get a temporary permit on Saturday, he pulled into the visitor's lot and took a ticket from the machine. Maybe his hospital ID and an explanation would get him out of paying as he exited.

Mark didn't bother to check the information desk. Kelly would still be in the ICU...unless she'd had a complication and required more surgery. But if that were the case, surely they would have called him. He consulted his cell phone to assure himself there were no messages or missed calls. No, nothing.

He entered the ICU waiting room and checked his watch. Visiting hours would start in ten minutes. Mark found a seat and looked around. He saw a familiar face in the far corner, and it took him a moment to place the man. Mark was used to seeing him in an entirely different setting.

Mark walked over and stood before the man. "Steve, it's good to see you. Visiting someone here?"

The pastor looked up at Mark and smiled. "Actually, the same person I'm sure you're here to visit." He indicated the empty chair beside him, and Mark sat. "I talked with Kelly earlier, and decided to hang around for a bit, hoping to see you."

"I know she appreciated your visit." Mark wondered how to put this, then just blurted it out. "Look, I'm sorry I haven't been back in church yet. But I guess you know I've had a lot on my plate."

"We'll be happy to see you when you make it," the pastor said, "And I'm glad to hear from Kelly that you're trying to let God be a part of your life again." He half-turned and leaned closer to Mark. "If there's anything I can help you with, I hope you'll call me. Like doctors, ministers don't keep banker's hours. Call me anytime."

"Thank you," Mark said. "You said you saw Kelly. Is she doing okay? Did she say anything about me?"

"She seems to be fine, and she was looking forward to seeing you." He rose. "Is there anything I can do for you before I leave?"

"Just…" The words almost wouldn't come out. Finally, Mark said in a hushed voice, "Just pray for me."

Before the pastor could respond, the nurse stuck her head out the door and signaled that ICU visitation was about to start. Mark rose and shook hands with Steve, who gave him a smile and an encouraging nod. Then Mark took a deep breath and headed for the double doors leading into the ICU.

⁂

It started with a murmur of voices. Shoe leather scuffed on vinyl tiles. An occasional sob broke through, but was quickly muted, as though it had occurred in church. The visitors were here.

Mark paused at the open door. "I'm back," he said in his best Terminator imitation.

"That's the worst impression I've ever heard," Kelly said.

He smiled down at her. "You're looking better."

"I'm afraid that's a relative term."

Mark sat down at her bedside. "Your surgeon says he should be able to pull that chest tube soon. Then maybe a day or two in a regular room before you can go home."

Kelly nodded. "The main improvement I see is that I can hold a reasonably intelligent conversation and remember most of it." She beckoned him closer. "I think the last time you were here—or maybe it was the time before—anyway, I believe you were about to tell me something, but you got interrupted."

Mark knew this was his cue. All the words he'd carefully crafted flew out the window. Instead, he spoke from his heart. "I've already told you how disappointed I was with my own selfish reaction when that gunman burst into the ER. But now I'm convinced that was just human. God has forgiven me, and I believe you have as well."

"Of course."

"I experienced another emotion after it was all over. I realized that I could have lost you if things had gone badly right then." He looked around to make certain they were still alone in the ICU room. "Then, when you were shot—well, there was no doubt in my mind anymore. I don't think I could live without you." He took a deep breath. "Kelly, I love you. Just you. Only you."

Tears dotted Kelly's cheeks. He wasn't sure whether they were tears of sadness or of joy, but her words removed all doubt. "And I love you, Mark."

It seemed like only a few seconds until the nurse tapped on the doorframe. "Sorry, Dr. Baker. I'm going to have to run you out."

Mark whispered to Kelly. "I'll be back in a couple of hours. We have a lot to talk about."

Mark decided a cup of coffee would be nice. As he exited the ICU waiting room, his cell phone rang and he answered.

"Dr. Baker, this is Carter Reitzman."

Mark didn't recognize the name and said so.

"I'm Dr. Anna King's ex-husband." The words were spoken with a heavy Boston Back Bay accent.

"I'm sorry for your loss, Mr. Reitzman. Are you calling about Anna's memorial service?"

"I guess you could say that," Reitzman said. "Her parents want her body shipped back to Iowa, where they'll arrange her funeral. Because she has so many friends here, we decided to hold a memorial service tomorrow afternoon at the Drayton Community Church."

"I appreciate your letting me know. I'll certainly be there."

"That's why I'm calling," Reitzman said. "I don't want you anywhere near that service."

22

MARK SNIFFED THE MUG OF RICH COFFEE HE HELD IN BOTH hands before sipping from it. He wasn't sure if this room should be called the den or library or what, but Steve Farrington had certainly put his stamp on it. The desk and chair where the pastor prepared his sermons was in one corner, but it was obvious this room was also where he liked to read.

Every available square foot of wall space around Mark was taken up by bookshelves, but the contents weren't exactly what he expected. Charles Swindoll's *Grace Awakening* tilted slightly to lean on James Scott Bell's *Try Dying*. A copy of *The Message* translation of the Bible sat beside Poland's book of baseball devotionals, *Intentional Walk*. It was a mishmash, yet Mark felt certain that the pastor could put his hand on any given book in just a few moments.

The two men were in overstuffed leather chairs, facing each other at a slight angle, a lamp and small side table between them. Mark pictured the man sitting here for hours on end, reading and meditating. He wished he could do the same—turn off his phone, ignore the doorbell, and simply let the circus running wild in his brain calm down and settle into place. But that would have to come later. Right now, he needed the answer to a single question. And for some reason, he thought he'd come to the right place for it.

"I know you're busy preparing for services tomorrow, so I'm really grateful to you for seeing me," Mark said.

"How can I help you?" the pastor asked, leaning back in his chair as though he had all the time in the world.

Mark told him about the phone call from Anna King's ex-husband. "I'm crushed, obviously, because Anna was a colleague—more than a colleague, really—and I wanted to honor her memory one last time by attending her memorial service." He hunched forward and rested his elbows on his knees. "I had no idea that Anna even attended this church, but when I heard that her service would be here, I hoped you'd know enough about her to answer my questions. What I'm trying to find out…if you know anything about Anna that I don't, can you tell me what would make Carter Reitzman want to keep me away?"

The pastor put his cup on the table and folded his hands in his lap. "Some of this is common knowledge—at least to a few people—and some of it will come out as Dr. King's death is investigated further. But I have to ask you to be circumspect about sharing it."

Mark nodded. "I know, of course, that the police have this crazy notion that I might have shot Anna, but my attorney assures me that won't hold up. Is that why Reitzman doesn't want me there?"

"No, there's more. Anna didn't attend church here, but she had been meeting with me for some weeks for support and counsel. She was working to stay clean and sober, hoping to get her visitation rights to her daughter restored. To do that, she turned to what Alcoholics Anonymous calls her

'Higher Power.' At one of her meetings with me, actually less than a week before her shooting, she became a Christian. She made no secret about it, and when I heard of her death, I called her ex-husband and offered to hold the memorial service for her."

"I'm happy she did that, of course," Mark said, "but—"

"What I didn't share with her ex is that Anna told me there was another sin that accompanied her drinking, one she also was determined to put behind her."

Mark sat stock still, hardly even daring to breathe.

"She'd been having an affair—one that just ended," Steve said.

Mark nodded slowly. "When I talked with her the night she was shot, she painted her ex as a pretty vindictive man, one who was determined to fight her efforts to see her daughter. But Anna didn't give me any—."

The pastor put down his coffee cup and folded his hands. "What she probably was going to tell you was that not only did Reitzman suspect she was having an affair, but he thought the man involved was you."

Kelly was less drowsy, more awake, this afternoon. She deliberately avoided asking for the analgesics her surgeon ordered. She could take a bit of pain if it allowed her to be more lucid. And this was especially important to her after Mark's confession of his love earlier in the day. Each time he came back, they talked a bit more about it. They hadn't gotten around to planning a future yet. That would come after she was further along her road to healing, and they were no longer the targets of the cartel that apparently wanted to kill them.

She was napping, waiting for Mark to come back, when she heard a familiar female voice. "Some people will do anything to get a few days off."

Kelly opened her eyes and saw her best friend, Tracy Orton, at her bedside. Tracy wore a blue hospital scrub suit. Her dark brown hair was tucked into a scrub cap of the same color. A fingertip length floral smock covered the outfit.

"Are you working tonight?"

"Yep." Tracy consulted the clock on the wall behind her. "I'm due in the OR in ten minutes, but I wanted to check on you first."

"Did you scrub on my case?"

"No, I was off that night. Remember?"

"Oh, of course," Kelly said. "I still haven't got my days straight. Mark has been trying to fill me in a bit at a time, but since he can only be with me for short stretches, and I'm just now coming out of the fog, it's taking some time." She looked at the clock. "And speaking of that, why are you here? Visiting hours don't start for another—"

"Since when do rules bother me?" Tracy said, with the impish grin her friend knew so well. "But I gotta go to work. I'll keep checking on you."

After Tracy left, Kelly lay in her bed thinking back to the chain of events that brought her here. If Tracy hadn't been sick, would the shooter have attacked Kelly as she rode with her friend? What if Kelly had accepted Carl's offer of a ride? And what if, when Kelly was shot, Mark had reacted differently and not rushed her to the ER?

Kelly shook her head. There were too many what ifs. All that really counted was what actually happened—then and later. A verse from the book of Romans came to mind, one she'd heard frequently, and had reason right now to apply to her own life. She didn't have the exact words on the tip of her tongue, but she knew the gist of the passage: God can and does use everything, even the bad things, to ultimately work for the good of His children.

She wasn't certain how that one applied to her getting shot, but then again, maybe God wasn't through using the episode. She'd have to wait and see.

———— ✺ ————

Mark was having an early supper in the hospital food court, preparing to swallow a large bite of tuna sandwich, when his cell phone rang. He started to walk to a more secluded place to take the call, but noticed that no one was seated near his table. He chased the bite of sandwich with some Diet Coke, then answered. "Dr. Baker."

"This is Abe Nunez. I hope I'm not calling at a bad time. I got your cell phone number from Detective Jackson."

"What's up?" Mark asked.

"It came down the way I predicted. The police stopped the man who shot at you last night. He still had the pistol in the car with him. He tried the old 'I don't know anything,' and 'I don't speak English' excuses, but after a night in a holding cell he broke and gave us some pretty interesting stuff."

Mark picked up some potato chips but didn't put them in his mouth yet. "Like what?"

"I'd really rather tell you in person. Can we meet?"

"I've been at the hospital with Kelly most of the day, but I suppose I can get away soon." He swallowed the potato chips and took another sip of Diet Coke. "Where shall I meet you?"

"Can you come by the police station?"

"I suppose so," Mark said. He looked at his watch and did some quick calculations. "I imagine after the six o'clock visitation Kelly will tell me to go home anyway. How about seven?"

"Fine. See you then."

Mark ended the call. He picked up the remaining portion of his sandwich, then dropped it back on the plate. His hunger had disappeared, to be replaced by curiosity when Nunez uttered the words, "Interesting stuff." Maybe this thing was finally drawing to a close.

"Don't you get tired of sitting in the ICU waiting room?" Kelly inched upward in the bed, pleased that she was able to change positions without the level of pain that stopped her previously.

Mark leaned so close she could feel his warm breath as he spoke. "If you mean 'Would I prefer to be at your bedside constantly?' then yes. But I know rules are in place for a reason, and if I insist that the nursing staff make an exception for me, I'd be standing in the way of your care. Besides, it sets a bad precedent for other patients and families."

Kelly had similar thoughts when Tracy visited, but her friend had always been of the opinion that rules were made for other people. Since Kelly also knew that Tracy would do anything for her, she chose not to mention her opinion during today's visit.

"I need to go pretty soon," Mark said. "I have a meeting with Abe Nunez."

"Abe...Oh, the DEA agent. Is Carl going to be there?"

"Abe didn't say," Mark replied.

"I wonder why the Drug Enforcement Administration is chasing the Zeta cartel here," Kelly said. "I could understand if it were Immigration or even the FBI, but if the DEA's on the case they must have a strong suspicion that drugs are involved. "

"Oh, I guess I didn't tell you," Mark said. "They suspected the Zetas were using this hospital as a way station for drug traffic." He pursed his lips. "Carl was already working here when that gunman broke into the emergency room. He and Abe just took advantage of what followed."

"And they've been watching us since then?" Kelly asked.

"Carl and Abe told me they'd been following us in order to protect us, but I asked them point-blank if they weren't really using us for bait."

"And what did they say?"

Mark shook his head. "They danced all around it. Abe said that if they hadn't been around, you and I might already be dead."

"On the other hand, if we hadn't been working in the ER that Saturday night, neither of us would feel like we have to keep looking behind us." She felt tightness between her shoulder blades, tightness that shifting her position didn't change. "Even here in the hospital, I worry that someone with a gun may come through that door at any time."

"You know—"

"I know," Kelly said. "I'm safe here. But I'm so ready for this to be over."

Even though last night's shooter was in police custody Mark figured there could be more than one of them. Matter of fact, a dozen more people could be hiding not far away, seeking revenge for the deaths of the Garcia brothers. Darkness had not yet fallen, and he had been careful to park in a well-used area of the hospital parking lot. His masculine pride wouldn't let him ask one of the security guards to walk him to his car. Besides, he couldn't bring himself to ask someone else to risk their life to protect his. Sergeant Ed Purvis had done just that and paid the ultimate price for it.

At first the idea of the Zetas seeking revenge by killing those involved in the deaths of the two cartel members seemed so far-fetched that Mark couldn't bring himself to believe it. Now, at least two people were dead and another lay in the hospital recovering from wounds sustained in a shooting. No, this was quite real. And he couldn't believe the danger was over yet.

Mark beeped the locks open on his rental car and peered through the door to check the back seat for someone hiding there. When he was certain everything was clear, he climbed behind the wheel of the red Corolla and locked the doors. He drove cautiously toward the police station, staying on main streets and constantly looking around for suspicious vehicles.

He parked in a visitor's slot at the Drayton Police Station and fell in beside two uniformed officers who were headed for the front door. Once inside, the police officers peeled off down a side corridor, while Mark stopped at a window behind which sat an older officer. Mark put his mouth near the round metal speaker in the center of the glass. "Dr. Baker to see Abe Nunez. He's a DEA operative who's—"

"Yeah, I know." The officer held up one finger, gesturing Mark to wait a moment. He picked up his phone, punched in two numbers, waited. "Dr. Baker for Nunez." He nodded, hung up the phone, then pointed to a row of well-worn chairs along the wall on either side of the outer door. "Have a seat. Someone will tell him you're here."

Mark wasn't certain which was worse: being in a location where he had strong memories of interrogation by detectives asking him to confess to a shooting he didn't do, or awaiting a discussion with a federal agent about a plan of a huge drug cartel to kill him and someone he loved. And although he knew that a police station was probably the safest place he could be, thoughts came unbidden of killings of prisoners by other prisoners, evidence of the reach of organized crime even into places like this.

He was staring at the gray tiled floor, reflecting on the scuffed trail the footsteps of countless men and women had carved, when he sensed someone standing over him. Mark looked up to see not Abe Nunez, but instead, Detective Ames.

"You here to see Abe?" the detective asked.

Mark nodded, but remained silent.

"He's stretched out on a bunk in the back. I'll make sure he knows you're here."

Ames made no move to leave. Instead, he looked down at Mark and continued. "I sat in on the interrogation of the guy we picked up last night. He didn't want to talk at first, but eventually he gave us some information." His facial expression started out as a smile, but quickly turned to a smirk. "Actually, quite a bit of information."

This time Ames did turn and take a couple of steps away from Mark. Then he stopped and said over his shoulder, "What he told us didn't clear you for Dr. King's murder. I hope you still have your lawyer's phone number on speed dial."

23

Mark, in a back office of the Drayton Police Station, tried without success to find a comfortable position in the hard folding chair across the desk from Abe Nunez. The DEA agent leaned back in a swivel chair, his feet on the scarred surface of the desk next to a phone and computer monitor. He wore the same clothes Mark had seen him in twenty hours ago, but now his tie was pulled down, his collar was open, and the sleeves of his wrinkled shirt were rolled to just below his elbows.

"You're sure nobody in that lineup looked familiar?" Nunez said.

Mark shook his head. "A bunch of young Hispanic males? No, I could make some guesses, but I'd probably pick out one of your detectives or a guy who came down here to deliver a pizza." He sighed. "Sorry."

"No, that's okay. I figured you didn't get a look at the shooter last night, but it was worth checking to see if maybe you'd seen him sometime in the recent past. You know, it's likely he followed you around trying to pick the best spot to hit you."

"So what do you know about the guy?"

"Name's Alejandro Rojas." Nunez's feet thudded onto the floor as he leaned forward and put his elbows on the desk. "When the officer that stopped him approached the car, he saw the driver trying to jam something between the seats." Nunez looked at the ceiling and recited, as though reading from a card. "In fear of his safety, the policeman ordered the man to raise his hands. When he did, the officer saw a weapon still in the driver's left hand."

"And—"

"It was a gun—a Beretta Bobcat."

"How did Rojas explain that?"

"He claimed to speak no English, or at least only a few words, so the patrolman brought him here, which was the idea anyway. I talked with him in Spanish, but initially he refused to answer my questions." Nunez leaned back again and smiled. "While that was going on, the Drayton detectives who were helping us checked your car at the Toyota dealership where the wrecker took it. There were two bullet holes in the passenger seat back, but only one bullet went through and hit Miss Atkinson. The other was still lodged in the back of the passenger seat. It was a .25 caliber round, exactly what that Bobcat is chambered for."

"Have they fired a comparison from the pistol?"

"Earlier today...and they match. When I confronted Alejandro with that, he finally admitted to shooting at your car."

"All the shots? The shot that hit Kelly and the others aimed at me?"

Nunez nodded.

"So..." Mark said.

Nunez spread his hands. "So the charge has escalated from possession of an unregistered firearm with no permit to assault with a deadly weapon. When we get the slug the surgeon removed from Ms. Atkinson, it probably goes to attempted murder."

"What about Anna King and Buddy Cane? What about those bullets?"

Nunez rose and moved toward the door. "Sorry. The rounds that killed both of them came from the same gun, but it was a .22, not a .25 like Alejandro was carrying. Close, but not the same." He opened the door. Detectives Ames and Jackson were standing in the hallway. "That's why these men want to talk with you some more."

<hr />

Gwen Woodruff had her wine glass halfway to her lips when her cell phone rang.

Her dining companion frowned and leaned across the linen-covered table, careful to avoid the candle burning in the center. He looked around to be certain that the diners at adjoining tables weren't listening. "Gwen, can't you turn that thing off? We're supposed to be having a quiet dinner, and frankly, I don't want to have to share your attention with whoever's on the other end of that call."

Gwen put down her glass and shook her head. She'd deal with Roger in a moment. The only people who had her cell number were people whose calls she needed to take, no matter the time of day or the circumstances. She lifted the phone to her face. "Gwen Woodruff."

"Gwen, it's Mark. I'm sorry to bother you, but—"

"Don't apologize," she said. "What's the problem?"

She listened, ignoring the frowns Roger threw her way. When Mark finished, she said, "So they want your permission to search your home. Right?"

"They say they can get a search warrant, but it would be easier if I just let them do it."

"That's right," Gwen said. "Are you willing to let them search?" What she meant, but didn't want to say, was, "Will they find anything incriminating?"

"I don't have a problem with it, but thought I'd better check with you first."

"Go ahead. Stay with them, though. Make sure they don't split up. I doubt they'd plant anything, but like one of our presidents said, 'Trust, but verify.'"

After asking Mark if he wanted her to be present and receiving assurance that he didn't feel it was necessary, she ended the conversation with, "Call me when it's over. And don't hesitate to phone before then if there's a problem."

She stowed her cell phone in her purse and looked up to meet her date's frown. "Roger, I'm sorry. But I'm an attorney, which means that sometimes my clients have to reach me at inconvenient times—just like a doctor."

After more soothing words from her, he seemed to calm down, but Gwen was certain that this first date with Roger would probably also be her last with him. She didn't really care. The man didn't understand her situation, and she wasn't about to give up her professional life to be the significant other of a CPA—or almost anyone else, she supposed. *I still wish it could be Mark across the table from me.*

<hr />

"Satisfied?" Mark asked the two detectives as they stood in the doorway of his home.

"I'm not sure satisfied is the right word," Jackson said. He stripped off his latex gloves and shoved them into the pocket of his rumpled suit. "We've done what we came to do. Just because we didn't find a gun doesn't mean you're innocent. It's simply one more step in our investigation."

Ames frowned, but didn't add to the conversation.

"Look," Mark said. "I've answered every question you asked me. My attorney has pointed out that all you have are suspicions, yet it seems the only thing you've done is stay right on my heels, waiting for me to make a mistake. Why aren't you investigating other explanations for Anna's shooting?"

Jackson stepped through the door, and once everyone was outside, Mark closed and locked it. The three men started down the walk to the street where their cars sat.

"I asked you a question," Mark said. "Why aren't you looking elsewhere for Anna's killer?"

Jackson paused with the door of the unmarked squad car open and said, "Doctor, I can't go into detail, but I can assure you we're looking in other directions as well."

"Where?" Mark asked, his voice sharper than he intended.

Ames and Jackson looked at each other and shrugged. Then Ames ducked into the car and slammed his door. Jackson followed suit.

Mark stood at the curb and watched the car disappear down the block. He pulled his phone from his pocket, intending to call Gwen. But what could he tell her? The police searched his home and didn't find a gun. He knew going in that they wouldn't. Although they had assured him the investigation of Anna's death wasn't totally centered on him, where else were they looking? And what did it mean that both Anna and Buddy Cane were killed with the same caliber weapon, but not the one used to wound Kelly and almost kill him?

He hoped Gwen had some answers, because he certainly didn't.

The windshield of the silver Lexus parked down the street was tinted just enough to catch the last rays of summer sun and reflect them back into the eyes of anyone who might be looking at the car. On the other hand, sunglasses and the windshield tint made it relatively easy to see Baker as he stood next to his car, talking on his cell phone.

The detectives had already left. They should have taken Baker with them, preferably in handcuffs. Incarceration by the police wasn't as satisfying as his death, but it seemed to be an appropriate alternative. With Baker behind bars, the nurse in the ICU (where anything could still happen), and both Buddy Cane and Anna King dead, the planned scenario would be almost complete.

But apparently the police weren't going to cooperate. This called for more direct action. It was a shame, but things didn't always go as planned. The mark of a good manager was to adjust, and that was what would happen next.

Baker ended his call and drove off in his car. The Lexus followed at a discreet distance, the driver steering almost without conscious thought while working out the details of the next phase.

Kelly's eyes were closed, but she knew—knew of a certainty—that someone was standing at her bedside. She didn't think they'd made a sound. Perhaps there'd been the faintest disturbance in the air circulation in the room, maybe a whiff of aftershave, but whatever the signal, she knew there was an intrusion into her space. Suddenly she was wide awake, her heart beating a trip-hammer rhythm as she eased her lids apart to peer at the intruder.

It was dark in her ICU room—or, at least, as dark as it ever got. True, the nurse's station right outside was brightly lit, but the blinds on the plate glass window of her room were drawn. A nightlight burned in the bathroom only steps away, but most of her room was bathed in shadows.

Through slitted lids, Kelly could discern that the person at her bedside was a man. Maybe this was a nurse—a male nurse—who'd come to check her IV and chest tube. But when you've come within a few inches of having your life snuffed out, she supposed it was okay to have heightened suspicions of anyone who stole into her room in the dark.

Finally, Kelly said in what she hoped was a reasonably normal tone of voice, "Can I help you?"

"Kelly? I didn't want to wake you." The voice was familiar, but it took her a moment to identify it as belonging to Eric McCray.

She took a deep breath, then regretted the action as her lungs and chest muscles reminded her forcefully that she'd been shot recently. "Eric, what are you doing here?"

"I'm about to go on duty in the ER and wanted to check on you. I hoped you'd be awake, but since you weren't I was going to pray over you before I left."

Kelly, you're getting paranoid. This is Eric. You work with him every day. "That's so thoughtful. I'd like that," she said.

There was a commotion outside and two nurses hurried by. Probably something going on elsewhere on the unit—maybe a code. With everyone occupied, Kelly felt more vulnerable. She found the switch and turned on the light above her bed. At least she wasn't alone in the dark now.

Eric frowned at the action, but maybe it was only a reaction to the light. He raised his eyebrows in a gesture that went with his next words. "Shall we pray?"

Kelly said, "Certainly." But during Eric's prayer, her half-open eyes darted here and there, constantly on the alert for danger.

Allen Goodrich was sitting in his living room when the phone rang. He put his coffee cup on the end table next to the overstuffed chair where he sat. The administrative intern was on call this weekend and had strict instructions not to bother Goodrich at home unless the situation was catastrophic. Other than a telephone solicitor, he had no idea who could be calling him on a Saturday evening. Well, whoever it was, he'd soon give them a message they wouldn't forget.

He lifted the receiver. "Doctor Goodrich," he said, emphasizing—as he always did—the first of the two words.

"Usted sabe que es esto."

Goodrich translated the phrase easily. "You know who this is." Not a question—a statement. He understood the words. Moreover, he recognized the voice, and his resolve melted. He wasn't going to give this person an earful. He hoped he wasn't going to get one, but in his heart he knew that hope was groundless.

He dropped back into his chair, the receiver in a death grip. "Yes."

The voice continued in Spanish. "Can you talk freely?"

"Yes, Mildred is visiting her parents this weekend. I'm alone in the house."

"The attempts to remove Dr. Baker have been unsuccessful. The goal was to sever his association with the hospital and the police attention that came with it. The best you've been able to achieve is to get him temporarily out of your hospital's emergency room. Something more permanent must be arranged. And it should not bring any more attention to Memorial."

"*Pero*—"

"No 'buts.' At this point, it's up to you," the caller continued. "By Monday, I want him out of the picture."

"But I can't—"

"He is to be terminated! His body isn't to be found near the hospital. And it's to look like he took his own life in remorse." The speaker allowed a moment for the words to sink in. "*¿Es que claro?*"

Was it clear? He wished it weren't. Goodrich opened his mouth, but apparently the question had been rhetorical. Before he could respond a click told him the person on the other end had hung up.

He leaned back in his chair, the phone still in his hand, his coffee forgotten. Dr. Mark Baker's death sentence had just been pronounced. It came from the highest level. And it appeared that Goodrich was to be the executioner.

24

THE RATTLE OF A LARGE CART, ANNOUNCING THE ARRIVAL of breakfast trays on the unit, jolted Kelly out of a half-sleep. She yawned, brought her bed to a sitting position, and swiveled the rolling table next to her across her lap.

There was movement in the door of her ICU room, but when she looked up she didn't see a dietary worker bearing her breakfast. Instead, Dr. Tom Sellers, her thoracic surgeon, stood smiling at her. "Are you up to receiving company?"

"Of course," Kelly said. "You're a little later than usual making rounds today."

"That's because it's Sunday." He pulled a stethoscope from the pocket of his suit and Kelly went through the routine of lean forward/take a deep breath/cough. After a few moments, Sellers told her to lie back and relax. "Sounds good. You seem to be healing well. No fever. No drainage from your chest tube."

"They took me downstairs for a chest X-ray early this morning. Have you seen it?"

Sellers nodded. "You've expanded that lung quicker than most patients do. Usually chest tubes have to stay in four or five days. We only put it in—" He did a quick calculation. "It's been in place less than sixty hours."

Kelly crossed her fingers. She knew things were going well. What she wanted to know was when she could get out of here.

"Let's get another chest film tomorrow morning. If it looks good, I may pull the tube then." He stuffed the stethoscope back into his pocket, but before he left the room, he surprised Kelly one more time. "Oh, and after you've had your chest film tomorrow, they'll be taking you to a regular room." Sellers smiled. "We need that bed for some people who are a lot sicker than you. It was touch-and-go for a bit, but you're going to make it, young lady."

"Glad to hear it." The familiar voice made Kelly smile. Mark stepped into the room and shook hands with Sellers. "Tom, I only caught the tail end of what you said. Are you going to move her out of ICU?"

Kelly relaxed back onto the bed while the two doctors spoke briefly. When Sellers was gone, Mark walked over and used his foot to hook a chair and pull it to her bedside. "You must be even tougher than you look," he said with a grin.

"I had good care...beginning with a doctor who got me to the emergency room quickly, without regard to his own safety."

Mark shrugged that off. "I guess I should bring you up to date on events since I was here last."

She listened silently as he explained that, although the cartel shooter had indeed targeted both Kelly and him, a different gun was used to shoot Buddy Cane and Anna King. "The police searched my home, but, of course, there was no gun."

"So you're still under suspicion for those shootings?"

"For some reason, the police don't seem to want to turn loose of that idea," Mark said. "But Gwen thinks they're reaching and I have nothing to worry about."

Kelly felt another visit from the little green monster of jealousy coming on. "When did you talk with Gwen again?"

"I called her last night before I let the police search my house." Mark frowned. "Kelly, she's still my attorney, and I have to trust her. But believe me, there's absolutely nothing between us. That ship has sailed."

That's okay if the ship keeps going in the other direction. Frankly, Kelly wondered if Gwen Woodruff might still have ideas of getting back together with Mark. If that was the case, it was going to put the two women on a collision course. And Kelly intended to win that battle.

Mark slid into the back row of the Drayton Community Church as the choir entered the loft. Pastor Steve Farrington was already in his chair on the platform, his Bible open on his lap.

Mark's church attendance had been hit-and-miss since coming to Drayton, with few hits. But somehow, he felt right being here now. Maybe Eric had been right. If Mark put God in charge of his life, things would take the right course. He hoped so.

Once the service began, Mark gradually slipped into the rhythm of worship. He concentrated on the words of the hymns as though singing them for the first time. When the pastor read from Psalm 139, it was as though the words came from Mark's own heart: "Search me, O God, and know my heart; test me and know my anxious thoughts."

After the service, Mark lingered, hoping to get a few words with the pastor. He was waiting at the rear of the church when someone behind him said, "Mark, I'm so glad I ran into you."

Mark turned to see a woman about his age. Her short blond hair was perfectly styled. Glasses with designer frames did nothing to hide eyes so dark brown they almost appeared black. He was no expert, but it seemed to him that her makeup was perfect. And he guessed that the black dress she wore, accented by a short string of pearls and small pearl ear studs, probably cost more than his entire wardrobe. The voice was familiar, but he couldn't identify the woman who stood before him.

"You don't recognize me, do you?" she said, smiling. "It's Margaret. Margaret Cane."

The Margaret that Mark remembered from Buddy's funeral was a plain woman with mousy brown hair. She'd been dressed in black at that time, but the resemblance ended there. This woman had undergone a significant makeover, with notable results.

"Margaret, I'm sorry. I guess…"

"It's my hair, isn't it? After I lost Buddy…" She dabbed at her eyes with a lace handkerchief. "After he passed away, I decided I needed to do something to get me out of my depression, so I did this." She indicated herself with an open hand.

"Uh, well Margaret, I'm sorry for your loss. And if there's anything—"

"There may be." She looked around to make sure no one was in earshot. "Can I call you and talk about it?"

"Of course. You have my number?"

"I'm sure it's in Buddy's address book." She started to turn away, then looked over her shoulder at Mark. "Thanks."

As Mark watched her walk away, he saw that the pastor had finished with the last person at the back door and was moving briskly up the aisle. Mark stopped him. "Can I have a word with you?"

"Sure, Mark, but it will have to be quick. I have a memorial service here in about an hour and a half, and I need to get a quick bite and go over my notes."

"The service is what I want your advice about." Mark gestured to one of the pews. "Can we sit down for a moment? I promise this won't take long."

When the two men were seated, Mark said, "It's that call I received from Anna King's ex-husband, Carter Reitzman. You know the story there, of course. He made a point to tell me he didn't want me at Anna's service."

"Yes, and I told you why."

"But it eats at me that I can't attend the memorial for a friend and colleague."

"Are you certain Anna wasn't more than a friend?" the pastor asked gently.

"Do you believe Reitzman's silly theory about my being the other man in the affair Anna was having?" Mark said. "Because, if you do—"

"No, I believe you when you say you weren't having an affair with Anna. But did you have deeper feelings for her, feelings you've buried? Are you mourning the loss of a woman you thought someday you might love?"

"Absolutely not," Mark said. "I'd seen a side of Anna I wasn't particularly fond of. I'd already made up my mind that I'd dated her for the last time. But I was talking with her when she was shot. And somehow I feel guilty about it. I don't guess I'll get over that until the real killer is discovered and brought to justice."

The pastor looked at his watch. "Mark, I'm going to have to go. Here's what I'd advise. I know that in all the mystery novels and TV shows the killer generally shows up at the funeral of his victims, and for that reason I'm guessing there'll be one or more detectives here this afternoon... either in the church or outside. Leave the detective work to them. Don't go against Reitzman's wishes. Don't make a scene. That would dishonor Anna, and I don't think you want to do that."

Mark stood alone in the aisle, watching the pastor disappear through the door that led down a hall to his study. Then he sat back down, put his head on the pew in front of him, and closed his eyes. *Anna, it looks like I won't be at your memorial service. But that doesn't mean you're forgotten. Someone will pay for your death.*

—⟨⟩—

The one saving grace for Allen Goodrich was that his wife was visiting her parents. Though it was Sunday noon, he was still in his pajamas and robe. Unshaven, hair uncombed, he paced back and forth in his kitchen, his mug of coffee long grown cold as he tried to figure how he could possibly pull off his assignment.

There was no doubt in his mind that he had to... he couldn't say it, couldn't even make himself think it. However he chose to phrase it, he'd been given the order to eliminate Mark Baker. No longer was it someone else's responsibility. It was up to Goodrich. And if he should fail, he was certain his own life would be forfeited as a penalty.

The first question, he supposed, was how to do it. Could he arrange to poison Baker? With a whole hospital at his disposal surely he could find some medication, some substance that would be lethal but not be discovered at autopsy. And there was certain to be a postmortem examination of Baker's body, given the amount of attention the police had focused on the doctor.

If Goodrich set it up correctly, the police would accept the obvious explanation that Baker killed himself in a fit of remorse after shooting Anna King. The police would close that case, the authorities would look elsewhere for the Zetas, and the hospital could go on... *he* could go on with business as usual.

Thinking of the Zetas made Goodrich wonder about setting up something that would suggest Baker was ambushed and killed by a weapon of some sort—shot, stabbed, even strangled with a garrote. Could he do that? And even if he could bring himself to carry out the execution, where would he get the weapon?

No. He shook his head. The orders had been to make it look like Baker took his own life, perhaps despondent because he'd killed his colleague. So, in the end, Goodrich was faced with two problems: getting a weapon and setting up a scene that would be interpreted as suicide.

Goodrich walked through his house, opening closets, pulling out drawers, knowing before he finished his search that there was no gun, no knife more lethal than the ones in the kitchen drawers. Of course, he could use almost anything to set up a hanging: an electrical cord, the clothesline that lay coiled in the hall closet, even a belt. But could he do it? No, he decided. He couldn't.

He'd had the TV going, mainly because he seemed to think better when there was conversation in the background. Goodrich started to flip it off when an item on the noon local news caught his attention. And suddenly he knew how he was going to get rid of Dr. Baker.

⟨⟨⟨⟩⟩⟩

Mark Baker sat in his car in the farthest corner of the church parking lot. He'd been there since he left his conference with Steve Farrington after church. Mark knew he should go somewhere and eat a bite of lunch, but the thought of food turned his stomach. A colleague had died. Her memorial service would begin in half an hour, and he'd been specifically forbidden to attend it. It wasn't so much the words of Anna's ex-husband as the reason behind them. Bad enough to be excluded from the service, but it ate at Mark when he thought Reitzman suspected him of an affair with his ex-wife, the mother of their child.

Mark wondered if perhaps he could sit here in his car until everyone arrived and was seated. Then he could slip unobserved into the church. Maybe he could find a spot in the balcony. Unless the attendance was higher than anticipated, that space would probably be roped off. He'd sneak in and sneak out, and no one would be the wiser. But he'd feel that he had truly paid his last respects to Anna. For some reason, it was really important that he do so.

Mark thought back to just a week ago. He'd dreaded the act of visiting Sergeant Purvis's family. He'd avoided that funeral, and would have skipped the one for his colleague, Buddy Cane, if he hadn't been asked to serve as a pallbearer. Why the difference in his attitude? Was the pastor right when he suggested that Mark's feelings toward Anna were deeper than friendship? No, he was certain that wasn't true. It was more a case of seeking justice. And that seemed quite important to him.

⟨⟨⟨⟩⟩⟩

Allen Goodrich pushed through the crowded aisles and hurried from the church. He'd barely heard the words of the pastor as he told how Anna King had only recently taken the most important step in her life, but almost waited too late to do it. The words and music of the service washed over him, as he mulled over the plan he'd hatched in desperation.

He unlocked his car and crawled into the driver's seat. As people straggled out and drove away, he surveyed the rapidly emptying parking lot. There, in the far corner. Wasn't that Baker, in the red car? *He must have sprinted to the parking lot to get here ahead of me.* There was no hearse, no trip to the cemetery. Once the police released the body, it would be shipped to Dr. King's parents in Iowa. The ex-husband—the name escaped Goodrich at the moment—wouldn't be going. His excuse was that he didn't want their daughter further traumatized by yet another service and by the sight of the actual burial. Goodrich thought it was more likely the man wished to put all this behind him as quickly as possible.

Goodrich glanced down at the long bundle lying on the floor of his car in front of the passenger seat. He'd driven to a nearby city to purchase the shotgun and a box of shells from a sporting goods store, paying cash and giving a false name. Fortunately, there was no waiting period for buyers of long guns. No licensure necessary.

Unfortunately, there was no resemblance between Goodrich and Baker, but if things worked out well, if Goodrich set the scene correctly, the police would never try to trace the ownership of the weapon. What did the provenance of a shotgun matter when it was used in a clear-cut case of suicide?

The parking lot was almost empty now. Baker's red Toyota started and moved slowly toward the street. Goodrich eased his car out behind him. Soon this would all be over—for Baker and for him.

As he drove, Goodrich went over the scene in his mind. He'd ring Baker's bell, the doctor would invite him in. Goodrich would ask some sort of question that would make Baker turn his back. Then it was a matter of wrapping his fist around the roll of quarters in his pocket, delivering a hard blow to the back of Baker's head where the skull and spinal cord met. That should put the meddlesome doctor down for the count. Drag him to a chair, put the shotgun on the floor between Baker's knees, the barrel under his chin. Put the man's finger—or more likely, his thumb—on the trigger, pull, and that would be that.

The damage from the gunshot would cover up any bruises from the blow that knocked out Baker. Then Goodrich would compose a suicide note on the doctor's computer, explaining this was the result of overwhelming guilt over killing his colleague, Anna King.

Goodrich emerged from deep thought when he realized that Baker's car wasn't headed home. No, he was going to the hospital, probably to visit his nurse girlfriend. That was okay. Goodrich had time to wait. So long as this was done by tomorrow, he'd have complied with the orders of the *Jefe*. If Baker was still alive on Monday, though...well, that wasn't something he wanted to contemplate.

25

I'M GLAD YOU FOUND ME," KELLY SAID. "THEY TRANSFERRED me to this room after I had my chest film this morning."

Mark hitched his chair closer to Kelly's bedside. He spoke in low tones, even though her new room on the post-surgical unit was a private one. "No problem. I'll confess that, sort of through force of habit, I went to the ICU, but they directed me to your new room. How are you doing?" He squeezed her hand. "Must be okay, since Tom moved you up here."

"He said he'd be by later to talk with me."

Mark nodded. "I imagine Tom will take out the chest tube in the morning, do a follow-up film tomorrow afternoon, and let you go after that."

"Do I hear my name being bandied about?" Tom Sellers came in, shook hands with Mark, and smiled at Kelly. "Your chest film shows complete expansion of that lung. I'm amazed at your progress, but I think we're ready to get rid of your chest tube." He paused. "You okay with that?"

"You mean now?" Kelly asked.

"Why not? Some of my colleagues don't like to do this on a weekend, so they don't get an emergency call back. Personally, if I had one of those tubes in, I'd like it out as soon as possible." He smiled. "Besides, you've got the next best thing to a special duty nurse right here." He directed his gaze at Mark. "They tell me you've been practically living around here. Plan to stick around tonight?"

"Sure," Mark said. "Pull the tube tonight, get a chest film in the morning, discharge if she's doing okay?"

"You got it," Sellers said. "Give me a few minutes to get this set up. In no time at all, you'll have one less tube and the stuff that goes with it. By tomorrow, you'll be headed home."

But will I be safe? Kelly looked at Mark, who obviously was thinking the same thing. Then she saw his expression change.

He smiled and nodded to her. "I'll be glad to stay here tonight. That upholstered recliner in the corner makes into a bed."

"That's not really necessary, is it?" Kelly asked.

"Maybe not, but I'll feel better if I do it. Then, when it's time for you to go home, I'll take you." As though reading her mind, he added, "And don't worry. I'll make sure you're safe."

Mark had slept on hard lumpy mattresses in hospital call rooms, snatching a few winks when he could. He'd fallen asleep in med school late at night to the sound of his roommate sitting in the corner, memorizing the bones of the wrist: "navicular, lunate, triquetrum, pisiform…" After one particularly tough double shift in the ER, Mark had fallen face down onto the couch in the break room and been awakened four hours later by a nurse asking if he wouldn't rather go home to sleep. But despite his past ability to sleep almost anywhere, Mark couldn't find rest in the reclining chair in Kelly's hospital room. Eventually he slid aside the thin blanket with which he'd covered himself, made sure that Kelly was still sleeping, and tiptoed out into the hall.

His watch showed it was just after midnight, early Monday morning. Mark counted in his head. It had been a bit more than eight days, one hundred ninety-four hours to be exact, since the scene in the emergency room that changed his life. And not only his life, but Kelly's as well. At one time, he would have added two more names—Buddy Cane and Anna King—to that list, but that was when he thought the gunshots aimed at Kelly and him by the Zetas were also directed at these two colleagues. If the story from the cartel gunman was to be believed, that wasn't the case. It appeared the difference in the weapons used in the crimes backed him up. And that meant that, although one shooter was in custody, another was still free.

Mark strolled down to the unit's kitchen and helped himself to a half-cup of coffee that appeared to represent the remains of a pot made long ago. *Should have just cut off a piece and chewed it.* That was okay. He liked strong coffee—it helped keep him going. And the way he felt right now, sleep was a long way off.

He approached the nurse who sat at her desk, typing into a computer terminal. "Would you have a blank piece of paper and a pen I could use?" he asked.

She smiled. "Of course." She opened a drawer and handed him a blank pad and a disposable ballpoint pen. "Is everything all right with Kelly?"

"She's fine. Since Tom...since Dr. Sellers removed her chest tube, she seems much more comfortable."

"You know, there's really no need for you to sleep in her room," the nurse said. Her white lab coat had "Cheyenne Williams, RN" embroidered on the pocket.

"I know. But I feel better being here." He was willing to admit to himself that the reason for his presence was more to protect Kelly than provide medical care. But she hadn't argued with him. If his being here helped, he'd hang around as long as was necessary.

Mark sipped on the coffee, made a face, and tossed the remains, Styrofoam cup and all, into the nearby wastebasket.

Cheyenne rose. "I was about to make some fresh coffee. Why don't I bring you a cup?"

"That would be nice, but if it's okay with you, I'll wait here for it. While you're gone, maybe I can use this pad to make a to-do list for tomorrow." He looked at his watch. "I mean, for today."

Mark pulled out a chair and began to write. It seemed there was something he'd intended to do, but events kept him from getting around to it. What was it? Oh, yes. He scribbled, "Call Ames pediatrician re: possible abuse."

A sleepless night was nothing new for Mark, although this morning he seemed to be yawning a bit more than usual. He found a quiet corner of the food court and pulled out his cell phone. He'd offered to go to radiology with Kelly this morning, but she assured him she'd be fine. She'd slept well last night, seemed to have no difficulty breathing, and her vital signs were so normal an observer might wonder if the nurse had skipped taking them and simply entered norms from a textbook.

Despite her being a nurse in this hospital, the odds were pretty good that Kelly's chest film would take a while. There'd be time spent waiting for an X-ray room to come open. After getting Kelly into a room and helping her into the proper position, taking the film would be over in a matter of seconds. Then the finished product would have to be reviewed to make certain it was satisfactory. On some occasions, the radiologist called for a retake or additional views. While all this happened, Mark figured he had time to grab a quick breakfast and make this call.

He'd spent a little time in the record room during his sleepless night, reviewing the ER visits for Addison Ames Jr. There had been three visits in the past twelve months, all because of injuries due to trauma of some sort. Because none of the injuries was serious, and a different doctor was involved each time, there was no mention in any of the emergency room records of a contact with Child Protective Services to rule out child abuse. Mark wondered if the child's private pediatrician had any knowledge that would shed more light on the situation.

Searching the most recent emergency room record, Mark jotted down the name of the Ames's pediatrician, one of the partners in a respected practice in this part of town. He found a copy of the county medical society directory on one of the tables in the record room and got a phone number for the group. Now it was time to make the call.

After he'd polished off a plate of scrambled eggs and toast, Mark shoved the plate aside, consulted his watch, and punched in the number scribbled on a scrap of paper.

"Drayton Pediatrics Group, this is Carolyn. How may I help you?"

"Is this the office or the answering service?" Mark asked.

"This is the office, sir. How may I help you?"

"This is Dr. Mark Baker. I need to speak with Dr. Krempin. It's about one of his patients. Is he available?"

"I'm sorry, sir, but Dr. Krempin is still making rounds. If you'll give me the child's name, I'll pull that chart. Are you currently treating the patient?"

"Not presently, but I'm an ER doctor who's treated the child in the recent past. I need to discuss the case with Dr. Krempin."

"If you'll give me your number, I'll ask the doctor to call you."

Mark left his cell phone number. He knew he might be walking close to the edge of acceptable practice according to the federal regulations aimed at protecting patient privacy. Then he remembered something one of his mentors had told him early in his medical career. *Do what's best for the patient and worry about regulations later.* This was probably a case of it being better to get forgiveness than permission. At least, he hoped so.

Mark arrived at Kelly's room almost simultaneously with her return from radiology. He stuck his head through the door and caught a look from Kelly's nurse, a look that said, "Give us a minute." He nodded and moved down the hall toward the waiting room for the unit.

The room was empty at that hour of the morning, and the TV set on the wall had been muted. Other than the faint clatter of the carts doling out breakfast trays on the ward, this was an oasis of silence, something Mark appreciated right now.

He'd no more than settled into a chair in the corner of the waiting room than his cell phone buzzed. Was Dr. Krempin calling back so quickly? Without checking caller ID, he answered.

"Is this Dr. Mark Baker?" The woman's voice wasn't one he recognized.

"Yes. Who's calling?"

"This is Clara Purvis."

Wow. With everything else going on, Mark had totally forgotten the possible malpractice suit from Sergeant Purvis's widow. He still thought any such action was groundless, but on the other hand this was modern America, where anyone could sue anyone else, especially if a doctor was on the receiving end. Was that what this was about? His pulse quickened, and he had to swallow twice before he responded.

"What can I do for you?"

The pause on the line seemed to go on forever. Just when Mark was about to take the phone from his ear to see if the connection had been dropped, he heard, "I've been wondering how to do this. Finally, I got your cell number from a colleague of...a friend of Ed's." She stifled a sob. "I only now found out you were given the impression we were considering a suit against you for failing to save Ed's life. That's not going to happen. It wasn't even my idea—it all came from T.R. I think he was simply lashing out—reacting to the death of his friend."

"Who?"

"I guess you know him as Detective Jackson. His full name is Tyrell Rashard Jackson, but don't ever call him that." There was a hint of a smile in her voice. "He and Ed went through the police academy together, and they stayed close friends. Didn't T.R. say anything about that?"

"No, but it explains some of his attitude."

"I'm glad that my husband was able to save you...and that he shot the man holding you prisoner. I know that's not very Christian, but I'm feeling very Old Testament about the whole thing. Maybe when the pain lessens, I can be more forgiving."

"If it helps any, the authorities are working to roll up the entire local network of the cartel those men were part of," Mark said.

"I hope they do," she said. "Would you let me know if that happens? I think it might help bring a bit of closure."

Mark didn't know what else to say. Apparently neither did she, and in a few moments the conversation ended. *I need to call Abe Nunez or Carl Ortiz to see if they've learned anything more from the gunman they captured.* He sighed and added that call to his mental list. Meanwhile, it was time to get back to Kelly's room.

Kelly hated that she had to be in a wheelchair, pushed like an invalid to the car where Mark waited under the hospital portico. Then again, she was familiar with hospital regulations that specified such a procedure for discharge of a patient. According to her doctor, so long as she took things easy, there was no reason she couldn't recuperate outside the hospital. Now she was on her way.

Mark hurried around to open the passenger door of his red Toyota Corolla. He and the nurse helped Kelly into the car.

After several exchanges of "thank you" and "take care of yourself," the nurse headed back inside, trundling the empty wheelchair, while Kelly settled into the passenger seat of Mark's car.

She fastened her safety belt and sniffed. "It even has a new car smell. You may not want your old car back."

"I may not get it back. It wouldn't surprise me if it's totaled." He buckled in and turned toward her. "The insurance adjustor should be looking at it soon, but meanwhile this is your magic carriage." Mark's voice took on a serious tone. "Are you sure you want to be alone in your house?"

Kelly had thought of this. To tell the truth, she was concerned about being out of the relative safety of the hospital. "Honestly, I have mixed emotions. I guess, since the Zeta shooter is in custody, you and I are safe for now."

"Yes and no." Mark started the car but didn't move forward. "There's nothing to say that the Zetas won't send someone else."

"So we have no way of knowing if there's another shooter out there."

"No. Besides which, someone else beside that shooter—Rojas, I think his name is—someone else apparently shot Buddy Cane and Anna King. And they're definitely still running around loose."

Kelly turned this over in her mind. "I'm capable of taking care of myself at home, so long as I don't do any straining or heavy lifting. Maybe if I lock the doors and keep the blinds closed…"

"You could stay at my house." Mark apparently saw the look on Kelly's face. "I have two bedrooms, two baths. I assure you, it's only to give you protection, as well as having someone around to help until you recover fully."

Kelly was saved from answering by a tap on the window of the car. It was Carl, the surgical technician. She felt ashamed that she'd suspected him of being a shooter sent by the Zetas, when actually he was a DEA agent, trying to protect her. She rolled down her window.

"I see you're breaking out of this place," he said with a smile.

"I want to tell you how grateful I am for all you tried to do," Kelly said.

He grinned. "Just doing my job. And, speaking of that, I guess it goes without saying that you can't tell anyone who I really am. I'm still undercover here at the hospital."

"I've been meaning to ask you about that," Mark said.

A honk from behind them made Kelly look around. "We'd better move. Can we talk later?"

Mark started the car's engine and put his hand on the gearshift lever. "I'll give you a call later this morning," he told Carl.

"Sure," Carl said. "Meanwhile, I'm going to nose around and see if I can find out what's going on with Dr. Goodrich."

Kelly gave him a puzzled look. "What's that?"

"Oh, I guess you haven't heard. Dr. Goodrich didn't show up for an appointment this morning. Evidently, he's gone missing."

26

Responding to another honk from behind his car, Mark stuck his arm out his side window and waved the driver around. Then he leaned toward the open passenger window where Carl still stood. "What? Tell me about that."

Carl opened the back door and climbed into the car. "You're blocking traffic, and I feel sort of vulnerable standing out here. Let's drive."

Mark put the car in gear and edged into the street. "Okay, we're moving. Now what's this about Goodrich?"

"His secretary got concerned this morning when he didn't show up for a ten o'clock appointment. Sometimes he comes in late, especially when Mildred—that's his wife—when she's gone. But he's never late for an appointment."

Mark wove through traffic and got in the turn lane. "So what did his secretary do?"

"She called the head of hospital security, Bill Wilkinson. Actually, she wanted to call the police, but Goodrich had made her absolutely paranoid about keeping the police away from the hospital. Finally, Bill told her to hold off until after lunch. If Goodrich is still gone with no explanation by then, he'll notify the police."

Mark looked at the clock that was a part of the car's display. "It's about noon now."

"Head back for the hospital and let me out. I'll call you when I know something."

As they approached the hospital, Mark said, "What about the cartel shooter the police picked up? Anything more from him?"

As soon as the car stopped, Carl had one foot out the door. He turned back and said, "Lawyered up. I don't think we'll get any more out of him, but Abe's still trying."

Mark looked at Kelly, who'd sat silent throughout his exchange with Carl. "You look sort of pale. Are you worried about your safety?"

Kelly shook her head. "Maybe a little. But mainly I feel like I could throw up at any moment."

Immediately Mark's doctor brain kicked into gear. "Are you in pain? Short of breath? Do you feel—"

"I'm weak, that's all. I just got out of the hospital, and I've been sitting here in the car for a half hour or so. I want to go home and lie down. That's all."

Mark waved to the departing Carl, then put the car in gear. "For now, I'm taking you to my house. You can lie down on the bed in the guest room."

"That may not—"

"Don't worry. I'll be a perfect gentleman, but you need someone to take care of you for a day or two until you start getting your strength back." He reached over and touched her lips with a finger. "No arguments."

Kelly pulled the covers up to her chin and tried to relax. Mark had given her one of his scrub suits, which now served her as pajamas. Her brain still whirled with thoughts of shooting and disappearances and police investigations, but for now she was safe. She should put those thoughts aside and concentrate on her convalescence.

Mark's voice from outside the bedroom startled her. "Are you okay in there?"

"I'm fine. You can come in now."

He opened the door and stood in the doorway. "I'll let you rest, but if you need anything just sing out."

"No, come in for a minute. I need to ask some questions."

Mark sat on the side of her bed. "I may not have the answers, but ask away."

"Carl and Abe told you they thought the Zetas were using the hospital in a drug scheme. Do you think this has anything to do with Goodrich's disappearance?"

"It's possible. That might even explain some of his recent actions."

Kelly started to scoot up in the bed, but before she could move, Mark was up and bending over to help her adjust her position. She looked him in the eye. "Thank you…but you have to stop treating me like I'm made of china and might break at any moment." She tried to think of the best way to phrase it. "You and I worked together for quite a while. We respected each other as professionals. Now we're in a totally different relationship. If you try to take over doing everything—"

"I get it," Mark said. "I need to let you be independent. It's just that—"

"You want to do things for me, and I appreciate it. Tell you what. If I need anything, if there's something I can't do for myself, I'll ask. Fair enough?"

Before Kelly could answer, Mark's cell phone rang. He pulled it from his pocket and checked the caller ID. "I have to take this."

He started to leave, but she signaled him to stay. He sat in a chair in the corner of the room and answered the call. Kelly could only hear one side of the conversation, but it wasn't hard for her to put the pieces together.

"Dr. Krempin," Mark said. "Thanks for calling back. I'm an ER doctor at Drayton General, and I recently had occasion to see Mr. and Mrs. Ames's son, Addison, Jr. with an apparent injury to his right arm. There was no real damage, but I noticed some old bruises at that time."

Apparently Krempin made some remark, after which Mark said, "Oh, I agree. Every two-year-old falls and gets the usual number of lumps and bumps. But I believe there's a pattern here. Just a few days later, Mr. Ames brought Junior to the ER with a possible head injury."

The person on the other end of the line said something, to which Mark replied, "No, I didn't go through all the ER records, but I found a total of three such visits in the past year."

Another burst of conversation.

"No," Mark said. "No one has notified Child Protective Services. I thought I'd start by giving you a call to see if you'd—"

Mark stopped to listen, nodding occasionally. Finally, he said, "I see. Well, I'm glad you're on top of this. If there's anything we can do, you have my number."

He ended the call and turned back to Kelly, who said, "Sounds like he was aware of the situation."

"Oh, yes," Mark said. "He's seen a couple of instances that could be child abuse. After the last one, he sat the parents down for a talk. They initially denied anything was going on, but finally one of them confessed to taking out their anger on Junior."

"So what did he do?"

"He got them both to agree to counseling. In addition, the parent who'd been hitting Junior is now enrolled in anger management classes."

"And..."

"And Dr. Krempin thinks Mrs. Ames is making progress."

<hr />

Mark pushed back from the kitchen table. He'd warmed some chicken noodle soup for Kelly, who assured him she wasn't really hungry. There was a bit left over, and he'd finished it off. He was already worrying that it might have been a mistake to insist that Kelly come here to convalesce for the first day or so—not because he minded taking care of her. No, what worried him was the tape of his mother's voice playing in a constant loop in his brain: "What will people say?"

Maybe he could call Kelly's friend, Tracy. If Tracy would stay with Kelly...No, Tracy had to work. More than that, her shift in the operating room would probably coincide with time when Kelly needed someone with her. Maybe if he stayed with Kelly from midafternoon to midnight...no, that probably wouldn't work either.

He needed to find a female who wouldn't mind taking care of Kelly as well as offering a safe environment in which she could recuperate. Mark's own sphere of friends was woefully lacking in such a person. And if he mentioned it to Kelly, she'd insist on going home, where she'd be by herself.

The ring of his phone interrupted Mark's thoughts. He sighed and answered.

"Mark, this is Margaret...Margaret Cane."

"Oh, yes." He'd already forgotten the way he'd crossed paths with Margaret at church yesterday. "What can I do for you?"

"I'm going through some of Buddy's papers, and I need your advice. Could you come over this afternoon?"

"Margaret, I can't leave right now," Mark said. He was about to ask if there wasn't someone else who could help with going through his colleague's papers, but then it hit him. Margaret had a house to herself. The cartel certainly wouldn't think of looking for Kelly there. Maybe she'd be the person to ask. "Perhaps you could come over here. I'd be happy to help if I can."

"Let's see," Margaret said. "It's two o'clock now. I'll see you in about half an hour. Okay?"

"Make it forty-five minutes. I need to shower and change." Mark ended the call, thinking that he might have just solved a major problem.

After a quick shave and shower, Mark, dressed in a clean tee shirt and jeans, headed for his living room. If he could intercept Margaret before she rang the doorbell, maybe Kelly wouldn't wake up. He'd just checked on her, and she was dead to the world in the guest room. Poor thing, he wished once more he could have prevented her being shot. He hoped Abe Nunez and Carl Ortiz would be successful in their efforts to put an end to the Zeta operation in this area. Maybe then he and Kelly would feel safe once more.

He heard a car stop at the curb. That must be Marge. Mark hurried into the living room, noting a stack of unopened mail on the end table. He reached the door and flung it open, then turned back and scanned through the letters in the pile.

When he'd assured himself there was nothing important, he looked again toward the open door. Mark had his mouth open, but the words, "Margaret, come in" never escaped.

That was because the person he saw wasn't Margaret. Instead, Dr. Allen Goodrich stepped through the open door and staggered forward to stand in the center of the living room. He certainly wasn't the person Mark expected to see, but the surprise didn't end there. Goodrich smelled like a brewery. His eyes were red-rimmed. He was unshaven and his hair uncombed. His suit was wrinkled, his tie hung loose around his neck. The man was the picture of someone who'd been on a bender, then slept in his clothes.

But Mark wasn't focused on Goodrich's appearance. The thing that got his attention was the shotgun Goodrich carried, the stock tucked under his arm, the barrel pointed at Mark like the open mouth of a tomb.

27

ONE THOUGHT DROVE ALLEN GOODRICH, ONE CENTRAL theme ran through his liquor-addled brain: kill Dr. Mark Baker. That was the order given him by the *Jefe*, and he knew failure to carry out the task would result in grave consequences for him. He seemed to recall something about doing it "by Monday," and he wasn't totally sure what today was, but Goodrich figured that even if he were late it would be better than failing completely.

He'd waited in the hospital parking lot until three A.M., at which point he decided Baker was going to spend the night there. That essentially trashed his plan to confront the doctor in his home and set up a death that would look like suicide. He wasn't certain where to go from there, so he drove home where he could think more comfortably.

The house had been quiet. Mildred was still visiting her parents, which was a blessing. Goodrich settled into a chair in his den and tried to think through his problem. After an hour of wracking his brain, Goodrich decided he needed a drink to help him concentrate. One drink turned into three, and soon more than half the bottle was gone. He fell asleep in his den, slumped in a comfortable chair, where he awoke several hours later. He couldn't recall the details, but it seemed to him that he'd dreamed a plan—an excellent plan, a foolproof one. Goodrich had several more drinks directly from the neck of the bottle of Jim Beam, grabbed the shotgun, and jumped into his car.

And now, here he was, face-to-face with Baker. Unfortunately, he couldn't recall the details of his plan. Only one thing resonated in his mind—Mark Baker had to die.

Baker pointed to the shotgun. "Dr. Goodrich, what are you doing with that?"

"I'm going to kill you. Isn't that obvious?"

"Why?"

"Because if I don't, *El Jefe* will tell everyone about what I did down in Mexico a few years ago. There are pictures, you know. If Mildred found out, if she saw the pictures, she'd leave me. And—" He winked. "And Mildred is the one with money. The house is in her name. The cars are hers. I married well, but it will all be gone if she finds out about Mexico."

"So this *Jefe* controls you?"

Why did Baker want to know all this? Couldn't the man just let him pull the trigger and get this over? "Of course. That's why I had orders to get you away from the hospital."

Baker appeared to be genuinely puzzled. "Why?"

"If I didn't, the police might start nosing around. They might ruin a good thing. I mean, what's a better place for the center of a drug ring than a hospital? That's why that man, Garcia, brought his brother to the emergency room when he was shot. It was one of the first places he thought of. He'd been there before to drop off drugs and pick up money for the Zetas."

Goodrich saw Baker's eyes widen. Maybe it was because he finally realized he was about to die. Then he heard a voice—a familiar voice—that froze him in his tracks.

"Necio, me dan el pistoletazo de salida."

Goodrich's numbed brain translated automatically. "Fool, give me the gun." His gut clenched, and he was afraid his bowels would loosen then and there. The *Jefe* was right behind him. And Baker was still alive. Goodrich was doomed.

⁕

Mark didn't know what happened, but at the sound of those words—words not covered by Mark's limited knowledge of Spanish—Goodrich went pale. The shotgun trembled in his hands. Slowly the man turned and handed off the gun.

But Mark's amazement didn't end there. The person standing behind Goodrich, the one who'd spoken the words in accent-free Spanish was Margaret Cane.

"Allen, get over there beside Dr. Baker." She held the shotgun like someone familiar with such a weapon, the gun angled diagonally in front of her with the barrel directed upward, her left hand supporting the stock. Marge reached toward the trigger area with her right hand, and Mark heard a faint click. "I can't believe you didn't even have the safety off." Then her left hand went through a rapid pumping motion, and Mark heard a metallic *chuk-chuk*. "And you didn't have a shell in the chamber." Marge shook her head.

"Marge, what's the meaning of this?" Mark knew it sounded corny, but those were the words that came out.

"I think Allen here told you most of it," she said, calmly. "The Zeta cartel has established a base here in this part of north Texas, with Drayton General Hospital as the focal point. Because we could blackmail good old Dr. Goodrich here into doing pretty much what we wanted, things were going well." Marge made a wry face. "Then you and that nurse let one of our people die, and to keep the respect of the rest of the rank and file we had to go after you for revenge."

"What do you mean, 'we'?"

"Haven't you guessed? I'm the *Jefe*."

Mark's head was spinning. "I thought—"

"Yes, *Jefe* is a masculine noun, but since 99 percent of the members of this cell have never seen me, and they wouldn't take orders from a woman anyway, it served me best to leave it that way."

Mark searched desperately for a way to get the upper hand on Marge. There was a pile of letters on the table, but throwing them at her wouldn't help. It would only hasten the time when she cut him down with the shotgun. Could he simply rush her—cover the distance between them before she could pull the trigger? No way.

He had to keep her talking and hope something changed. "I can understand the attempts on my life and Kelly's. The Zetas believe in revenge. I guess I can see how you'd order Anna's shooting. But how could you order the killing of your own husband?"

Marge grinned. "Actually, I'm the one who shot both Anna King and my husband. I used the .22 target pistol Buddy kept in his sock drawer for years."

"Why? Because they both were involved in treating the Garcia brothers?"

"No, because my husband and Anna were having an affair."

"So when Anna tried to say who shot her, but all she could get out was 'Mar—' it wasn't Mark, it was Marge."

"Killing those two was a double bonus for me," Marge said. "Everyone thought it was a revenge killing by the cartel. Actually it was personal."

"And the gun you used?"

"Safely buried in my late husband's coffin."

Mark recalled the time Marge asked to be alone with Buddy's body. Now he could see why.

Marge shrugged. "I was going to come over here, get you in the kitchen, and stab you with a knife. Then I'd tell the police you tried to force yourself on me—you know, recent widow, ripe for the taking." She raised the shotgun to her right shoulder and sighted down the barrel. "Now, I guess I'll set up a different scenario. You and Goodrich met here to discuss your getting back to work, and you stumbled into a burglary in progress. The burglars shot you and ran away."

"You're crazy," Mark said.

"No, I'm smart—smarter than anyone else around. That's why I'm the *Jefe*. That's why I have the money to buy the luxuries I wanted. You didn't think Buddy's income was enough to support my lifestyle, did you?" She paused. "I think you both had better move over here by the door. That sets up better for my little story."

For the second time in just a few days, Mark was facing death, staring down the barrel of a gun. But this time, he wasn't thinking of himself—not at all. If Marge killed Goodrich and him, the sound of the shot would certainly bring Kelly out of the guest room, and she wouldn't stand a chance. Marge would gun her down and think of something to explain her death as well.

The shotgun in Marge's hand didn't waver. Obviously, she knew how to handle it. And Goodrich would be no help—

right now, he seemed on the verge of tears. If something was to be done, it was up to Mark.

He looked once more at the table near his right hand. The lamp? No, by the time he could rip it free from the cord Marge would annihilate him with a barrage of shotgun pellets. The phone? Not heavy enough. Then he saw the Bible, the one his parents had given him, the one he'd read recently. It was thick and heavy. If he could just—

"Move, I said." Marge made another gesture with the gun.

Mark took a step forward as though he was obeying, then swept up the Bible and flung it—not at the gun but at Marge's face. Her left hand came off the stock of the shotgun in an automatic gesture aimed at knocking the book away, and Mark launched himself at her like the All-District tackle he'd been in high school football. He hit her in the midsection with his shoulder, heard the shotgun blast, and felt the discharge go over his shoulder, then he was wrestling with Marge for possession of the weapon.

That's when a deep male voice behind them said, "Police! Drop the shotgun! Hands above your head! Now!"

⸻

Kelly stood stock-still in the doorway leading to the living room and watched one police officer, a diminutive blonde, train her pistol on Margaret while her partner, who resembled an angry linebacker, applied the cuffs to the woman. Only when the situation seemed secure did Kelly move forward to grab Mark.

They hugged for a long moment, then he whispered in her ear. "You're the one who called the police?"

"Goodrich's voice woke me up. I knew I couldn't go up against a shotgun, so I used my phone to call 911. Then I tiptoed here and stood in the doorway just out of sight. I was listening when Marge came in." She held out a bookend. "This was on your bedside table. It was the heaviest thing I could find. If the police didn't get here in time, I was going to throw it at her."

Dr. Goodrich stood transfixed, a puzzled look on his face. Finally, he said, "Well, I guess I'll go now."

The blonde officer swung her pistol toward him. "I don't think so. We can start with the charge of assault with a deadly weapon. And I know Detectives Jackson and Ames have some questions for you. I'd guess by the time this is all over you'll be looking at a long, rent-free vacation courtesy of the State of Texas."

Her partner took a second pair of cuffs from a pouch at the rear of his belt and secured Goodrich's hands behind him.

"Looks like the party's winding down." The voice was that of Detective T. R. Jackson, who walked through the still-open front door, followed by Detective Addison Ames. Jackson addressed the two police officers. "A backup unit just arrived. Read these people their rights, put one of them in each car, and take them to the station. We'll be there as soon as we talk with Dr. Baker and Ms. Atkinson."

The two officers shoved Margaret and Goodrich through the door, and Jackson closed it behind them. Jackson looked at the shotgun, still lying where Margaret had dropped it. "We'll take that when we go. I'm sure it has prints from both of them all over it."

"How much do you know about what happened here?" Mark asked.

"Not much." He sat down on the couch and pulled out a notebook. "Why don't you tell us about it?"

"I can do better than that," Kelly said. She reached into the pocket of the scrubs she wore and pulled out an iPhone. "Right after I dialed 911, I recorded everything that went on."

A wide grin split Jackson's face. "We'll keep those two separated while we question them. I was willing to bet Goodrich would give up his partner in short order. This pretty much guarantees it."

For the first time since she'd interacted with him, Kelly actually saw a faint smile flit across Ames's face. Maybe that was a sign things really were turning around.

<hr />

Almost an hour after the last of the police had left, Mark and Kelly sat in his living room trying to come down from the adrenaline rush they'd experienced, when Mark's cell phone rang. He noted that he'd already missed two calls from the same "Private Number." He frowned and answered the call.

"Doctor, this is Abe Nunez."

"Abe, I'm sorry. Things have been sort of busy around here."

"I know. I talked with the officers who brought in your hospital administrator and that doctor's wife. They gave me some time with ... what's his name? Oh, yeah. Goodrich. He was anxious to confess. We rounded up an assistant DA and a stenographer, and he gave us pretty much everything we need to roll up the Zetas here in this area."

"What about Marge?"

"The detectives have applied for an order to exhume her husband's coffin. If the pistol that killed him and Dr. King is there with her fingerprints on it, I believe you can say that

El Jefe—or maybe it should be *La Jefe*—will be incarcerated for a long time."

"So Kelly and I don't have to feel like we're walking targets?"

"I think within a few days you'll be as safe as in your mother's arms." There was a smile in Abe's voice. "I'll keep you posted."

"Does this mean Carl won't be at the hospital anymore?"

"Carlos—I mean, Carl—will probably be gone within a couple of weeks. We'll both be heading back down to the border."

"I'm sorry we didn't have time to get to know each other," Mark said.

"Just glad we were around to help," Abe replied. "See you down the road."

Mark ended the call and pocketed his phone. "Abe tells me that they're winding things up. We should be safe now."

"I'm afraid it's going to take me some time to stop looking behind me for potential shooters," Kelly said. She rose slowly from her seat on the sofa and eased over to where Mark's Bible still lay on the floor. "I suppose it's okay to straighten up now."

"I would think so," Mark said. "But you don't need to do it."

"No, no." She picked up the book and thumbed through it until she found the passage she wanted. "Here it is."

"Here what is?" Mark asked.

"A passage I thought of when I was in the hospital after I'd been shot. I guess I was trying to feel sorry for myself. Then I remembered this one: Romans 8:28. 'And we know that God causes everything to work together for the good of those who love God and are called according to His purpose for them.'"

"So you're saying all this was good?" Mark asked. "I don't see how."

"No, people died as a result of the actions of some evil people. God doesn't cause bad things like that. But He can use even the bad stuff, just like He used this to help you make a change in your life and me to deepen my faith."

"Eric says the key is giving up control of our lives. So long as we feel like we're at the helm, God isn't. And I guess that's one reason I thought about my own safety first when we faced the gunman in the ER. But I've tried to change that."

"And I saw the results," Kelly said. "You put your own life in jeopardy to protect me when you were facing Marge holding a shotgun."

For a moment they were quiet, each lost in their own thoughts. Then Mark said, "There's one more thing I was hoping would come out of all this. But I don't know how to—"

The ring of his cell phone stopped him. He pulled it from his pocket, read the caller ID, and said to Kelly, "I think I'd better take this. But I'll put it on speaker."

He punched a button and said, "Hi, Gwen."

"Have you heard anything more from the police," Gwen asked.

Mark explained to her what he'd just experienced. "The police assure me they'll have this wrapped up in a few days. So I guess I won't be needing your legal services in the future."

"I'm glad," Gwen said. "But there's another reason I called. I can't tell you why I feel this need, any more than I can tell you why I've fought it and put it off so long." She paused. "Could you give me the phone number of your pastor?"

Mark grinned. "I'm going to give you two numbers. One is my pastor, the other is a doctor who's helped me a lot—a real man of faith."

He read off the phone numbers of Pastor Steve Farrington and Dr. Eric McCray. "Wait about a half hour before calling, so I can contact both men and tell them to expect your call."

"Thank you," Gwen said in a quiet voice.

"No thanks necessary. I'm glad you're taking this step," Mark replied. "Is there anything else Kelly or I can do for you?"

The answer was slow in coming, and when it came it brought smiles to both their faces. "Yes. Pray for me."

Group Discussion Guide

1. As you consider their backgrounds, what events in the early lives of Mark and Kelly might have shaped their relationship with God? If their backgrounds had been reversed, how might this have affected the way they behaved?

2. What was your impression of Dr. Eric McCray? What factors influenced his behavior?

3. Who in the story seems to have the best grip on their personal relationship with God? Who has the most accurate ideas about God? Why do you say that?

4. How would you compare the strength of character of Kelly and Tracy? Of Mark and Eric? Did these change over time? How?

5. Did your opinion of Carl (Carlos) change as the story developed? What influenced your original feelings about him?

6. What factors seem to have affected Gwen Woodruff to shape her current mind-set?

7. Discuss your feelings about the two detectives. Did you sympathize with either? Did your emotions change as the story unfolded?

8. Did you have a suspect in mind for *El Jefe*? Who? Why?

9. What was your opinion of Dr. Anna King? Did that change as the story unfolded?

10. Can you think of a takeaway message for the book in one sentence? Is there a Scripture passage you think applies to the book?

Want to learn more about Richard L. Mabry, MD
and check out other great fiction from
Abingdon Press?

Check out our website at
www.AbingdonFiction.com
to read interviews with your favorite authors,
find tips for starting a reading group,
and stay posted on what new titles are on the horizon.

Be sure to visit Richard online!

http://www.rmabry.com/

http://rmabry.blogspot.com/

We hope you enjoyed Richard Mabry's *Fatal Truma*. Here's a sample from his next book from Abingdon Press, *Miracle Drug*.

1

Dr. Ben Lambert stood at the bathroom sink washing his hands. He sensed more than saw the movement behind him.

"You're not supposed to be in here," he said without turning. The intruder didn't respond. Lambert repeated the words, this time in Spanish. "*Supone que no debe estar aquí.*"

When there was still no answer, Lambert, his hands wet, the water still running, turned toward the intruder. That's when he felt it—a sharp pain in his left upper arm. Within seconds, a burning pain swept over his extremities. His vision became fuzzy. He tried to reach out, but the commands his brain sent went unheeded by his arms and legs.

With agonizing slowness, Lambert crumpled to the ground. He felt his heart thud against his chest wall in an erratic rhythm, at first a fast gallop, then slower and more irregular. He tried to breathe but couldn't satisfy his hunger for air. His calls for help came out as weak, strangled cries, like the mewling of a kitten.

Then the next wave of pain hit him—the worst pain he'd ever experienced, centered over his breastbone as though someone had impaled him with a sword. Lambert struggled to move, to cry out for help, to breathe. Through half-closed eyelids, he could barely see a patch of worn linoleum, topped by an ever-enlarging puddle beneath the soapstone sink. Then that vision and the world around it, faded to black, and Ben Lambert died.

Dr. Josh Pearson tapped on the office door. "Nadeel, you wanted to see me?"

Dr. Nadeel Kahn half-rose from behind his desk. Kahn was a small man—probably five eight compared with Josh's six feet plus. His accent was almost non-existent, probably worn off through years of medical school, residency, and practice. Normally, Josh's interaction with the managing partner of the Preston Clinic was limited to an occasional "Hi" as they passed in the halls, plus phone calls about hematology patients Josh referred to the subspecialist. This summons to Kahn's office had come as a surprise.

Kahn motioned Josh inside. "Thanks for coming. Close the door and have a seat, would you?"

Josh did as Kahn asked. "What's up? I think this is the first time I've ever been called into your office." He tried to summon up a grin. "Am I in trouble?"

Kahn's expression never changed. "We'll wait to decide that until you hear both pieces of news I have for you." He leaned back in his desk chair and tented his fingertips under his chin. His dark eyes fixed Josh's. He took a moment, apparently deciding how to deliver his message. When he spoke, his tone had turned serious. "As you know, our colleague, Ben Lambert, left a few days ago to accompany ex-president Madison on a trip to South America. The delegation was to consider locations for a free clinic Madison's foundation was considering setting up. Before he left, Ben approached me and said he thought it appropriate, as he got older, to prepare a younger colleague to care for David Madison should the need arise."

An idea took faint shape in Josh's mind, but he quickly rejected it. *Surely not.* He shook his head.

"Yes. He named you," Kahn said. "Ben told me he had already discussed it with Madison. They'd known each other for years—actually grew up together—and Madison trusted his friend. He said he was willing to go along with Ben's recommendation."

"I'm . . . I'm flattered, I guess, but I have no idea why he'd choose me."

"Unfortunately, we can't ask Ben that question. I just got a phone call that he died earlier today of an apparent heart attack." Kahn rose from his chair. He reached across the desk and put his hand on Josh's shoulder. "I don't know whether to offer congratulations or sympathy. Josh, you're now the personal physician for David Madison, former president of the United States."

Tears formed in Rachel Moore's eyes as she stood on the tarmac of El Dorado International Airport in Bogotá, Colombia, watching the special metal coffin holding the earthly remains of Dr. Ben Lambert disappear into the cargo hold of the private jet. *Dr. Lambert, I'm so sorry. I wish I could have done more.*

An older man, the silver waves of his hair blowing slightly in the wind, stood beside her. As though he could read her thoughts, he said, "Don't beat yourself up, Rachel. No one could have predicted this. And you and the others did everything humanly possible. Ben was probably already dead when you found him." Then David W. Madison, ex-president of the United States, put his arm gently around her shoulders and hugged her.

"I guess I know that," she said. "But no one expected it. I mean, we all had physicals along with our immunizations before leaving, and he told me he was in tip-top shape for a man over sixty. Then, when we were eating lunch at the church, he was in the bathroom . . ."

"I know. It's a shock. Ben Lambert was an old friend. We grew up together. And now he's gone." Madison took his arm away and looked down at the nurse. "You know you don't have to be the one to accompany his body back to Dallas. One of the other members of the party could do it."

"No, I think I need this to achieve some closure. You'll be coming back in a couple more days, and if there's a medical problem after I leave, you still have Dr. Dietz and Linda Gaston."

The door to the cargo hold closed with a thud, and Rachel shivered despite the tropic heat. She lifted her carry-on bag and started to turn away, but Madison stopped her.

"Ben must have sensed something like this might happen, because before we left he spoke to me about another physician he thought should take care of me if he couldn't." Madison hesitated. "I think you know him. Matter of fact, I imagine he's the one meeting you at the airport after you land."

"You mean Josh?"

"When you see him, please tell Dr. Pearson I need to see him as soon as I return."

The Preston Clinic utilized cutting-edge technology in every aspect of its practice, and records were no exception. All the records were computerized, the information encrypted, ample backup in place. The primary difference between David Madison's records and others was that the former president's were more strongly encrypted and only available to the medical staff on a need-to-know basis. Now Josh had that need.

Most of the physicians had gone home for the day, but Josh was still at his computer studying David Madison's medical records, trying to prepare himself for what he anticipated was going to be his biggest job ever as a physician.

Did Ben Lambert have a premonition something like this might happen? Was that why he named Josh as his successor before leaving on the trip? Maybe there was a clue in his medical records.

Closing down Madison's record, Josh opened the one for Ben Lambert. His pretrip physical had been just as thorough as the ex-president's . . . maybe even more thorough. Then why would he have suffered a sudden heart attack and died? Josh figured it was something weird like a rhythm disturbance. He shook his head. No need for him to agonize over something that had already happened. Maybe the autopsy would tell them, maybe not.

But, no matter what was in Ben Lambert's medical records, whatever his autopsy would show, one thing remained a certainty. Dr. Ben Lambert was dead, and Josh Pearson was now the personal physician for the immediate past President of the United States.

It would be wonderful to get back home to Josh, Rachel thought. They'd been dating for a year, and this was the longest they'd been apart. A mutual friend had introduced them, warning her that he was still a bit fragile from the death of his wife a couple of years earlier. Well, since her fiancé had dumped her before she moved to Dallas, perhaps she and Josh would be kindred spirits. They proved to be more than that, though. And this absence from him cemented it—her feelings for him were more than friendship. She'd fallen in love with Josh. And she could hardly wait to see him, to pick the right time to let him know.

Rachel looked out the window of the plane, trying to discern landmarks below. She'd always envied people who could look down at the metropolitan sprawl that was Dallas and say, "Oh, I can see my house," or "There's the building where I work."

Sometimes, if she was lucky, she might recognize the sprawling campus of the University of Texas Southwestern Medical Center. On rare occasions, she might even be able to spot the Zale Lipshy Hospital where she worked—but not today. She wished she were there right now, checking on patients in the ICU, instead of escorting the body of a colleague back to his loved ones. A wave of guilt washed over her like the rain that streaked past the windows of the plane. *Get over it, Rachel. You did all you could.* But if that were true, why did something about it all simply feel wrong?

The plane dropped lower, and through the rain she was able to make out street lamps and car headlights. The touchdown was relatively smooth, and soon she heard the roar of reverse thrusters and the squeal of brakes as the pilot brought the jet to a slow rollout. This area of Love Field was reserved for VIPs, and certainly a plane chartered by former president David Madison qualified. She wondered who would meet her—besides Josh, of course. Exactly how would she accomplish the handoff of Dr. Lambert's body?

The jet rocked to a stop and the engine noise died. Rachel looked out the window and saw that the plane was probably a hundred yards from the terminal building. The male steward unfastened his seat belt and made his way back toward her. "Miss Moore, we're here. Are you ready to deplane?"

Rachel rose from her seat, took her carry-on bag from the steward, and moved toward the forward door, which had already been folded downward to form a short staircase. She grasped the wet handrail and descended the steps, which were already slippery from the rain. She avoided looking to her left as the airplane's cargo door opened. Dr. Lambert's coffin would be off-loaded soon, and she knew that seeing it would tear at her heart.

Then she saw Josh hurrying toward her, oblivious of the rain. His raincoat flapped behind him, the rain on his bare head turned his sandy hair to a helmet from which water streamed down a handsome face. Josh opened his arms toward her, and, for the first time in what seemed like days, Rachel felt the clenched muscles in her shoulders relax.

As Josh had prepared for his trip to the airport to meet Rachel, he once again took a personal inventory and realized how blessed he was to find love once again. When Carol died two years ago, Josh felt as though his world ended. He was certain he'd never love again. But Rachel changed that. She'd brought sunshine into what had been, to that point, a dark world. Josh was determined not to let her go.

In his vehicle, he tried to imagine how she must feel. Josh knew it was up to him to comfort her and guide her through the next few hours and days. He just hoped he could do it.

He snagged a parking place in the short-term garage at Love Field. Despite a few wrong turns and false starts, Josh managed to navigate the route to where the private jet bearing Rachel would land. He planted himself where he had a good view of the tarmac outside, then stood peering through the large, rain-streaked plate glass window, as though by his actions he could make the plane arrive more quickly. Finally, he saw the small private jet land, traverse a couple of runways, and come to a stop. As soon as the plane door opened and the steps unfolded, he hurried across the tarmac to Rachel, ignoring the rain. He kissed her, then pulled her close to him and clasped her tightly, her head resting comfortably on his shoulder. He nestled his face in her soft brown hair and whispered, "I've missed you so."

"And I've missed you." He held her as though he'd never let go. Eventually Rachel pushed back and said, "I . . . I guess I should see about—"

A middle-aged man in a black trench coat and dark felt hat approached them. He opened a black umbrella and held it over Rachel to shield her from the spring shower as he talked. "Excuse me," he said, in a voice as somber as his attire. "Miss Moore? I'm Bill Smith. President Madison's office arranged for us to meet the plane and take the body of Dr. Lambert."

"Oh. We . . . we hadn't talked about the details." She looked uncertainly at Josh. "I guess it's okay."

"Could we see some identification?" Josh asked.

"Of course." Smith pulled out a wallet, which he opened to show a Texas driver's license bearing his name and photo. Then he brought out a card identifying him as a member of the National Funeral Directors Association.

"Thank you," Josh said. He turned to Rachel and gave a small nod.

Smith raised a clipboard in the hand not holding the umbrella. "If you'll just sign this form, we'll do the rest."

Rachel took the pen from under the clip and signed the paper. "And that's all?"

"Do I need to call someone to pick you up? Anything else we can do?" the man asked.

"I'll take care of her," Josh said.

As the hearse pulled away, Josh took Rachel's arm. "Let's get in out of the rain. What about your luggage?"

"I only have this carry-on. Mr. Madison said not to worry about the rest of my things—someone would pack them and send them back. I guess all I have to do right now is clear customs." She took Josh's hand. "I thought that once someone else took charge of Dr. Lambert's body, I'd feel some relief, but I don't . . . I . . . I . . ."

"Later. We'll talk about it all you want, but right now let's get you home."

As they arrived at the glass door into the terminal, it slid back to reveal an older man wearing a black suit and a somber expression. "Miss Moore?"

"Yes. Did President Madison arrange for you to meet me?"

The man nodded and stepped back so Josh and Rachel could enter. "I apologize for being a few minutes late. There was an accident on Mockingbird Lane that held us up." He handed her a business card, then reached into the breast pocket of his coat and produced a three-page document. "I'm Vernon Wells with Sparkman Hillcrest Funeral Directors. The coach will be pulling around next to the plane in a moment. If you'll sign this, we'll take possession of Dr. Lambert's body."